Also by Caleb Wygal

Mytle Beach Mystery Novels

The Brass Key (Short Story Prequel)

Death on the Boardwalk

Death Washes Ashore

Death on the Golden Mile

Death on the Causeway

Death at Tidal Creek

Lucas Caine Novels

Moment of Impact

A Murder in Concord

Blackbeard's Lost Treasure

The Search for the Fountain of Youth

DEATH ON THE
BACK NINE

DEATH
ON THE BACK NINE

A MYRTLE BEACH MYSTERY

CALEB WYGAL

FRANKLIN/KERR
KANNAPOLIS, NORTH CAROLINA

Published by Franklin/Kerr Press
1040 Dale Earnhardt Blvd. #185
Kannapolis, North Carolina 28083
www.FranklinKerr.com

Edited by Lisa Borne Graves
Cover art and design by Mibl Art
Author photo by Pamela Hartle
Interior design by Jordon Greene

Printed in the United States of America

FIRST EDITION

Hardcover ISBN 979-8-9887979-3-7
Paperback ISBN 979-8-9887979-2-0

Fiction: Cozy Mystery
Fiction: Amateur Sleuth
Fiction: Southern Fiction

This book is dedicated to the pickup line at Lakewood Elementary School in Myrtle Beach. Much of this book was written while waiting to pick up our son from school.

*"Time is a precious thing.
Never waste it."*

– Gene Wilder –

CHAPTER
ONE

MY OLDER BROTHER is a jerk. Especially when it comes to respecting other people's time.

When Bo and I were kids, and he got his driver's license, Mom and Dad would have him drop me off at my first job as a bag boy at the grocery store. It was his job to pick me up. Sometimes, I'd have to wait for almost forever for him to get me after I clocked out.

He'd pull up to the doors, screech to a halt in his Pontiac sports car, and apologize because he was out with his girlfriend and lost track of time. The girlfriends varied, but the excuse didn't.

Here I was again, waiting for him. I checked the time on my phone. He was a solid ninety minutes late. This time, however, it wasn't his fault.

I waited at the bottom of the stairs for arrivals at the Myrtle Beach International Airport near the bright new Visit Myrtle Beach kiosk, tapping my toes and trying to decide if I wanted to hit the coffee bar for a second cup. The airline had delayed his plane during his layover in Kansas City as he traveled cross-country from his estate in La Jolla, California, on the world-famous Torrey Pines Golf Course. He retired early after being on the ground floor with Uber and selling his share of the company last year. Now, he traveled the world on thrill-seeking adventures. If the activity called for a helmet, Bo wanted to do it. From mountain climbing in Nepal to whitewater rafting the Upano River in Ecuador, he's traveled the world over.

The world over, except to visit Myrtle Beach and his family. Mom was at home, preparing his favorite meal from our days of growing up in Southern Ohio: a bowl of chili with peanut butter sandwiches. Dad had made a trip to Total Wine to get a selection of beers—Bo's beverage of choice.

The only thing I had done to prepare for his visit was to dust off my golf clubs. When he called to say he was coming, he told me he wanted to take me out for a round of golf. I played at the Dunes Club a few weeks ago at the invitation of Emilie's dad. He had backed up his promise to take me out on the prestigious course after I solved the murder of his daughter. Other than that, the only time I played was when old college friends would pop into town once or twice a year.

I wasn't any good, but it would be fun to knock some balls around a course on Bo's dime.

A flurry of passengers from an offloaded plane swarmed down the stairs before me. I craned my neck, searching for Bo, but he was not among the throng. Most of the new arrivals made a beeline for the baggage claim area while a few headed straight for the exit. One or two hefted carry-on bags over their shoulders and made for the exit.

I settled back into my place, leaning against a wall beside the Visit Myrtle Beach kiosk. It had been two months since I'd solved the murders of Emilie Smith and Stanley Griffin at Tidal Creek Brewhouse. The summer had stayed hot. Tourists had flocked to the Grand Strand in record numbers. My relationship with Andrea leveled off. I couldn't place my finger as to why that was the case, but we still saw each other most days as she owned the furniture boutique next to my bookstore. We ate dinner together at least once a week. She would be my date for dinner tonight. It was the first time she would meet my parents and Bo.

Andrea and I led busy lives. She had a daughter to take care of by herself and a business to run. I was about to open my second bookstore and was knee-deep in writing my second novel.

We set a date to open the second bookstore, Garden City Reads, on the Friday before Labor Day Weekend. The date fast approached. My hand-picked manager for the store, Winona, had left my store and now worked full-time stocking and organizing the new spot next to the Garden City Pier. With my help, she hired three people to help prepare the store and continue to work after it opened.

Back to Andrea. I hadn't dwelled on the stagnation in our relationship. We needed time to level off and get to know each other better. She and I had both dealt with the sudden loss of our spouses and were in no hurry to walk down the aisle or stand before the justice of the peace anytime soon.

Part of me wondered if the cooling off had been all me. After solving the last murder, I attended a ceremony in my honor to receive a commendation from the mayor. Before the ceremony, I finally met Detective Gina Gomez's fiancé, Lucien. It turned out he was the one who last had possession of my dead wife's, Autumn, cell phone before it was stolen from his forensics lab. I had found threatening text messages from an unlisted number to her the night before she died. Messages she never told me about.

I had tried to research the number as much as possible, before I resorted to asking Gomez and Moody for help. Gomez had offered to let someone she trusted examine the phone and discern if they were able to pull more information from the phone that might lead to the mysterious messenger.

She had said she would give the phone to a forensics tech and see what else they might extract from it, and attempt to identify the sender of the threatening messages. It wasn't enough to open a case, so she was doing me a favor by going through a backchannel.

That was the last I saw of the device.

I didn't trust Lucien from the moment I met him. There was something about the way he shook my hand that sent alarm bells ringing in the back of my head. Not only was he devilishly good-looking, but something about him also reeked of dishonesty.

I didn't tell him that I made out with his fiancée, the lovely Detective Gomez, in her car before she told me she was engaged. That would have been a real icebreaker.

That marked the last time I encountered him or Gomez.

As I had the last forty minutes to ponder the weight of the world while waiting for Bo, it occurred to me that the plateau with Andrea might stem from meeting him and realizing that whatever led to Autumn's death might go deeper than I imagined. If he was behind the disappearance of her phone, then that hinted at a . . .

"Clark!"

I broke from my reverie and from staring at my feet when I heard my name called.

"Clark!" the voice shouted again.

I looked up the stairs to see Bo waving an arm in the air and smiling in my direction.

Little did I know that this would be the beginning of another long weekend I'd wish to forget.

CHAPTER
TWO

THE LAST TIME I saw Bo in the flesh was a decade ago. He didn't even come to visit after Autumn's death. That was around the time he sold out and made his fortune. He was in Nepal at the time.

The last time I laid eyes on him, his hairline had started to recede, and flecks of gray snuck into the hair on top of his head and on his chin. He'd put on extra weight after spending hours at an office in San Francisco helping with the early coding of what would start as UberCab and eventually become the Uber platform. Bo was one of the first employees.

He cashed out and would qualify as one of the richest people in Myrtle Beach if he lived here year-round. I'd settle for him being here three days max.

Bo and I had a contentious childhood. He was older by three years and lorded it over me. He was always taller, smarter, more athletic, more popular at school, and some might argue, better looking than me.

When he reached the bottom of the stairs, he whipped off a pair of designer sunglasses and flashed two rows of pearly white veneers. These weren't the slightly crooked teeth from his childhood. His hairline had miraculously grown back, better than ever. Wavy hair with blonde highlights tumbled over his eyes. He swept his hair back and I swear I saw one of the female passengers bite her lip as she passed by.

I wasn't in bad shape myself but seemed flabby compared to his chiseled frame. It was amazing what a couple hundred million dollars could do for a person versus your average person paying ten bucks a month for the local gym.

As I pondered the positive side-effects of his income bracket, I reminded myself that he accepted the invitation to stay at my place, mom's invitation to a homemade dinner at their house, and my offer to pick him up from the airport. I figured that one of the people who created Uber ought to get unlimited free lifts for life, but here we were.

We were two grown men who possessed similar genealogical attributes hugging within the concourse of the Myrtle Beach International Airport like we were children again being forced to by Mom after being in a fight.

Except there was no fight this time. We broke the hug, looked each other in the eyes, and gave a silent nod.

We both sensed it. A clean slate.

"You look well," he said. He had a voice suited for movie trailer voice overs. Deep and sonorous, one that made people take notice. "How's life treating you?"

I shrugged. "It's okay. Considering." This wasn't the time to get into the misery I went through during the first two years after Autumn's death before finding the body of Paige Whitaker behind my bookstore. After that, things took a turn for the…well, more interesting, for starters. I took a step back from him. "You look better than ever."

I meant it. Sounds of cash registers at skin rejuvenation spas rung through my head.

He grinned. "Appreciate it."

He picked up his duffel bag off the ground and we walked side-by-side to the baggage claim to retrieve his luggage. A couple dozen other passengers stood around the conveyor belt awaiting the parade of luggage to pop out of the chute on the wall.

"I had to check my clubs," he explained.

"What? No rental clubs for you?"

He chuckled. "No. Bo doesn't roll that way. Gotta have my Itboris. They're hand-made in Japan, you know. What are you playing with nowadays?"

"Same ones I've had. Some old Adams set you gave me when I graduated."

Bo looked at me like I was the saddest person on earth, and he was the happiest, which he might be. "Then we've got to do something about that. Can't have you out there with me, playing with clubs from the Stone Age."

"If you can call the early 2000s the Stone Age, then sure."

"We'll run by a golf store on our way home."

I've never bought a new set of clubs in my life. When I was a teen, I'd inherited a set with actual persimmon woods from a relative whom I can no longer recall. I had that set until Bo gifted me a new set upon graduating from Coastal Carolina. The "new" set had been used a dozen times in twenty years.

"There's a PGA Tour Superstore near here."

"That's our first stop," he said.

After we collected his golf club travel case, we delicately placed them and his travel bag in the back of my Jeep before going to the golf store where he lived up to his word and bought me a brand spanking new set of Callaways.

As this was a Friday afternoon, two weeks shy of Labor Day, traffic stunk. We sat in a jam on the 17 Bypass between the Coastal Grand Mall and Farrow Parkway. Tourists would never learn to merge correctly when it goes from three lanes down to two. Flashing lights up ahead in the median hinted at a fender-bender.

We took the time to catch up. Despite our differences and time apart, it was nice to see him again. The way we interacted, instead of bickering the entire time like we used to, hinted at a maturation on both of our ends. No, I'm not a little kid anymore.

We pulled into my parents' driveway in Surfside Beach in the Ocean Commons neighborhood near the Wyndham Resort. They had a big two-story home with stone accents and a two-car garage. The fronds of a palmetto tree identical to the ones in front of every house in the subdivision swayed in an air of slight saltiness. If the wind blew right, as it did today, you smelled the beach from the front porch.

We climbed out of the Jeep, and Bo took in a deep breath of air.

"Ah," he said. "The last time I smelled the Atlantic was when I went cave diving off the coast of Portugal."

"Sounds nice," I commented.

"You should have been there. It was magical."

"I bet."

"And the *mulher bonitas* were to die for."

"I'm assuming you mean women."

"Correctamundo." He looked down the quiet street, no doubt lost in fond memories of the high-maintenance women who inhabited his life.

As we began walking to the front door, a red Hyundai sedan pulled to a stop on the street near us.

"There she is," I said.

Bo turned and tried to see who was inside the car, but the tinted windows prevented that. "Who is it?"

"Andrea."

Andrea exited the car from the driver's seat. She flashed a thousand-gigawatt smile. "Hey, Clark."

"Hello yourself," I said. "Libby in the back?"

The car had tinted windows, so I wasn't sure.

"Sure is. She's excited to see you."

I strode across the lawn to the rear passenger side of the door and opened it. Bo hung back while I helped Libby out of her car seat. She was almost big enough to sit in a booster seat. The little girl with long curly blonde hair wrapped her arms around my neck as I raised her up after unbuckling her straps. "Yay! I'm so happy to see you!"

I lifted her up out of the car and set her down on the grass with care. "I'm happy to see you too, Junebug. What have you been up to?"

"Helping Mommy make lemonade." Her smile revealed a missing front tooth. She'd lost the first one while eating a corndog last week at Nacho Hippo in Market Common.

"That had to be fun," I said and looked across the car at Andrea.

"Oh, yeah. A real blast."

She said it in a way that I'd become well-acquainted with since being around her and Libby increasingly. "A real blast" was parent-speak for "It was a blast for her but nerve-wracking for me."

Andrea came around the car, toting a jug of pink lemonade under one arm and enveloped me in a hug with the other. I took the beverage off her hands, like the gentleman I am, and we turned to Bo. He waited in the yard. I knew from experience that he was evaluating Andrea from head-to-toe.

"Andrea, Libby," I said, "This is my older brother, Bo. Bo, this is Andrea and Libby."

Bo gave Andrea a momentary look like a predator gives his prey before moving in for the kill. Except this time, he was a good boy.

He shook her hand. "It's a pleasure. Clark has told me so much about you."

That was a lie. I had told him as little as possible, only that she would be present this evening and she owned the store next to mine.

"Good things, I hope," Andrea said.

Bo glanced at me, wiggled his eyebrows, and went back to Andrea. "Only the best, except he didn't tell me you were so beautiful."

Andrea blushed. She wore a white dress with a yellow flower pattern on it. The hem ended an inch above her knees. Braids kept her blonde hair in place, while two locks on either side of her face fluttered down past her eyebrows. A pair of smart, black-rimmed eyeglasses made her look like the hot librarian in every schoolboy's dreams.

She tucked one strand of hair behind an ear. "Thank you."

Bo kneeled in front of Libby. "And you. You're one of the cutest little girls I've ever seen."

If it would have been socially acceptable to faint and fall in the grass, I might have. This wasn't the self-absorbed Bo I remembered. Maybe he had changed. Good.

Libby's face lit. "Thanks, Mister. You're tall."

Bo stood up to his full height and said to Andrea, "And she's observant as well. Nice to meet you both."

"Same." Andrea reached down for Libby to hold her hand.

Mom had come out on the front porch, wearing a Betty Boop apron, covered with flour. She awaited us under the overhang.

Bo saw her, grinned from ear-to-ear, and ran toward her. He shouted, "Mom!" like he had gotten off the school bus for the first time in kindergarten.

"Bo, my boy!" Mom said with seldom used enthusiasm.

Did I mention that Bo was always Mom and Dad's favorite? Although they would never confess to it. Andrea, Libby, and I followed Bo to the porch.

He picked Mom up in a bear hug and twirled her around once before placing her back on the ground. She put her hair back into place and stared up at her oldest boy. They had only seen each other on video calls over the last decade.

"I would say you've grown," she said, "but I know you stopped doing that over twenty years ago. You look great."

Bo gave Mom another hug. "Thank you. You do too."

They broke the connection, and she stepped aside to allow him to enter the front door. "Dad's inside. There's a Braves game on."

Bo wiggled his head. "The more things change, the more they remain the same."

"Death, taxes, and the Braves," Mom said. "You know how it is. Don't just stand there, go on in and reintroduce yourself."

"Thanks, Mom," he said and entered the house, leaving us standing on the edge of the porch.

This was the first time Mom had seen Andrea in the flesh. I had shown Mom pictures of Andrea and Libby but had hesitated to let her meet the parents. Part of me hoped that this would change the stagnation that had arisen in our relationship over the past few weeks.

There was an awkward moment while my mother gave Andrea a scrutinizing once-over. Andrea did the same. They must have liked what they saw.

They shared a quick, loose hug and stepped back from each other. Libby waited patiently, holding one of her dolls by the hand as it dangled by her side.

"Welcome," Mom said. "It's nice to meet you after hearing so many great things about you."

Andrea glanced at me.

My cheeks warmed.

She placed a hand on my upper arm and then said to mom, "It's great to finally meet you as well, Mrs. Thomas. I can tell Clark thinks very highly of you."

The corners of mom's mouth lifted. "Please, call me Nancy." She lowered herself down to our little companion. "You must be Libby."

There were no awkward moments with Libby. There was no hiding for her. She wasn't shy. She grinned from ear to ear. "That's me."

"Well, aren't you adorable," Mom said. "I hear you like spaghetti."

"Uh-huh. It's my favorite."

Mom leaned down as much as her knees would let her. In a conspiratorial manner, she said to Libby, "Guess what? I made some just for you because I knew you were coming."

"Yay!" Libby shrieked. Her shout echoed off the homes across the street.

Mom ushered Libby and Andrea inside but held out a hand to stop me. When they were out of earshot, Mom whispered, "No one will ever replace Autumn."

My brain stopped. As my relationship with Andrea progressed, thoughts of Autumn became less prevalent. This newfound romantic entanglement, I think, finally helped me realize that life goes on. Autumn wasn't coming back, and I still had a whole life ahead of me. She and I might have been married for our entire lives, and I'm sure they would have been happy years. For the longest time after her death, I'd dwelled on the fact that we would miss doing so many things together, hopefully with several children. We never had a child, although I learned she had been pregnant at the time of her death. We had been so close.

In the past three years, I've learned to not dwell on what might have been, but instead focus on the possibilities. Andrea and Libby presented new, exciting prospects. If Autumn could speak to me from beyond the grave, I was confident she would have wanted me to pursue a relationship with Andrea.

Mom was awaiting an answer.

"I know," I said.

Mom rubbed my arm in the same place Andrea had touched it a moment ago. "Life is long. We have to enjoy it while we can. Your dad and I are thrilled to see you making strides."

"Making strides toward what?"

"Being happy again."

I didn't know what to say to that. I bent down and gave Mom a hug. "Thank you."

After we parted, she said, "Come on. Dinner's ready. I made Bo's favorite. Don't want it getting cold on him."

I should have known that everyone's attention shifting to Bo was one of many signs. It turned out that what Mom remembered as Bo's favorite meal was no longer the case. That was the point the weekend started going downhill.

CHAPTER
THREE

THE THING WITH tumbling down a mountainside with no way of stopping is that there are the occasional upward bumps. Not everything is down, down, down. Even in an avalanche, bits of snow and ice will bounce up every now and then.

We had fun *that* evening. Bo caught up with Mom and Dad. Libby had a new audience with which to make friends. Andrea charmed my parents. Even Dad's attention to the Braves game waned as he got to know Andrea.

Mom had made Bo's favorite meal growing up: chili with peanut butter sandwiches. Here's the rub. At some point since we last saw him, Bo became a vegan but didn't tell us. The ground beef part of the chili was out, as was the cheese made from good old cow milk. Even the side dish of green beans was made with a little bit of bacon grease. The double chocolate cake dessert? Double nope.

Bo ate a peanut butter sandwich, but abstained from the chili. Mom about cried. Bo apologized and said that he should have alerted her before coming about the change in his eating habits but thanked her for going through the effort.

As I sat through dinner, watching Bo do his Bugs Bunny impression with the carrots to Libby, I mentally scanned my refrigerator and pantry at home, wondering if I had anything Bo would eat. Triple nope. I ate so much food that they had to practically roll me out the door to my Jeep.

After dinner, Andrea gave me a warm hug goodnight. We didn't want to smooch in front of Libby and the rest of my family. She whispered in my ear that she liked my parents. Mom sent me a text message later with the same thought about Andrea and Libby. Win, win. I took Bo to the Ultimate California Pizza in Surfside where he picked up a Berkeley with vegan cheese before going back to my place.

We had an early tee time, so we spent a few awkward moments in the living room. He ate half of his pizza before going to the bedroom on the opposite side of the house. Bo and I had gotten along well since he arrived at the airport. Once upon a time, he would verbally poke and prod at me until an argument arose. Not today. Maybe veganism caused him to mellow?

Although I couldn't hit a ball straight, the anticipation of playing on one of the top courses, not only in Myrtle Beach but also the country, kept me from getting a good night's sleep.

If I had known then what I know now, I would have stayed in bed.

* * *

THE PRIVATE SWAYING Palms Golf Club, located centrally in Myrtle Beach, was once in the running to host a large purse PGA Tour event. However, the Dunes Club located on the ocean won the prize. The rumor was that the powers-that-be in the PGA favored the Dunes Club over Swaying Palms because it had previously hosted Senior PGA Tour events and was beside the Atlantic Ocean. The back nine at Swaying Palms ran along the Intracoastal Waterway, close to the Grande Dunes course. When it came to thinking about

TV money, viewers preferred seeing professional golfers play with the ocean in the background as opposed to the waterway.

Ordinarily, Bo and I wouldn't have access to Swaying Palms. When he called and told me he was coming for a visit and wanted to play golf while he was here, I felt the pressure to impress him. He lived next door to the world-famous Torrey Pines golf course in La Jolla in a multi-million-dollar house (I know because I checked the home's value on Zillow) and was a member of the Torrey Pines Municipal Golf Club where he played in tournaments every week. There was no wait list for him.

The grand entrance for Swaying Palms and its surrounding neighborhood rested beside the Del Webb community on the 17 Bypass where I had met with Ed Banner's wife, Brenda, a couple of months ago. Banner had been the lead detective the evening of Autumn's death. The up-and-coming Detective Gina Gomez got called upon to be his partner that night, but she said he held her at arm's length during the investigation of Autumn's office at the city courthouse where she had been found dead. Gomez had said Banner acted odd that evening. He had taken and made several hushed phone calls. Gomez didn't know who he had been talking to.

When I'd met Banner's wife, she'd brought out his phone records from that month. He hadn't used a police-regulated phone to make the calls, instead using his personal cell. The list of calls from that evening revealed that he'd been in contact with an unlisted phone number. The *same* unlisted phone number that had sent Autumn the threatening text messages the night before her death. I may never know why she didn't tell me about them.

Banner's assigned partner during the time of Autumn's death had been the crusty Phil Moody. He was unavailable that evening, which was why Gomez tagged along with Banner. Moody was a man of few words and of many grunts — a man who also happened to be my ticket to get into Swaying Palms.

It turned out that the aging detective was an avid golfer. He grew up in Myrtle Beach and had many friends and connections. One person who fit both of those aspects as well was Thomas Williams. He owned a home on Swaying Palms and was a member. I had recalled that Moody mentioned Williams and their golf outings during a rare conversation that had nothing to do with a murder.

I had reached out to Moody to see if he would pull a few strings, and told him I would owe him one. Moody came through, and we had a 7:43 tee time at Swaying Palms.

The sun rose behind partly cloudy skies. A hint of a breeze caused the palmetto fronds to, well, sway. Dense humidity already clung to our skin on this early August morning. We were past Independence Day, but there was a noticeable lack of a drop in traffic, which usually happened after the middle mark of the summer.

We drove slowly down a long street lined with tall palms and oaks. Instrumental jazz music by John Coltrane played through the car speakers. Hints of green fairways and immaculate homes peeked out between tree trunks. I sipped coffee out of my Tidal Creek Coffee travel mug. Bo, who shared my love of coffee, drank his from my Benjamin's Bakery branded thermos.

Neither Bo nor I had said much since leaving the house. He'd spent the time on his phone, studying the layout of the Swaying Palms course. I was fine with that.

This course was designed by Clyde Woofley in 2003 to create what he called a Scottish-American design. Swaying Palms sits on a former plantation, nestled along the Intracoastal Waterway.

Surrounded by a coastal maritime forest, Woofley combined the dramatic contours and bunkering of a Scottish links course with coastal South Carolina's marshes and waterways to present a shot makers course that rewards players who can place the ball at strategic areas along the meandering fairways than those who hit for power.

The gorgeous scenery combined with the majestic golf course made it one of the top destinations for golfers when they come to the Grand Strand. A lengthy wait list that books up months in advance for tee times keeps most golfers who pop into the town for the weekend away, but for those with memberships, it is their preferred course on which to play.

"You ready?" Bo asked as the palms parted and the understated clubhouse appeared. The Cape Cod-style clubhouse sat in the center of the golf course. A large parking lot with several vehicles already parked lay in front of the clubhouse. Off to the side was a driving range. Seven golfers were there hitting balls, getting ready for their rounds. We were early enough that Bo and I were going to share a bucket just to get warmed up.

We pulled up to the right side of the building where a bag drop attendant unloaded our bags from the cargo hold and loaded them into a golf cart reserved for us. I let Bo out and drove around the lot and parked the Jeep.

Angling toward me through the parking lot, aiming for a nice Highlander were two familiar faces. One I didn't mind. The other I found annoying.

It was a husband and wife. The pretty red-headed wife walked in front of her tall husband. It was clear she was enraged by something.

"I can't believe you drug me out of bed for this," she said over her shoulder.

The guy wore glasses and a blue hat with a white egret silhouette on it. "I'm sorry, Sweetie. I got my weeks mixed up."

She wheeled on him and held up a finger. "Next time you book a round of golf weeks in advance, add it to our calendar, and make sure you get it right. You wasted perfectly good sleeping time for me."

The guy was an apologist. For the second time in as many statements, he said, "I'm sorry. The good news is, the tee time is for next week, and we can do this again."

"Fat chance," she said and stormed around to the passenger side of the SUV and left her goofy husband holding his golf bag.

I unsuccessfully tried to duck around a tall truck so he wouldn't see me.

"Clark! Is that you buddy?"

I've never been this goober's "buddy" and not sure that I'd want to be. But he'd caught me, and I had to say something to him. "Hey, Caleb. Tough morning?"

The rusty gears spun in his head. He seemed to get an idea on how to salvage his day with his wife. I didn't like it because I surmised that it involved me.

"You could say that," he said. "Look, I came at the wrong tee time. Tasha was going to drive the cart, and I was going to take her out for a nice lunch, but instead I got her to wake up earlier than usual and now she's mad at me. Do you have room in your group for another golfer? It'd really save my skin, man."

"Nope. Sorry." I walked past him and clapped a hand on his shoulder. "We have a full group. Show her you appreciate her getting up early and take her over to the Eggs Up Grill near here."

I left him standing there while he figured out how to fight a battle he was sure to lose.

By the time I stepped onto the sidewalk where our cart awaited, Bo had come back out the main entrance carrying two bottles of water and two packs of crackers in one hand and a bucket of range balls in the other. A healthy breakfast time snack while on the course.

He got in the passenger side of the cart, leaving me as his chauffeur for the day. I didn't mind. Bo drove with a heavy foot. The last thing I needed was for him to plunge us into the Intracoastal because he tried to zoom around a hump while searching for one of my lost balls.

"Hold on while I go in and pay," I said to him in passing.

He held out a hand, proffering one of the water bottles. "Paid for. Don't worry about it. I got it."

First, he bought me a set of clubs, now he was paying for a round of golf on one of the most expensive courses to play on the Grand Strand. I can get used to having this rich brother thing. Once he graduated college and got his first programming gig, he never lacked for money. He managed to find high-paying jobs from the get-go. Then came Uber and the rest was history. I must admit, he was good at what he did. Knowing Bo, however, there had to be a catch somewhere.

I accepted the bottle already wet with condensation from his hand and got in behind the steering wheel. Once I settled in, we headed for the driving range. Moody had sent me a text when he'd seen us pull into the lot, saying he and his buddy were already hitting practice balls. Our tee time wasn't for another twenty minutes. The plan was to hit from the bucket for ten and then move over to the putting green for five before driving over to the nearby first tee.

We drove along a paved cart path to the driving range. A thirty-foot-tall net spanning a distance of three hundred yards separated the range from the first hole. The practice area had several fake flags and bunkers set up for players to practice their "precision shots" and yardage markers ranging out to 350 for the drivers.

Normally Detective Moody wore a gray overcoat over mismatched slacks. He was short, stocky, and had wavy dark gray hair. He reminded me of a grizzled poodle.

I almost didn't recognize him out of uniform. As we approached the range, I spotted him and his friend on the far end. His longish hair ballooned out of a white Titleist golf hat. He wore a bright orange Nike golf polo shirt over matching golf shorts. He was a walking billboard straight out of *Golf Digest*. I fought the urge to rub my eyes like a person would after staring straight into the sun. I almost couldn't believe my eyes.

His friend was almost a polar opposite. He was tall and lanky with a prominent Adam's apple and hawkish nose, clad in a muted white golf polo, khaki pants, and a plain white hat. No logos.

The range had a dozen separate practice bays from which to hit from. A shapely blonde-haired woman, wearing a pink top and short skirt, took up the first spot. A large, overturned bucket of balls lay at her feet. White balls marked by black stripes to denote range balls from regular balls were grouped in clusters of ten. Judging by how large the bucket was to begin with and the number of balls remaining to hit, she had been here for a while.

Bo eyed her like prey as we passed by. The next four spots after her were vacant, followed by a foursome in various states of practice. Their golf bags rested on rolling carts, indicating that they would walk the course the old-fashioned way instead of riding in a motorized cart. That wasn't for me. Not in this humidity.

One of them was in the process of finishing off a can of beer. He crumpled it up and tossed it at a nearby trash can. It missed and clunked to the ground. It was five o'clock somewhere, I guess. Like my brother, he stared at the woman.

His friends were hitting what looked to be their last few balls as we drove past him. The early drinker nodded at us. He had gray hair on the sides under a black hat. A bulbous nose fronted a face pockmarked with acne or burn scars. He too wore a white shirt, but it had horizontal tan stripes racing across it. It didn't flatter his beer belly.

Bo and I returned the nod and pressed forward another twenty feet where I stopped the cart, and we got out as Moody whacked a practice drive long and straight. This was a side of the detective I hadn't seen before and a reminder that you can't judge a book by its cover.

Bo let out a whistle as Moody's drive landed past the 275 marker in the middle of the fairway. "Nice shot!"

Moody watched the ball roll to a stop and turned. "It'll do."

His friend hit a ball that sliced far to the right. He cursed under his breath as it sailed away.

"Come on, Tom," Moody said to his friend. "How many times do I need to remind you to not bend your knees so much and close your clubface when you follow through?"

"I know. I know." Tom stepped off the practice tee and placed the club in his bag. "I wouldn't have to bend my knees as much if I went and got custom fitted clubs."

Moody stuffed his club in his bag and picked up the club head cover. "You are a tall so-and-so. Those rack clubs are made for men of average height. You're what? Seven, eight inches over that. No wonder you slouch to hit."

"Your hips and hands also didn't follow through," Bo added.

Tom gave Bo a quick appraisal. "Thanks. I'll keep that in mind."

"You must be the brother." Moody picked up his tee and stuck out a hand.

Bo grasped it. "Yup. Bo."

"Phil Moody."

"Nice to meet you."

Tom joined the handshaking fray. "Thomas Williams, but you can call me Tom."

After we all pressed palms, Bo and I grabbed clubs from our bags and started hitting from adjacent tees. The pattern of the balls I hit would have been like buckshot on a target practice diagram. Bo's would have been centered right between the eyes. Moody helped Tom fix his swing.

The blonde-haired woman on the other end finished, gathered her gear and empty bucket, and walked back toward the clubhouse. She didn't have a cart at her station.

In the foursome between us and her, the beer drinker whistled loudly at the woman. "Lookin' good, Good Lookin'!"

She didn't turn to acknowledge the catcaller. Just shook her head and kept on going. I tore my attention from the grouping of balls at my feet and watched with idle interest.

"Zach," one of the men said to the ogler. This guy had dark skin and wore a creamsicle-orange Puma golf shirt and matching hat. "Leave her be."

Zach stuck out his tongue at his friend. "You're just jealous that she loves me."

"Whatever," another friend on the pudgy side said. "We all know she doesn't give you the time of day. Besides, your wife would kill you if she found you were whistling at another woman."

Zach smiled. "What Paxton doesn't know won't hurt her." He eyed each man in turn. "And she won't find out, will she?"

Puma hat walked to his pushcart and stuffed a club in his bag. "We know. What happens on the course, stays on the course."

The other men in the foursome finished hitting their balls, collected their clubs, and headed toward the first tee. I surmised that they would be the group ahead of us. If the one guy was already drinking and catcalling to women out of his league, not to mention his marital status, and they were walking, then this could be a long day.

CHAPTER
FOUR

SOMETIMES, I HATED being right. The foursome with the early morning drinker was indeed in front of us at the first tee.

A starter waited for us as we approached the first tee box. He was a sunburnt man with a Crocodile Dundee-style Australian bush hat. He guarded the tee box like a bodyguard out of an exclusive night club.

Bo wanted to give Tom some golf tips, so they switched golf carts before we left the practice range. Tom and Bo immediately found common ground. Both were affluent. Tom owned three gas stations and a home on this golf course. He was our ticket inside. I wasn't sure how he and Moody became good friends. It baffled me how anyone was a close friend with the constantly grumpy and grunting detective. Thus far, Moody seemed like a completely different person. Like actors who play a villain's role in TV or the movies, and then you meet them in real life and learn that they are the nicest people who don't have an agenda to take over the world.

Tom now drove Bo, and to my absolute chagrined delight, Detective Phil Moody sat in the driver's seat of my golf cart. I've never seen him drive, but I had a sneaking suspicion based on how he went about his life that we'd putter around the course like Grandma on her way to Sunday morning church.

We waited for the foursome ahead to tee off, but at first, they stood by the tee box watching a group ahead of them navigate the first hole. One guy trudged along a meandering creek on the left side of the fairway, searching for a lost ball.

That was fine. A soft breeze blew through the pines and palmettos, diminishing the humidity. Thick cloud cover had moved in overhead, keeping the normally blazing August sun at bay. The Chamber of Commerce couldn't have scripted a better summer day.

I had moved my schedule around to clear time to spend with Bo this weekend. A normal week saw me working at the bookstore six or seven days a week. Of course, sometimes "working" meant sitting in my office, drinking coffee, and writing a book. I didn't consider writing a job. It was more of a hobby now. A good royalty check meant treating myself to a ribeye at Chuck's Steak House. A normal royalty check would find me in line at the Taco Bell drive-thru. I found it fun to make stuff up and hoped it gave readers an escape from their lives for a few entertaining hours.

The early drinker had another beer wrapped in a blue koozie with a law firm's name printed on it. He studied one of his group mates with a scheming eye. "Hey, Archie?"

The pudgy fellow looked up from where he was doing a few practice swings off to the side. The man was vacant-eyed and had tufts of black hair poking out from under his hat. "Yeah, Zach?"

"Wanna make it interesting?"

Archie rested the club to his side and turned to face Zach. "I'm game. The usual?"

"A hundred a hole, if you think you can do it."

"Yeah, I can. You're on."

They shook hands on the bet while their friends watched with concern for Archie. Puma hat guy tightened his golf glove on his left hand. The fourth member oozed quiet confidence. He rested his hands on top of his driver like Sir Lancelot waiting for battle with his sword, Excalibur. The man wore a white Adidas hat. Blond hair fell from beneath the back of it. He had a chiseled physique under a blue polo and a square jaw. I figured ladies flocked to him.

I noted that Archie's side of the brief conversation wasn't laced with confidence. More like he would make the wager knowing he was about to lose money but did it to fit in with the guys and to keep this Zach guy from intimidating him. I wasn't sure about Archie, but if the guy placing a bet with me already seemed drunk, then I might take it, knowing Zach might not know which direction the hole was.

Detective Moody observed the entire conversation. Of course, what Zach and Archie just shook hands on was illegal. Moody could have warned them not to go through with it; otherwise, he might slap a pair of cuffs on them if he saw money change hands.

Moody grunted and turned his attention to the scorecard.

A soft, briny breeze whispered against my skin. Birds chirped in the pines. If he was going to let the gambling ride, it was up to him. It wasn't my job to bust criminals.

"Played here before?" Moody asked.

"I haven't."

"It's a tough course. Not a long one, but you gotta be able to place your shots."

After the shock of unsolicited advice from Moody wore off, I said, "I just hope to make solid contact."

He took his eyes off the scorecard and studied the perfectly manicured first hole ahead of us. "Just swing easy and try not to kill the ball. I know you'll want to try to hit it as far as I and what it seems like your brother can do. Don't try it. Be you."

"Yeah, thanks. At least we're not playing for money like those guys are."

Moody snorted. "Not today, at least."

"You play for money?"

He didn't make eye contact. "Harmless fun."

I nodded, taking his comment to be the end of the conversation.

Before long, the grouping in front of us had teed off and were up ahead preparing for their second shots. Zach had smoked one down the center of the fairway which ended in a "whoop," a fist pump, and an intimidating glare at Archie. Their friends watched with disinterest as though this was normal for their foursome.

Archie, to his credit, landed his ball near Zach's, just not as far, which led to a crude comment about always being longer from the red-nosed man. Moody laughed at the sophomoric humor. I found it cringy.

We moved our golf carts up to the first tee and prepared to tee off. We agreed that Moody would go first, followed by Bo, then Tom. I would go last. No pressure there. Bo said he normally played from the back blue tees, as did Moody, but would hit from the white middle tees so as not to make Tom and I feel like lesser men. Playing from the blue tees presented more of a challenge as you had to hit the ball farther to get a good second shot and sometimes those tees would be placed at a more challenging angle.

The first hole was a par 4 of 369 yards, meaning that a good golfer–not me–should be able to finish the hole in four shots. Tall pines lined both sides of a wide fairway. Two squirrels chased each other around a tree on the left side of the fairway near the tee box. A large deep sand trap guarded the green on its front left. Water lay to the right of the green.

While we waited, I asked Moody, "How's work?"

He kept his attention forward. Tom laughed at something Bo said in the cart behind us. After a moment, Moody responded, "It's the busy season. Nice to come out here and get a break."

"Any big cases?" I was mainly interested in murder cases. I didn't tell him that, but I was sure he knew.

He snorted and shook his head in slow, sad arcs. "The usual. Tourists."

"Gotcha." It was true that while everyone came to Myrtle Beach to escape and have a good time, some of them ended up on arrest reports. The same was true for any tourist destination. As a long-time resident, I understood this and had to begrudgingly accept that not everyone played nice, and a small amount of foul play came with the territory.

I couldn't help myself. While Moody studied his scorecard, I asked him, "How's Gomez?"

He didn't turn to face me. "Dunno. She's out of town."

"Right." I kick myself for making things awkward, but awkward was what I did best.

"What do you care?" he asked.

A sinking feeling settled in my chest. I didn't think of Andrea during this conversation. I should have, looking back on it. I hesitated, trying to think of a way to play it cool without arousing suspicion. "We're friends is all."

"A friend would know she was out of town." His pointed statement made its mark. Then he followed it with, "She's engaged, ya know?"

"I'm aware that she is happily engaged, yes."

A second passed before he said, "I didn't say 'happily' engaged."

So things weren't all hunky-dory for Gomez and Lucien. While I tried to sort out my feelings about Moody's statement, he said, "She's off at some big training conference in Maryland the new chief sent her to."

"Cool. Training for what?"

"Gang investigations."

I was aware of gang-related incidents in the Grand Strand over the past few years. The mayor had come out on it and reinforced Myrtle Beach's commitment to cracking down on them.

"That's good," I said.

He shrugged. "I guess."

I cocked an eyebrow. "So, you're the big dog right now in the detective room?"

"I guess. Been rolling solo when the calls come."

"How long has she been gone?"

"It's a week-long conference. She's due back tomorrow."

Today was Saturday. "Well, hopefully nothing big will happen this weekend, and you can take it easy."

He grunted. "That's a dream."

I had to go and open my big mouth.

CHAPTER
FIVE

AFTER THE FOUR guys hit their second shots and cleared the potential landing area for our tee shots, Moody got up and piped one down the center. Bo drove his ball past the detective's. Tom's shot landed to the right of the fairway, fifty yards shy of Moody's, before rolling into the rough.

After Tom collected his tee, he stepped back with Bo and Moody. I stepped up between the white tee markers with a shiny new driver in my hand. I hit with it three times on the driving range earlier. Based on that "extensive" practice, I wasn't confident. I imagined my tee shot fading to the left and ending up in some rich person's backyard. If it left the tee at all. One of my practice shots earlier glanced off the end of the club head and dribbled fifty feet straight to the left.

I plunged the tee and ball into the soft turf at the same time with one hand, leaving the ball high enough for my driver to hit it on an upward trajectory when it came swooping back through on the downswing. A soft breeze breathed against my back. Not strong enough to have a dramatic effect on the ball's flight. I took two steps back from the ball and took a half-power practice swing, just to get the motion down. Although I hadn't played much golf in years, muscle memory went a long way. I played baseball for Coastal Carolina as a walk-on and used to be able to hit the ball well over the fence. The difference between striking a ball on the diamond and the fairway was the baseball swing was more horizontal and a golf swing was vertical. In both sports, the key was focusing on the ball and allowing your body to take over at the point of impact.

Moody, Tom, and Bo stood and watched. The urge to think about them watching me tried to take over my mind, but I pushed those thoughts back and focused on what I was about to do. I don't give myself credit for much, but I could sharpen my focus when the need arises. Like it did now.

Taking a deep breath, I lined the ball up between my feet and looked out over the fairway, finding a target. The group in front of us were finishing their putts on the green. One tall loblolly beyond the end of the fairway seemed like the obvious place to aim. A mourning dove cooed in a tree behind me.

I got into my stance, waggled the club, and focused on the back of the ball. I took another breath and started to draw the club back.

At that exact moment, Phil Flippin' Moody said to Tom loud enough for me to hear, "Ah, we have a lefty with us."

All the mental clarity and my vision of the ball sailing high and long down the middle of the fairway vanished in an instant.

I groaned and stepped back from the ball, casting an evil glare at Moody. He didn't see me do it because he, Tom, and Bo were laughing so hard. My cheeks warmed in the morning sun.

The group waiting in their golf carts behind us were snickering at my expense. Even the Crocodile Dundee starter cracked a smile.

The gaff in golf etiquette from Moody should have made me mad, but after knowing him for over a year, this was a side of him I hadn't seen before. He was downright likable outside of his detective uniform. Talking in someone's backswing was like something I would have done.

After collecting myself and waiting for the laughter to die down, I got back on the tee, hit my shot, and climbed back in the golf cart beside Moody. My shot fell well short of everyone else's, but at least it was in the fairway.

Heat radiated off my cheeks as I stared forward out the front of the cart. I felt Moody looking at me.

I turned my head to find him staring at me with a crooked grin. "Sorry kid. Had to do that to you. You needed to loosen up."

He was right. I might have been a little tense. I admit, playing golf for the first time with a stranger, someone you only knew from crime scenes, and another who I hadn't seen in ten years made me nervous. Moody hit the gas, and the cart moved forward. As I sat there, the tightness in my shoulders had eased. I even cracked a smile.

Phil Flippin' Moody.

* * *

I MADE A triple bogey on the first hole. Moody made par and Bo birdied. Show off. Tom picked up his ball with a red face after several errant shots and climbed back in his cart. Must have made double par, which was usually the point where a golfer quit playing on a hole and moved onto the next to keep the pace moving. Since this was a Par 4, poor Tom would finish with a score of eight.

On the fifth hole, we waited for Bo to help Tom find a ball in the tall grass around a pond.

I sat there and tried to process Moody's comment about Gomez's engagement not being all that happy and what it might mean.

Moody glanced at the clock on his phone and said so only I heard, "C'mon Tom. Your five minutes are almost up. Let's get moving."

In golf, a rule of etiquette is that if you hit your ball into the weeds, woods, or water, you should only spend five minutes looking for it. That way the pace of play keeps moving. We would like to play "ready golf," meaning that, after everyone has hit from the tee, we would be ready to hit our next shot after the person farthest away from the green has hit theirs. This keeps the pace of the game moving for not only your group, but everyone on the golf course.

The problem with this instance was that Tom's tee shot didn't go far, and this hole had a dogleg, meaning that the fairway makes a bend. It would be my turn to hit next, but my ball would be directly where Tom would aim his second shot—hopefully. I've seen enough of his game to not want to be out in the open when he hits. Not that I'm Arnold Palmer, but Tom was a bit of a hazard.

Then Moody said something I never expected to hear him say. Maybe it stemmed from this newfound camaraderie we're sharing.

"What did you think of Gomez's fiancé?"

My breath caught. Autumn had been the furthest thing from my mind since Bo landed at the airport yesterday. The evening with Andrea and Libby had gone well. Playing golf was a nice distraction from the events of the world. I had to remind myself of this in the future. Might not be a bad way to spend what little recreational time I got. Or took.

Moody's question wasn't about Autumn, but I couldn't help thinking about her when the subject of Gomez's beau, Lucian, came up and him being the person she gave the phone to. He worked in forensics. He and Moody had to have at least a working relationship. That might be as far as it went, or they might be bosom buddies.

Without knowing that bit of information, I didn't want to give away my suspicions. "He had a strong grip."

When Lucien and I shook hands upon meeting each other, the power behind his handshake caused my fingers to *pop*. I flexed my hand at the memory.

Moody grunted. "Yeah, I normally fist bump him. He's a workout king, even though he's not on active patrol."

"Did he used to be?"

"Yeah, up until a couple years ago when he transferred to forensics. It was right around the time he and Gina started seeing each other."

"Does your PD frown upon relationships?"

"To a degree. That's why he transferred to a department where they would have less contact with one another."

"Ah. Have less contact so they can have more contact, so to speak?" I regretted the words as soon as I said them with the mental picture that came with them.

"Like that."

Bo found Tom's ball buried in the mud along the bank of the pond and tossed it out into the short grass.

Bo smiled at Tom. "A dirt weasel must have kicked it."

It took Tom a moment to catch Bo's joke. He snorted. "Right. Those crazy dirt weasels. Always kicking balls out of bad lies."

Typical Bo, breaking rules, but at least it was with good intent.

We resumed play. The rest of the first nine holes continued in the same manner. Tom finished most of them. Bo and Moody traded birdies and pars. My scorecard was all over the place. I made double par on a short Par 3 hole but made par on a long Par 5. Go figure. The rest were various bogies.

Throughout our journey over cart paths and on fairways, I marveled at the verdant beauty of the course and architecture of the colossal stately homes bordering the holes. Not a blade of grass nor a leaf on any bush was out of place. Even the flowers clustered around each tee box were in full bloom. Most holes were bordered by tall pines running the length of the fairways. The loblollies gave way to manicured palmetto trees around the greens. A soft breeze caused the palm fronds to sway, hence the name of the golf course.

In all, it was an enjoyable front nine. The weather remained fair. The pace of play moved along. Moody ordered a round of beers for us all from the beverage cart operator. I think he did it to impress the woman. He commented to me after she pulled away that it looked like she'd fallen out of the ugly tree and hit every branch on the way down, but that didn't diminish her gorgeous body. I didn't comment on his Neanderthal observation, nor was I going to complain or question a free beer.

I made my putt to finish the ninth hole, and we drove to the clubhouse for a short break. Moody tallied up our scores. Bo calculated his and Tom's. Bo ended up five shots ahead of Moody. Tom and I were bringing up the rear from way behind. I ignored my score. It didn't matter to me. I wasn't here for a competition. This was for fun.

There was much of that to be had.

Even in an avalanche plummeting downhill, there are times when rocks and snowballs bounce up. This was one of those times.

Little did I know that we were approaching the proverbial cliff.

CHAPTER
SIX

INSIDE THE CLUBHOUSE, the four of us used the restroom, washed our hands, and put orders in at the grill. I ordered a hot dog and a beer.

Many golf courses offer food in the clubhouses. Hot dogs are a necessity. Most of the places I've ever paid to play usually have that, along with burgers, packs of crackers, and cookies. Swaying Palms had all of that, but they also catered to the elite. This was no snack bar. The clubhouse offered a full menu. I glanced over it while waiting for my grub. Of note was prime rib and lobster. The offerings, and price, gave me a chuckle. A Thurston Howell III wannabe sat in the elegant dining room at a table wearing full golf attire and a bib for cracking lobster in between the front and back nine. Better than being stranded on Gilligan's Island. The restaurant also offered a French dip sandwich with au jus. I made a mental note about that selection for after we finished our round of golf. Might have to take out a loan or bum money off Bo to get it, though.

A short hallway connected the check-in counter to the restaurant on one side. Another hall connected the restaurant to a separate golf pro shop. The three spaces were laid out in a triangle. The clubhouses at many courses combined the pro shop with at least the check-in. At smaller courses, sometimes one or two people ran all three areas from a single cash register. Not at Swaying Palms. Each had their separate space.

The blonde woman we saw hitting balls on the practice range and the victim of Zach's catcalls, stood behind a counter in the pro shop, leafing through a ledger. Bo took a moment to poke around in the pro shop under the guise of looking for a new golf glove, but his true purpose was to speak to the pretty blonde. Bo didn't need a new glove because he bought a fresh one when we visited the golf store and bought me new clubs after his plane landed.

When he returned with his tail between his legs, he and Moody huddled together at a high-top table in the dining room in front of a window looking out over the practice green where two golfers were putting. Tom sat and listened to our partners discuss the events of the front nine over a beer. Moody gave Bo a scouting report of what was to come on the back nine, including the dreaded 11th hole. A pair of golf carts drove past the window, headed for the first tee. I spotted Myrtle Beach's mayor, Sid Rosen, as a rider in the lead cart. Greg Rowles was his driver. Talk about the elite.

The four in the group ahead of us were finishing their early lunch at a table near us. Zach was laughing and having a good time as only a man would after chugging what might have been his twentieth beer. Just estimating. He was having fun at the expense of poor, red-faced Archie. It sounded like Archie was down a paycheck on the betting side.

The young woman with brown hair who Moody bought the beers from on the front nine came through a door behind the bar and started talking to the bartender. Zach saw her come in and referred to her as a "Buttaface." She didn't turn in his direction, and I hoped she didn't hear him utter the hurtful comment.

His face turned red with drunken laughter as he explained his reference to his chums. "Everything about her is good, buttaface."

His friends did not laugh at the crude joke.

The guy who took our orders called our names to tell us our food was ready. Had we been here for a full lunch, the restaurant had a wait staff floating around. At least a few of the people sitting at tables were here for a late breakfast. One old codger wearing a fitted green tweed suit with professor patches on the elbows and a pocket square in the breast pocket sat with a woman who was either his gold-digging wife or daughter held a stacked bagel with lox between two hands while she used a knife and fork to cut up fruit into smaller, more petite bites. She sipped Perrier through a straw. He was dressed for the office. She was dressed for a night working in Amsterdam's Red-Light District with gold hoop earrings large enough to be rims on a compact car and a red dress cut so low that her belly button was almost visible.

She drew more than a few lecherous stares from the guys. The man paid no attention to the attention his date received. Either a man of unwavering confidence or a man with bats in the belfry.

I got up and went to retrieve our food at the same time Zach was returning an empty beer glass. As I reached for our trays on the counter, he stumbled and bumped my shoulder. He was a beefy man and had a good amount of inertia to him. He knocked me to the side so hard that I had to plant my left leg to halt my movement.

The guy behind the counter with the food said, "Whoa, buddy."

Being aware of Zach's inebriated state, I said in a tone not quite friendly, not quite annoyed, but a little sympathetic, "Take it easy there."

Zach wheeled on me. His face was red. "Watch where you're going, chief!"

Chairs in the dining area screeched as they were pushed back. I didn't look at them. My focus was on Zach.

I almost told him to watch where he was going, but I wanted to diffuse the situation before it got out of hand. I was here to play golf and have fun. Not get in a bar fight with a drunk yuppie.

"No need to get upset," I said with an outstretched hand, palm forward. "We both got here at the same time."

"No! I got here first. Whaddya doin' hittin' me like that?"

He clearly forgot what had just happened. I was the one who was moved off their center of gravity. I took a calming breath. "My apologies."

By this time, Bo was at my side. Zach glanced at him and back at me. "Don't let it happen again, plebeian."

"I'll make every effort not to." I held out a hand. "Let's just try to have fun. Cool?"

He eyed my hand but didn't shake it. "Whatever."

Bo stepped between us and grabbed the food off the counter. Zach gave me one more mean glare and stalked toward the exit where their golf clubs waited without another word. The door swung twice before stopping. The others in his group were on their way out behind him.

"Friendly chap," Bo said, handing me a hot dog and a can of beer. "I'm amazed he has any friends."

"Agreed."

This should be a *fun* back nine.

CHAPTER
SEVEN

WE HAD A repeat situation to start the second nine holes despite us taking a short break. Moody gobbled a hot dog loaded with chili, relish, and onions in one hand while holding a dewy can of Miller Lite in the other. My dog was lighter, topped with only ketchup and mustard.

We had plenty of time to eat because of a backup on the tee. The foursome two groups in front of us were up to their old escapades of searching for lost tee shots.

Zach and his friends waited on the 10th tee box for the fairway to clear. The red-faced bully supported his weight casually with the shaft of his driver while continuing to make Archie's life miserable. It seemed that, despite his insobriety, Zach made money off him in the first half of the round.

Archie, to his credit, wasn't backing down from Zach. If it were me, and I was a couple hundred dollars in the hole, I would stop playing for money. Simple as that. It didn't make sense as to why you would keep betting if you were losing to a guy drunk off his rocker. It surprised me that Zach hadn't fallen out of his golf cart at this point. One of his friends was his designated driver.

Moody watched the gambling take place with detached interest, but this was getting out of hand. I had to ask. "Are you not seeing any of this?"

His right shoulder rose and then dropped. "I am. You're wondering why I'm not stepping in."

"You would be correct."

Moody finished chewing the food. "One, I'm off duty. Besides, this goes on all the time. If I busted these guys for doing it, then we'd have to lock down on everyone. Sure, it might set an example and scare guys from doing it again, but for how long? You know how this tourism thing works. A million people come and go every week. These guys might live here." He tilted his head toward Zach. "This fella is someone not afraid to throw his money around. What's a couple hundred for a round of golf to a guy like him?"

"You know him?"

Moody wiped his mouth with a napkin. "Yeah. I've seen him around."

I chose not to comment on everything he said in his, for him, lengthy explanation. Instead, I focused on his question at the end. "So, what if he lives here? You go say something, and then he might think twice about doing it in the future."

"Do you think this is the first time he's done this?"

"Nope."

"Let's say he's been doing this for years. Maybe bet on hundreds of holes. I come out here once and say something. You don't think he'd take his chances that it wouldn't happen again? He is a gambler after all."

I looked at Zach and nodded.

"Sometimes, it's better to spend our time focusing on criminal matters elsewhere," he said.

What would Gomez have done had she been here?

"I see what you're saying," I conceded.

Behind us, Bo was regaling Tom with stories of playing at Pebble Beach, one of the most famous and picturesque golf courses in the world. Bo lived seven hours away from Pebble Beach but had played it twice.

Our attention returned to the guys in front of us after the first one teed off.

Zach pointed a club at Archie. "Whaddya say? Four hundred bucks on this hole?"

Archie took a step back. "Four hundred! That's quadruple the other holes. I don't know…"

"What are ya, chicken?" Zach folded his arms and flapped them like wings. "Bock! Bock! Bock!"

The other two mates laughed either at Archie's expense or at Zach. Might have been both. Archie cast glances at the two non-chickens, perhaps gauging what they would think of him if he backed down. The sort of machismo Zach displayed was better suited for neanderthals, but they acted like this was normal behavior.

Finally, Archie relented. "You're on."

A big grin broke out on Zach's face. "About time." He extended a hand which Archie shook. "May the best man win."

"That's right," Archie said, breaking their grasp.

Zach belly laughed with his club dangling at his side. "Of course, you have to qualify as a man first."

Archie's gloved hand balled up as though he was going to take a swing at the bigger man but didn't. "Whatever."

The 10th was a straight, short Par 4 with bunkers set up along the right side and a line of pines on the other. The handicap on the scorecard showed this to be the easiest hole on the golf course, which gave me hope. That might have been one reason Archie took

Zach up on his bet. I wondered why it was just Zach and Archie doing the wagers and not all of them.

Archie got up to the tee, driver in hand, and hit. His shot went dead straight and rolled to within a hundred and twenty yards of the hole. The other two congratulated Archie on the nice shot. I hoped mine would be half as good.

Now it was Zach's turn. He was the last in his group to tee off. His driver had the biggest club head I had ever seen. A bigger club head meant more forgiveness, longer drives, easier to hit. The US Golf Association had limits on how big a club could be, but we weren't playing in a tournament.

Zach planted his ball and tee in the ground and stood at address. Before swinging, he said to his playmates. "Watch this."

He then swung as hard as possible. I almost felt the wind coming off his club. The club head struck the ball with a loud *ping* and the ball blasted off a wooden tee that was obliterated in the process.

One of the guys whistled as they tracked the ball's flight. It started out straight.

"Come on!" Zach shouted. "Get on the green!"

Reaching the green in one hit on a 337-yard Par 4 meant a player had a chance at an eagle. A rare score on this type of hole.

As he urged the shot on, the ball went past everyone else's. At the last moment, it tailed off to the right and landed in a green side bunker.

"Wow!" Puma hat exclaimed. "That's the longest drive I've ever seen you hit."

Zach took his eyes off his ball's landing site in the distance and lowered his club. "Yeah, but it got dirty."

"No worries, mate. You're good out of the sand," the square

jaw guy said.

"Yeah," Zach sighed. "I'm sure it'll be an easy one."

Spoiler alert: it wasn't and that sent Zach over the edge.

CHAPTER
EIGHT

I MADE DOUBLE bogey on the 10th. My first shot dribbled into one of the fairway bunkers. It took three tries to get out of it. The third try might have been the best shot of my life. I'm not sure how I did it, but it rocketed out of a bunker over one-hundred and fifty yards away and stopped within seven feet of the pin. It took two putts from there.

A week from now, if I think back on this round, I wouldn't remember what I scored on this hole, but I would remember that shot from the bunker. That's the beauty of golf. I should play more.

Next came the most difficult hole at Swaying Palms. The 11th. Although I hadn't played this course before, the 11th hole's legendary reputation preceded it.

This challenging Par 5 golf hole presented a captivating sight with its dogleg to the right, bordered by charming homes and towering trees. As golfers navigated the fairway, they could appreciate the picturesque surroundings while strategizing their next shot.

The scenic beauty was further enhanced by the shimmering presence of the Intracoastal Waterway, gracefully flowing alongside the hole. Golfers needed precision and careful planning to overcome the obstacles and achieve success on this memorable and visually stunning hole.

As Moody navigated us down the cart path between the 10th

and 11th holes, he asked me, "Ever play this hole?"

"Nope."

He let out a low whistle. "It's a doozy."

The path bent to the left and as we rounded the corner, the full glory of the hole came into view. An elevated tee sloped down to a fairway with the Intracoastal running along its left side that disappeared with a sharp bend to the right. Tall pines obscured any views of the green.

We pulled to a stop a fair distance behind the group in front of us as they waited to tee off. Zach's face was beet red. Archie had a smile plastered across his, throwing little doubt on the outcome of their bet on the previous hole.

Moody paid them no mind. His gaze swept across the hole in front of us. He lifted a finger from where his hand grasped the top of the golf cart's steering wheel and pointed ahead. "What you gotta figure out is, do you get aggressive with a driver or strategize and use an iron off the tee?"

I studied the hole's layout. "Did you see the way I hit my driver on the first ten holes? Don't think 'aggressive' is a word in my golf arsenal."

He had a good chuckle at that. His finger pointed to the corner of the hole where the dogleg bent to the right. A stately home with stucco walls and Spanish roofing rose behind the trees, lining the backside of the hole. A deep, curvy bunker sat in the very corner of the dogleg.

"That is the challenge of this hole," Moody said, "and why it tempts aggressive players. Hit it just short, and you have a clear look at the island green. If the ball goes too far, then you're either sandy or in the jungle."

"No one wants to be in the jungle."

"That's right."

"The fun part is the island green. After you clear the turn in the fairway, you have to hit over water to get on the green."

I couldn't see the green from our vantage point, but a glance at the hole layout on the scorecard confirmed one of my biggest fears as a golfer: having to hit over water to reach a green. It didn't matter where I played in the past; on holes like this, I usually tended to lose a ball or two at the mercy of the water.

However, I relished the challenge. I squared my jaw. "Bring it on."

"That's the spirit." Moody released the brake and moved our cart forward as the grouping in front of us readied for their tee shots.

Archie must have been feeling his oats after a successful outcome on the last hole. He said to Zach, "Double or nothing on this hole?"

Their partners both went "Oooooo," at the same time.

Zach studied Archie. Sweat beaded on his thick brow.

"I know this is your best hole," Zach said. "I don't know why it is, but for some reason you're always good on this one."

"Ah, I see. Are you the one who's chicken now?" Archie asked.

Zach's eyebrows angled down. He turned and looked at the hole that confronted them. "You're on, loser."

They shook hands. I glanced over at Moody. He was playing Wordle on his new phone. He used a flip phone up until recently.

Puma hat went first. His tee shot sailed past the fairway but rolled short of the ominous bunker. He let out a relieved breath. Archie was up next. He set his ball on the tee, took a practice swing, and readied to hit.

As he stood over the ball, Zach said, "No pressure."

If it were me, I would have stepped back, said something to Zach about the lack of decorum, and tried again. Not Archie. He didn't react and kept his eye on the ball. The club head pulled back away from the ball, reached the top of the backswing, and came down and through the ball with a satisfying *ping* before soaring off the tee and knifing through the air. It was the best shot I had seen Archie hit yet. The ball landed in the middle of the fairway, short of the corner bunker.

Archie watched the ball land and pumped his fist.

"About as perfect as you can do here," Moody said.

Zach shook his head. "Lucky shot, I say."

Archie must have been feeling confident after that tee shot. "Let's see you top that, big boy."

Zach glared at Archie. "Whatever, pipsqueak."

All Archie did was shake his head in amusement and go stand with his mates while they waited for Zach to hit. The big man placed his tee and ball in the ground before standing straight and planning his shot. He held a 3-wood in his hand. Not the longest club in the bag, but one that was easier to hit and still get distance. Zach reconsidered, walked back to his bag, and switched out the club for the oversized driver.

"Whoa," Puma hat said. "You sure you want to do that with that bunker out there?"

Archie glared at Puma hat. Although I'm not a betting man, if I had a lot riding on this hole, I wouldn't want unsolicited advice coming from the peanut gallery.

Zach must've felt the same way, despite Puma hat offering reasonable advice. He didn't look at his mate. "Mind your business."

He stepped back and raised the ball a little higher on the tee to account for the larger clubhead. The idea was to hit the ball with the clubhead on an upward trajectory to get the ball airborne. The bigger club meant the ball needed to be farther off the ground to account for the size. Not doing so would make it difficult for Zach to get the ball high in the air.

When Zach contacted the ball, the strike echoed. The ball zoomed into the air like Tiger Woods had hit it in his prime.

"It's going over," Moody predicted beside me.

And it did.

The ball sailed over the fairway, over the bunker, and landed in the tall pines beyond. The trees separated the hole from two large houses bordering the Intracoastal.

"Welcome to the jungle," I said.

Zach screamed a word that would get censored from broadcast television and turned to glare at his mates. He pointed his club in their direction. In a threatening manner, he stated, "Not a word."

They bit their tongues.

Square jaw was the last to hit, his ball landed in the rough to the left of the fairway. He would have a clear look at the green from there, but he was a long way away.

They grabbed the handles of their pushcarts and made their way down the cart path in the direction of where their respective balls landed. Zach led the way. The other three smiled at each other behind his back. It was just as well. No need to poke the bear.

Puma hat was the furthest away from the hole, so he was the first in the group to hit his second shot. His first shot hadn't quite cleared the dogleg. The second might have a look at the green or at least the left side of it. While he selected his club, the square jaw guy found his ball and eyed his second shot.

Archie stopped at his ball and surveyed his next shot. Zach plodded around the large bunker in the corner. His head swiveled in both directions searching for his ball, hoping it had stopped before entering the woods. After a moment with no such luck, he pulled a club from his bag on the pushcart and disappeared into the woods.

Archie and Puma hat hit their second shots, stowed their clubs back in their bags, and moved up to where square jaw hit. We couldn't see where their balls landed around the sharp dogleg from our vantage point, but Archie smiled, and his partners gave him high-fives. Must have been a favorable result. Archie and Puma hat rounded the curve in the dogleg and disappeared from our view. The square jaw guy took his cart and legged it to where Zach had disappeared into the woods.

Gray clouds gathered on the horizon as we waited. No one from the group in front of us was in view. The only indication that anyone was playing was Zach's and square jaw's abandoned carts on the other side of the corner bunker. Moody, Tom, Bo, and I waited in our carts for several minutes. Well past the five-minute period to look for lost balls.

Just when I was getting ready to joke with Moody that we needed to send out a search and rescue crew, a blood-curdling scream came from where Zach and square jaw had vanished into the trees behind the bunker.

CHAPTER
NINE

MOODY TOLD TOM and Bo to stay put as he put the pedal to the metal of the golf cart. Of course, "pedal to the medal" is a relative term in the golf cart world. Our top speed was thirteen miles per hour.

An elevated tee box led to a gentle downhill slope before the shape of the hole rose as we got closer to the corner sand trap. Moody got this thing up to at least fifteen MPH going down the hill. His longish hair fluttered behind him under his hat like a superhero with a thick, graying neck cape. I gripped a handle in my right hand to keep from getting thrown from the cart over bumps in the cement cart path.

The square jaw guy who went into the trees after Zach emerged at a dead run, shouting at his friends, and gesticulating back to where he had come from. With caution, the two friends left their bags and walked toward the square jaw guy. Moody and I couldn't make out what the man was saying, but from the pale look on his face, it wasn't good.

As we approached the group, Moody slammed on the brakes, causing the cart to skid, leaving behind brown tire marks in the otherwise impeccable grass. I was sure the course manager would have the groundskeeping crew out here *toute suite* to repair the damage.

Unless the marks wound up being behind yellow police crime scene tape.

Moody sprung from his seat before the cart came to a complete stop. He didn't caution me to stay, so I hopped out and joined him in his brisk march to the bewildered men.

The men swung to look at us. Their collective jaws were on the turf.

In an authoritative manner I didn't think he was capable of, Moody held up a hand and declared, "Detective Moody. MBPD. What's going on here?"

The three men looked at each other, seeing who had the courage to speak first.

It ended up being square jaw guy. He surprised me with a Kiwi sounding accent I hadn't caught before. Not quite Australian and not British. Likely, New Zealand.

"It's our mate, Zach," the square jaw guy said. He took his hat off and revealed wavy blond hair. He had a diamond stud in one ear, and wore white, polarized sunglasses. "Someone whacked him real good."

"Is he injured? Unconscious? Dead?" Moody asked.

Square jaw sputtered, "I dunno. Looks pretty bad...he looks dead."

Moody squared his shoulders. "Were you the one who found the body?"

Square jaw gave a timid nod. "That's right."

Moody inclined his head toward the man. "Show me. You other two stay here. Call 911."

They complied. When I noticed Moody didn't include me in the command to stay outside the woods, I followed. My natural curiosity got the best of me. I hated it when that happened.

* * *

THE KIWI TOLD us his name was Gideon Ashdown. He led us into the woods, moving past where Zach had left his golf pushcart. A deer trail wound its way through thick undergrowth, a natural barrier between the course and the waterfront estates behind it. Birds twittered. Small bugs danced and jumped from the trees, bushes, and ground as we made our way. Woodsy pine trees mixed with yellow jasmine made for a pleasant smell. Clouds drifted across the sky beyond the top of the tree canopy.

Gideon gulped and called in a thin voice over his shoulder, "He's, uh, right here."

He wrung his hands most of the way. The only time they separated was when he needed to push aside a stray branch.

I held out a hand to push a branch out of the way to stay behind Moody. He put his head down and made his way through like a Sherman tank. A stray golf ball lay next to the path. As was my nature, I thought, "free ball!" but didn't bend to pick it up. You never know when something might be evidence. It might have been the ball Zach never found, but that didn't make sense. It was clearly visible on the ground between him and the edge of the woods.

We went ten, then fifteen yards into the woods. There was no way his ball would have gone this far. It had rolled over the bunker and into the woods. The ground cover along the edge would have stopped the ball.

We crossed over a thin stream. Gideon stopped and pointed a shaky finger at the ground in front of him. "H-here he is."

A leafy bush lay between where I stood and Zach. I moved around it and stood shoulder-to-shoulder with Gideon.

The back edge of the forest was a hands-breadth away. His body lay between the property lines of two grand houses. A cart path running the perimeter of the golf course separated it from the residences. A row of low, well-groomed boxwoods delineated the imaginary line between the properties and the golf course. One backyard had immaculate landscaping. The other was shoddy and overgrown. Both had pools. The one on the right had a shed at the rear on the other side of the shrubbery. Not a creature stirred at either residence. The Intracoastal streamed beyond the homes.

Moody bent over the body. His back was to us.

Zach lay belly down with his face turned in our direction. His eyes were still open as was his mouth. The club he had taken with him into the woods lay nearby. Its shaft was bent.

Gideon let out a deep breath at seeing his friend in this state. I placed a hand on his shoulder and suggested that he go back and join his friends. At this point, he didn't know if I was also a member of the police. From his vantage point, he might have thought that if I was in a pairing with Detective Moody, that I might also be a member of the MBPD. Now wasn't the time to make formal introductions.

He nodded and trudged off to rejoin his friends.

After checking for a pulse and doing a brief initial examination, Moody stood and shook his head.

I didn't need to ask. I had a flashback to the morning I discovered the body of Paige Whitaker and saw the indentation in the back of her head that caused her death. Zach had a similar mark on the side of his misshapen head.

No doubt about it. Zach was indeed dead.

Moody and I stared down at Zach's body.

I said, "Harmless fun, huh?"

He grunted.

I take back what I thought earlier. I shouldn't play golf as much.

CHAPTER
TEN

ZACH WAS THE sixth dead body I had seen in the past eighteen months. After not seeing a deceased person outside of a funeral home — besides Autumn — my entire life, to see this many this close together was almost starting to become normal. *Almost.* My hands shook, but I tried to hide that by stuffing them in my pockets.

This time was different. Zach was body number six. He was the first one I had seen moments after seeing him alive. The suddenness of his death shook me more than anything else. Yes, I had a brush with him in the clubhouse. No, I never imagined us becoming close friends. After the first couple of hours being near his presence, I felt guilty because in the back of my mind I had hoped to never see him again.

They say to be careful what you wish for.

I didn't know much about his personal life other than that he was married. One of his golf partners mentioned something about his wife back on the practice range. He wore a gold wedding band on his left hand. It was unknown at this point if he left behind kids. If he owned a business, then he might have employees who could suffer the consequences.

"What do you make of this?" Moody asked, breaking me from my trance.

A tremor shot up through my shoulders before I regained focus. He was pointing at the side of Zach's head where the killing blow had been placed. Without going into gory details, let's just say that the indicated side of his head now took on a different shape.

I looked from Zach to the bent 3-iron nearby and squished my eyebrows together. The fact that Moody asked the question of me showed that he somewhat at least trusted my untrained opinion. It was an unexpected sign of respect.

I said, "Must have been a heckuva hit to do that to him, but it wasn't done with the club laying over there."

Moody grunted and stood. "Agreed. The murder weapon is somewhere else."

The two of us were alone with Zach. A lawnmower started in the distance. A chickadee warbled nearby. The *click* of a released brake on a golf cart echoed through the trees. Wind pushed the branches around at the top of the tree canopy.

Moody took out his phone and made a call. He didn't shoo me away, much to my surprise. He spoke into the device for a moment, made another call, grunted a few more words, and returned it to his pocket.

He gazed up at the sky and rubbed his face. "I hate this part of the job, but I'll love catching whoever did this."

What he said rang true. How would a person ever enjoy seeing a murder victim?

"I've found in the cases I've been around that bringing closure to the families of the victims is the only positive. Makes me feel like I've done something to somehow help them." I pointed at Zach. "I know how his family is going to feel when they learn of this, and I don't want them to have to wonder about how he died for any longer than they need to."

He studied me. After a moment, he said, "Like with Autumn."

I tried to fight it but couldn't. A tear formed in the corner of my eye. "Yeah, like Autumn."

He patted my elbow like a kind uncle might do but didn't reply to my comment. He understood. Getting back to the topic at hand, he nodded at the body. "Know who he is?"

"I don't. Didn't you say you'd seen him around?" I wiped away the tear.

"Yeah. Ever hear of Lawson Luxury International?"

"The highfalutin real estate company?"

"That's the one."

"I've heard of it. They only sell homes with values over a million dollars and do it all over the world."

Moody pointed at the body. "Meet Zacharias Lawson. The owner of Lawson Luxury International."

I let out a long, low whistle. "Dang."

"That's putting the fallout from this nicely."

Beyond the head trauma, there weren't any other visible marks indicating foul play visible from my vantage point.

Moody was reading my mind. "Looks like someone just came up and whacked him."

I pointed over my shoulder. "Could it have been Gideon?"

"When would he have done that?"

As the foursome played this hole prior to Zach's death, Moody had been more interested in his phone. I said, "Gideon went into the woods after Zach to try and help him find his ball."

Moody grunted as was his habit. "How long were they in there together?"

"A minute or two."

"Did you see what direction they went after entering these

woods?"

"I didn't."

"What about the other guys?"

"They had already hit their shots and rounded the dogleg. They were out of my sight after that."

He pointed at the asphalt track beyond the trees. "One of them could have gone in and came back along this cart path."

"It's possible." The reason this cart path was here, I surmised, was to give access for the groundskeeping crew to service the greenspaces during the day without having to bother any golfers. A thoughtful addition.

"Hmph."

Footsteps trampled through the undergrowth, heading in our direction. That brought a question to my mind.

"Over here!" Moody shouted.

While whoever it was followed the detective's voice toward us, I asked, "Wouldn't Zach have heard the would-be murderer coming?"

We listened as our visitors came near. Dead, crisp leaves and pine needles being trampled. Branches being pushed aside causing *whooshing* sounds.

"The undergrowth is thick on either side of this deer track. Coulda been hiding."

"True," I concurred as the person pushed through the trail and came into view.

It was the mayor of Myrtle Beach, Sid Rosen. His golf partner, Greg Rowles, was nowhere in sight.

He turned to Moody. "I came as soon as you called. What happened?"

Moody pointed down at the body behind us. We stood apart to

allow Rosen a good look—although I'm not sure why he would want to. The mayor uttered a curse under his breath. His eyebrows furrowed. Lips tightened. Then, "Is that Lawson?"

"Yes, sir."

Another curse word followed, this one not under his breath. "What happened?"

Moody pointed at the golf course beyond and the dreaded 11th hole. "His tee shot went over the bunker and came into the trees. He entered the woods to search for the ball. One of his partners, Gideon Ashdown, entered the woods to search for the ball after he hit his shot. A minute later, Gideon screamed and said he found Lawson like this."

The detective maneuvered in front of Zach to spare the mayor from having to view the body any more than necessary.

"I'm familiar with Ashdown," Rosen said. "Owns a surfboard company. Australian."

"New Zealand," Moody corrected, "but close enough."

"Think it was him who did it?"

To this point, Rosen hadn't acknowledged my presence. He stood stiffly and avoided eye contact with me.

"He was spooked," I said.

Now, he turned to me. "Here we go again, Clark. How do you keep getting mixed up in these things?"

"I wish I didn't, sir."

He crossed his arms and regarded me with a strained smile. "Goodness, you've been through a lot in the past couple of years."

"You're telling me, Mr. Mayor."

Rosen held up a hand. "Please, save the formalities. It's Sid. You've done some remarkable things for this city, helping the police and these victims' families. Autumn would have been proud." The mayor scratched his clean-shaven chin and searched my eyes long enough to make me feel uncomfortable.

His words hit a soft spot deep within me. "Thank you."

Before running for mayor, Rosen had been a prominent attorney at a prestigious law firm in Myrtle Beach. Many wondered why he would run for the position with already having a full-time and surely well-paying position. He answered that question in the leadup to election day, stating that he was born and raised in Myrtle Beach and took considerable pride in the city and wanted to increase its standing as a world-class tourist destination.

In his time on the job, he had done just that.

Returning his attention to Moody, Rosen asked, "Have you called your partner yet?"

Moody pursed his lips. "Nope. Gomez is outta town at that conference."

"Oh, right," Rosen said.

"Two others are with her there, so we're a little short staffed this weekend."

Rosen glanced at the body behind Moody's feet. "Good timing."

We waited for Rosen to do or say something. Moody tapped his foot on the ground and put both hands on his hips. I shared his agitation. Whoever did this might be getting farther away while the flies would be coming closer as the body lay there in this heat while Rosen stood there.

Finally, he snapped to a decision.

Rosen glanced at Moody, opened his mouth once, closed it, and then said to me, "Okay, Clark. You're officially on the case."

CHAPTER
ELEVEN

I BLINKED RAPIDLY while processing what the mayor had just said. When the words wouldn't compute, I said, "What do you mean?"

Rosen glanced at Moody who showed only an eagerness to return to his investigation of the body.

"As mayor, I have a certain amount of say in police matters. I hold certain privileges, such as the ability to hire special investigators to help on police cases. Normally, those people are from SLED or the FBI, but you're different."

"That's what my mom always told me."

Rosen gave a tight grin and continued, "Both of us know how much you've helped the police in the past year. For someone untrained, you've done splendid work."

Moody gave a favorable grunt. "Got us out of some tough spots."

"Right," Rosen said. "You're turning into a regular Jessica Fletcher. Murders seem to pop up wherever you go."

He referenced the mystery writer character in the show *Murder, She Wrote*, played by Angela Lansbury, who lived in a quaint coastal northeastern town by the name of Cabot Cove, where murders occurred every week. The residents of the town never noticed that their friends and neighbors were dropping like flies.

"I'd rather they didn't," I said.

"Definitely," Rosen agreed. "You've been riding with Moody

all morning. From what I can gather, you witnessed and saw everything he did with the victim beforehand. His partner is out of town, and you've helped to solve, what, five murders?"

"Eight," I corrected. But who's counting?

The mayor's eyebrows arched in tandem. "Goodness. That's more than I figured. What I'm getting at is, we need your help on this, and I have the power to hire you as a consultant for the case."

Moody grunted. "Without asking the police chief?"

"I'm sure Miller will go along with it," he said.

Sue Miller was recently selected by the mayor as the new chief, replacing the retired Sharon Kluttz as the head of the police department.

When I didn't comment, Rosen said, "We'll pay you, of course, for your time and trouble."

The truth was, I didn't want to be paid. Zach had a wife, possible family, and business he'd left behind. All those people would want answers as to why he was murdered. Autumn entered my mind while looking at Rosen as he awaited my response.

He mentioned the Angela Lansbury character a moment ago, but what he was asking was straight out of the Nelson DeMille novel, *Plum Island*. In that one, the hilarious character John Corey had been hired to help solve the murders of two researchers and payment had been offered.

Thinking of Corey's response, I answered, "If you must pay me, I'll do it for one dollar."

Rosen puckered out his bottom lip and stuck out a hand. "That's admirable of you."

I shook it, sealing the deal.

He traipsed back through the forest a moment later after giving

Moody last-minute instructions.

As I watched him go, I had the distinct feeling that I was about to get in way over my head.

The good thing was, in the past year, I'd learned to swim.

CHAPTER
TWELVE

MOODY MADE TWO calls. First, he called the clubhouse and spoke to the superintendent, Warren Boyette, informing him of the murder and to shut down the course. Boyette had no qualms in doing so, not that he had a choice. It would be unbecoming of such a prestigious golf course to have golfers play around police tape strung across the fairway on their signature hole.

His second call was to police headquarters. Course rangers set about going from hole-to-hole, informing golfers of the course's sudden closure. During this time, approaching sirens sounded in the distance. The golfers were allowed to finish the holes they were on but were told to return to the clubhouse, and to avoid driving past the 11th hole. They would be given rainchecks to return at a later date. They weren't allowed to give a reason for the closure.

Moody had the course rangers instruct the golfers in the groups ahead of Zach and behind us to go to the clubhouse dining room to await questioning as soon as they were done. Moody instructed Boyette to close off the men's and women's locker rooms as well. It wasn't apparent to me at the time why he issued that order. I'd find out later.

Within minutes, a dozen police cruisers and two Suburbans entered the property. The coroner's van followed close on their heels. Officers locked down the clubhouse and grounds, holding every employee for questioning.

With the perimeter cart path outlining the golf course, it made for easy access to the back of the 11th hole. It was possible that anyone immediately ahead or behind Zach's grouping had snuck back and did the deed.

While all of this occurred, Moody told me to go back where we had entered the woods and tell Zach's partners what was going to happen. Not that I knew the exact protocols, but as they say, fake it until you make it.

As I pushed through the last of the branches and emerged back out onto the course, two of Zach's grouping raised their gaze from staring at the ground. They all seemed shell-shocked. Gideon's eyes were rimmed with tears. Archie's mouth hung open in disbelief. Puma hat, whose name I didn't know at this point, had his arms crossed, head bowed, and eyes closed.

I placed myself in their shoes. This entire crazy string of getting involved in murder investigations began when I discovered the body of my friend, Paige Whitaker. I understood the emotions these men were going through. Archie's hands shook with fright. Puma hat's eyes were closed tight. He pinched the bridge of his nose. His lips moved in what appeared to be a silent prayer. Gideon had a befuddled look on his face. I was sure I appeared the same way the first time I met Detectives Moody and Gomez.

I approached them and gave them an update. They took it in silence, not knowing what to say. Bo and Tom had driven up and parked beside mine and Moody's cart. I gestured for them to come to us.

While they climbed from the cart and navigated around the sand trap, it might be useful to break the ice. I said to Zach's partners,

"My name is Clark Thomas." The next words out of my mouth felt very odd to say, "I'm a consultant with the Myrtle Beach Police Department on this murder investigation."

This caused Gideon to start sobbing outright. Archie's eyes welled as he put an arm around Gideon's shoulders. The third guy drew closer as well as a tear started streaming down his face. Reality comes at you fast, and the word "murder" tends to speed it up.

Bo and Tom came and stood beside the other three. They had heard Gideon's screams. A course ranger's voice echoed via a megaphone or some other voice amplification device through the trees, giving instructions to golfers to finish up and head for the clubhouse. Puffy clouds grew tall and gray in the distance beyond the Intracoastal. A foreboding sign.

I took a breath and said to the two men I hadn't met, "I already have Gideon's name. What are yours?"

Puma hat started to hold out a hand but pulled it back. Up close he looked vaguely familiar. Wavy dark hair poked out of the back of his hat in a ponytail. "Percy Blythe."

I'd already heard the other guy's name from eavesdropping on their betting conversations, but for appearance's sake I let him say, "Archie. Archie Bristol."

He did offer his hand, which I shook. I didn't notice any blood on his bare left hand. A golf glove still covered his right one.

I tried to think of what Detective Gina Gomez might ask in this situation. Moody's questioning likely involved a high level of grunting. The move here would be to not try to influence what they said. Let them speak with little direction from me. If I had to fill in blanks, then I would ask a direct question. This would likely be a quick round of questioning to gain a picture of what happened when Zach and the gang disappeared from my view. We'd go back and speak to each of these three in-depth later. The important thing for me to do now was to pay close attention. That way if one said something contrary to what they told me now when we spoke again, I could call them out on it.

At this point, I wasn't sure if they'd seen Moody and I trailing them in the group behind them. If they had, then they might believe that we overheard their gambling conversations. If not, I wanted to see if they divulged that bit of information. I needed to pay close attention to their body language. If their hands shook, for example, was it because they were rattled over Zach's death and being questioned in relation to the crime, or because they'd just killed one of their friends? I had to remind myself that, odds were, the killer was standing in front of me. Archie's hands had been shaking when I returned from the woods.

After watching them all morning, I would have put money on Archie caving Zach's head in after being antagonized and berated by the dead man. Not to mention it seemed like Archie had lost a good deal of money to Zach. Yet, Archie was in a place to win back a huge part of it with many holes left to keep doing so.

It would be helpful to know if the betting today was a one-time thing, or if this was an activity this foursome participated in on a regular basis.

They waited for my first question. Instead of a question, I said, "Tell me what happened."

Couldn't get much vaguer in leading the conversation than that.

Percy led first. He left out the whole illegal betting part. "Uh, Zach hit his drive over the bunker." He pointed over my shoulder at the woods. "The ball went in there, I think."

He turned to Gideon for confirmation.

"Yeah," the Kiwi agreed. "He and I entered through this little gap right here. We split up. He went left. I went right. I heard him shout something."

"What did he say?" I asked.

His forehead tried to wrinkle, but a healthy amount of Botox kept it from moving. "First, there was, like, a shriek of surprise."

"Like he had been hit over the head?"

"No. Maybe. I don't know." Gideon shoved his hands in his pockets. Was that to keep me from seeing them shake? "It was odd. Zach shouted. Said something like, "How dare you?" A moment later, he cried out again, but it was from farther away."

"Show me."

I told the others to remain where they were and had Gideon lead me through the trees. We entered the tree line, shoving stray branches aside to make our way deeper. He moved with the ease of a high-level athlete.

We reached a point in the trail where it diverged.

"Here is where we split up. He went that way," Gideon said and pointed to the left facing the trail from the golf course. It meandered along a narrow stream in both directions. The perimeter cart path and private estates ran parallel to the sliver of water. Beyond that lay the Intracoastal.

With this being my second time treading this ground, it was becoming familiar. I grew up with a thick patch of woods behind our house in Southern Ohio. Bo and I used to go exploring often with other friends from the neighborhood. Our adventures sometimes got us in trouble, but boys will be boys. Traipsing through the woods was a familiar experience with the smells and sounds and topography.

"Where do you think Zach was when you first heard him?" I asked.

Gideon stroked his chin and narrowed his eyes back along the path. "This way."

I followed him fifteen feet or so deeper. He scanned back in the direction where he would have been standing when he heard the shout and then where we stood.

"Right about here, I think."

My head bobbed as I examined the area. A cluster of bushes and ground cover bordered one side of the path. The sun shimmered through the trees above our heads. A piney scent tickled my nose. Birds chirped. Squirrels stirred.

On the ground a few feet away was the golf ball I noticed when Moody and I first came in this direction. I brushed past Gideon and bent to examine it. The dimpled ball lay on top of a bed of pine needles. The brand of the ball was tilted away, but enough of the letters were visible to know what type it was. It was a Srixon.

I glanced up at Gideon. "Did you happen to notice what kind of ball Zach was playing today?"

"He only plays Titleists."

He made the statement in the present tense. I didn't have the heart to tell him that Zach would forever have played Titleists in the past. Too soon.

At first glance, it appeared fresh. Like it had only been hit a few times and had a short life from its original owner. I resisted the impulse to pick it up and put it in my pocket. Finding such a good ball in the woods was like finding gold for a golfer. It might be a random lost ball, but I would point it out when forensics got here.

The ground a few feet away had been recently trod, and not

from where Moody and I came through earlier. As I examined it, the few leaves of grass popped back into place, slightly bent from the way they had stood a few minutes ago. Marks in the dirt indicated indentations left from the cleats in the bottom of golf shoes. The small holes were fresh and led in the direction of Zach's body. I tilted my head and ran an eye down the path. Zach lay fifteen feet away from the ball. Moody was bent over the body. He didn't see us.

Another set of tracks stopped several feet short of the body. I pointed at them and asked Gideon, "Those yours?"

His square jaw fell open. "Y-yeah. They are."

"Thanks." They were too far away from the body for Gideon to have hit Zach with the club, but forensics would tell that tale.

Various broken branches lay along the path. Like a deer or bull had stormed through it. Or a big man like Zach.

Gideon watched me without a word. He didn't dare move so as not to disturb the crime scene.

I stood and instructed Gideon to return to his mates and stay put once there. He complied and moved off through the brush.

The crime began to form a picture in my head. Zach and Gideon entered the woods and split up to search for his ball. Zach got to this point, or somewhere hereabouts, when something happened to cause him to yell, "How dare you?" Then he ran through the woods toward his antagonist only to be met with a club upside the head.

I followed the path back to the body, being careful not to step on any existing tracks. Moody didn't acknowledge me. He was in the process of rolling Zach over on his back. Bits of leaves, pine needles, and grass were stuck to the blood-matted side of his head.

I cringed and looked away. The medical examiner would tell us more after his or her examination.

At present, I was more concerned with how the crime took place. Once the hit was made, Zach couldn't have gone far. I pictured him getting whacked and falling to the ground like a sack of potatoes.

The deformation on his head made it appear like the club struck him at an angle. It wouldn't make sense for him to allow the attacker to walk up in front of him and swing the club like a baseball bat and hit him with such a solid blow. He was big enough that he might have moved or deflected any would-be blow.

Which meant the attack had to have come from behind.

Near Zach's feet were two pine trees close together. Bushes covered the bottoms of their trunks. I padded around to the other side and discovered what I already figured would be there.

A patch of recently beaten down ground where the killer may have hidden.

The implications turned everything on its head. And we were just getting started.

CHAPTER
THIRTEEN

A FAINT TRAIL led to the hiding place, leading away from the course in the direction of the cart path, homes, and Intracoastal. I followed it to where it ended at the cart path. This provided several possibilities. If I were Archie or Percy trying to run away from Zach's body as fast as possible to get back into an unsuspicious position, then I would follow the path of least resistance. A smooth patch of asphalt would be that.

I put a hand over my brow to shade the sun to closely observe the two homes in this area of the golf course. They weren't true waterfront homes. A street lay in between the front of the houses and the Intracoastal. Their backyards faced the tree line at the edge of the course.

There weren't any visible security cameras. The grounds of the house to my left, the last house on the street, were unkempt and overgrown, suggesting either lazy homeowners or vacancy. The home on the right was the opposite. The grounds were immaculate with freshly mown grass, trimmed bushes, and flowering vegetation. A poster image for *Better Homes & Gardens*.

No one was visible at either location. Moody and I would knock on their doors later to learn if they were home and saw anything.

My first inclination upon discovering Zach's body was that one of his partners with murderous intentions had found an opportunity to club him over the head when no one was watching. Having the perimeter cart path nearby gave them the excuse that the murderer may have come from there. Which was also plausible.

Zach and Gideon disappeared into the woods after Percy and Archie rounded the corner of the dogleg and moved out of our sight. Would one of them have had the time to plow through the woods, come back to the corner, and hide in the bushes while waiting for Zach? What made him call out before pounding through to the eventual spot of his demise?

Percy's physical appearance suggested a man in good shape. Archie possessed a bit of pudginess, suggestive of a dad bod and desk job.

The problem with all of that, as I replayed the events that happened just before Zach's death in my mind, was it didn't seem like there would be enough time between Percy and Archie rounding the corner and hearing Zach's scream for them to have circled back unless the plan was to come back after they were out of view in case someone was watching from the tee box like I had.

Which left Gideon.

Which seemed implausible as well. There was a visible trail leading in the direction he pointed to where he said he and Zach split up. It's possible he made that part up and followed Zach. I didn't recall Gideon having a club with him. He would have had to get Zach's club from him somehow to be able to use it as a weapon. Gideon could have told Zach he found his ball and needed to use his club to hook it out from under a bush or something. At first glance, it had appeared that Zach had plowed through the woods like a juggernaut, but near where his body ended up, there didn't seem to be signs of a struggle. Only the blow to the head. Again, this is where the report from the medical examiner would come in handy.

I struggled to imagine how that scenario would have played out with Gideon murdering Zach with the scant evidence we had at this point.

There was another possibility beyond one of the three members of the group being the murderer. Someone else wanted Zach dead and knew when and where to find him.

I reentered the woods and rambled back to the other side where the golfers waited.

Gideon chewed on a thumbnail. Archie's eyes were moist with tears as he stared into space. Percy was looking at his cell phone.

Here was an example of not knowing the exact police protocol. If a witness was told to wait for questioning outside of an interrogation room, were they allowed to do what Percy was doing? I almost told him to give me the phone, but he put it away after a final tap on the screen.

"Sorry," he said. "Had to send our nanny a message telling her I might be late in arriving."

I waved a hand. "No worries. Just keep the phone in your pocket until we're done. I'll ask detective Moody about it, Percy, but we might have to confiscate your phone to make sure you weren't messaging a potential co-conspirator."

Percy's mouth fell open as his mates took a step away from him. Bo and Tom had returned to their golf cart and were having a conversation. A stray seagull squawked overhead.

He held out a placating hand. He pleaded, "No, sorry. Honest. That's what I was doing."

"We'll see," I said.

He was on edge, and the gravity of the situation fell upon Archie's and Gideon's shoulders. Now was the time to ask probing questions.

I stepped forward and centered myself in front of the three. "Have you four golfed together before?"

Percy was the first to speak, possibly out of feeling a need to redeem himself after looking suspicious with the phone. "Yeah, we play every week on this day and time. Have a standing tee time."

"What happens if one of you is sick or on vacation?"

"Then it's just the three of us," Archie said.

"Do you ever invite someone to fill in when one is going to be absent?"

Gideon scratched his arm. "Nah, we're old fraternity mates from uni."

"Ah. Where was college?"

Archie hooked a finger over his shoulder as though the college were directly behind him. "Out here at Coastal."

He meant Coastal Carolina University. My alma mater. None of them looked familiar, but they seemed a few years older than me, and it was a mid-sized school with few thousands of students when I had attended, about double that now.

"Always nice to talk to a fellow Chant," I said. Although it wasn't nice in this case. The Chanticleer, a proud and fierce rooster, was the mascot of Coastal Carolina University.

"How often did Zach hit it over that bunker?" I asked.

Archie glanced at Gideon and Percy before answering, "Eight times out of ten, he'd either hit it in or over. Zach wasn't the type of golfer to play the smart shot and lay up. He lived life on the edge, and his golf game mirrored that."

"Yeah," Percy said, "Zach was like a matador. Always grabbing life by the horns." He choked up a little, covered his mouth, and turned away to hide the tears after referring to Zach in the past tense.

He stood in between the other two. They rubbed his back in sympathy. Percy's sobs caused Gideon's eyes to well. Archie rubbed Percy's back but was staring at a spot on the ground behind me. Not at anything specifically. It was a look of concentration. Like he was trying to work something out in his head. I let him focus and gave them a few seconds to mourn.

Percy scanned over my shoulder in the distance. I turned to see a trio of golf carts, led by the course ranger, rush through the trees and into the open. The rear two carts were loaded with police officers. Both had one driver and passenger. The third cart had an additional officer standing in the well on the back of the cart where golfers normally stowed their clubs. His head poked up over the cart's roof. It was Officer Dame, who I had encountered twice in recent months.

The commotion of the police arriving brought the three men to attention. Bo and Tom also climbed out of their carts to watch the procession come toward us.

Two carts rolled around the bunker in the grass and stopped near my cart. The lead cart with the ranger kept moving. He tipped his hat and continued on his way. His mission had only been to usher the police to our location. Dame hopped off the back of one cart, alleviating the suspension. The cart bobbed now that it was lighter.

The driver was Officer Battles. He was a few inches taller than Dame and about the same bulk but made almost entirely of muscle.

He whipped his head around to glare at his partner.

"Dang, Dame. Take it easy," Battles said, rubbing the back of neck. "Give a man whiplash jumping off like that."

Dame laughed. "Sure." His tone was not serious.

I didn't recognize the officer in the passenger seat. She was young, thin, wore reflective sunglasses, and had dark hair pulled back into a tight bun. Most of her gear was stored in pockets on the front of her light-duty body armor. The other officers were older and wore what I thought was a more traditional style belt with their equipment attached. She didn't smile at the exchange as she climbed from the cart.

Officers Nichols and O'Brien climbed from the other cart. They were the first officers on the scene after I had found Paige Whitaker's body. It seemed like that happened years ago, but only a little over a year had passed.

"Fancy seeing you again," said Dame after they stood in front of us. Nichols and the new face had gone off to the tree line where she began stringing up yellow "DO NOT CROSS" crime scene tape. She held plastic posts under her arm as she ran the tape from one spot to my right, out to an area around Zach's abandoned golf clubs on the pull cart, and around to the other side where the left boundary of the course ended. She used the stakes to guide the tape around the clubs.

We stood beyond the new crime scene boundary.

Dame looked at the three suspects and then eyed me up and down. "You keep showing up like a bad penny every time someone gets killed in this town."

I knew from watching the news that I wasn't around *every* murder that occurred in Myrtle Beach. Just more than I would have liked. A number I would have liked to have been zero.

Battles and O'Brien came and stood beside Dame. Battles tilted his head at the three suspects (at least they all were in my book, at this point). "These the guys?"

"Yeah," I said. "They were the victim's playing partners."

"Understood," Battles said and stepped closer to them. He was bigger than the three golfers combined, and the intimidation factor of seeing such a burly officer in uniform while wearing body armor became evident when they shrunk away from him as one.

Dame hooked a thumb on his duty belt, causing the holstered taser on his left side to shift. A Glock hung off his right hip next to a pair of handcuffs. "Word came down when we got the call that you've been contracted by the mayor to work this case." He glanced at his partner then back at me. "That true?"

"It is," I responded.

O'Brien whistled. "They must be payin' you well."

I grinned thinking about the handshake agreement between Mayor Rosen and me. "Not as much as you might think."

We stepped to the side out of earshot from the suspects where I brought them up to speed on the circumstances surrounding Zach's murder and how I came to be involved. When I finished, the three officers huddled together. Nichols and the newbie rejoined them with a half-used roll of police tape tucked underneath her arm. Of the four, Dame seemed to be the one in charge.

The other four officers obeyed whatever command he issued and then stalked off into the woods. Dame came, touched my elbow, and drew me away from Bo, Tom, and the cluster of suspects. I glanced at Bo. He wore a stiff smile, and his bottom lip puckered out. It almost seemed like admiration for his kid brother. I didn't dwell on impressing the impossible-to-impress Bo. I had a case to solve.

Dame inquired, "Were you engaging in investigative detention with these men?"

The term rattled around my brain once or twice before I understood the jargon. "You mean like when you and your partner tackled me on the Boardwalk and questioned me as to why I was chasing a pretty blonde?"

I referred to the time I helped Shelly Garland try to find her fiancé Brian before all that ended on the dock of a cruise line in Charleston. Another brief image sprung to mind of Gomez pinning me against the glass of the passenger side door of her car in an all-too -brief moment of passion on the way home that day.

My eyes closed as I cleared away that thought. Tried to, at least.

Dame helped. "Yeah, that's what I mean. Learn anything useful?"

"Not yet. I really was just getting started."

"Okay then," he said, and turned to face the suspects. "Let's make a bust. Should be simple."

The outcome proved to be anything but simple.

CHAPTER
FOURTEEN

OTHER VOICES ECHOED through the trees from the direction of Zach's body. The crime scene technicians must have arrived via the outside cart path. If Gomez's fiancé were here, what would it be like to work with him? I didn't have a good impression of him at our first meeting down at City Hall before the commendation ceremony following the deaths at Tidal Creek case.

He seemed too polished. Too slithery. Like a snake. The last time I had that impression of someone upon first seeing them was when I met my new friend and business consultant, Chris McInally. He went on to prove that you couldn't judge a book by its cover. Who I'd assumed was distrustful at first sight ended up being one of the nicest and most charitable human beings I've ever met.

Gomez had to find something endearing in Lucien to want to marry him. Maybe it was his devilish name or chiseled jaw that I didn't like. A little voice in the back of my head suggested jealousy, but I chose to ignore it.

I would find out soon enough if Lucien was here. Zach's partners were waiting. Dame and I returned to where they stood. Now that they'd had a while to process their friend's demise, they were more composed. There were two lines of thought about having time to gather their stories. Directly after the killing, the murderer might have been shaken enough to make a mistake during questioning by either telling a lie he couldn't wiggle out of or outright tipping his bloody hand. Now that whatever surge of endorphins the murderer might have had coursing through their veins after the slaying dissipated, they might have a clearer head. I preferred suspects to be off guard.

When Dame and I reached the men, I picked up where I left off. "You said that Zach had an aggressive nature. Did that extend to the gambling?"

Dame shifted his weight beside me. I hadn't mentioned this part to him. He went, "Hmm."

Percy and Archie's mouths fell open. Gideon didn't flinch. "What gambling?"

"Betting on the holes," I said.

Gideon shook his head. "Not sure what you're talking about, mate."

"Come on," I said. "Don't play dumb. I was in the group behind you all. I heard it when we had to wait behind you on the tee boxes. Zach and Archie had been going back and forth the entire morning. Archie, I believe you won the hole before this?"

His eyebrows raised. "I did."

"Did that anger Zach?"

"Yeah," Percy answered. "Zach thinks he's better than everyone, especially Archie. He got hot-headed over the smallest of things."

"Was Zach the best of you four?" Dame asked.

"Nah," Archie said, pointing a thumb at Gideon. "He is."

Gideon didn't gloat or change his expression. He must have been confident in Archie's assertion.

I asked, "And Zach bet double or nothing on this one?"

This time, it was Archie's Adam's apple that moved up and

down. "He did."

"How long has the wagering been going on?"

They glanced at each other, waiting for one to answer. Gideon took the lead as he had mostly to this point. "Not sure how long, exactly. A couple years, I reckon."

Percy and Archie nodded in confirmation.

"It's not like we're the only ones," Percy said.

I shifted my stance. "What do you mean?"

"It's this course," Archie said. "Most of the members here do it."

"Yeah," Gideon agreed. "It's a well-known fact that if you play a round with another member of the club, money is going to change hands."

"You know that's illegal, right?" Dame asked.

"Yeah," Gideon said, "but there are politicians and cops who play here. *They* all gamble."

After seeing them earlier, I wondered if the mayor and Greg Rowles were in on the gambling. Rowles had a spotless image in the Grand Strand. If he participated, it would be a bad look. Their actions didn't upset Moody, causing me to wonder if he and his buddy, Tom, had the occasional friendly wager with each other.

"Interesting," Dame said.

I said to Archie, "Who was winning the round up to this hole?"

"Zach was," he answered.

"How far in the hole were you?" I asked.

His lips puckered as he did the mental math and before revealing the embarrassing total to his friends. "About thirty-five hundred dollars."

I whistled. "That's a lot of dough to wager on one round of golf." I paused. "Wait a second. I thought one of you said at the start of the round that your usual wager was $100 per hole?"

Archie's eyes glazed over. "Uh, yeah. Normally."

"What happened to run up the number?"

When Archie looked at his friends for help, they didn't come to his defense. I wouldn't have either. "We, uh, raised the stakes a couple times during the round."

I raised my brows. "I wish I had that much money to throw around."

"That's the thing," Archie said. "I don't. Of everyone here, I have to admit that I probably have the least amount of money."

Percy and Gideon didn't react. They must have known already.

"What do you do?" I asked Archie.

"I own a landscaping business," he answered. "We hold contracts to some of the mega neighborhoods in the area, like Clear Pond, the Dunes, and Berkshire Forest."

Those were, in fact, three very nice areas in Myrtle Beach. Clear Pond was farther inland. Berkshire Forest was big enough that it had its own elementary school, and Dunes was by the ocean near the Golden Mile.

If Archie says he didn't have the money to wager, two questions sprung to mind. I asked him, "If you're not as well off as your friends and other members here, why do you do it?"

"To not look poor in front of Zach and the others," Archie answered matter-of-factly.

I turned to Dame. "I think his definition of 'poor' is relative, don't you?"

"I wish I had thirty-five dollars to throw around, much less thirty-five hundred."

"Me too," I said.

This exchange, I hoped, would go to show these affluent men that, even though they were wealthier, they still had to answer to me and that Dame had the power to snap the cuffs on them and haul them to jail. Even the playing field.

When they didn't give a comment, I kept going. I'd focus on Archie later when we were in private. Which led to the second question that had sprung to my mind that I wanted to learn the answer to sooner rather than later.

"If you didn't have the money," I said, "I can't imagine that Zach would let you owe it to him. Where were you going to get that sort of money? It's possible you may have lost more than that by the end of the round."

Archie scratched the side of his chin. "I can dig it up from various places if need be."

I would take him at his word. For now. "In being near you all at various times this morning, it seemed that Zach liked to antagonize you."

"He did," Archie confessed. "Off the course, he was an okay guy, but on it? He was a different person."

"Why do you think that was?"

He jerked his shoulder. "I'm not sure what the other guys think, but out here, we're on our own, away from society. He didn't have to play nice. He could be his true self."

"I've known Zach the longest," Percy said. "Zach was a star soccer player in college until he blew out his knee. Being the big man on campus gave him a big head. Bigger head, that is. Modesty was never Zach's strong suit, except for when he engaged in charitable activities."

"He might have been a big head and been more well off than any of us," Gideon said, "but he had this generous side to him unlike anyone I've ever met."

Percy said, "Even had his own foundation where he raised awareness for autism."

"He has an autistic son," Archie added.

"Ah." I leveled my gaze at Archie. "Some might consider picking up a quick debt totaling in the thousands of dollars to someone as motive, especially if said someone saw it as taking it away from his foundation. You know. So, you wouldn't have to pay up."

Archie paled. It was obvious he hadn't thought of that. "Whoa, whoa. You're not suggesting that I did this, are you? I wouldn't place the bets with Zach if I was aware that he was using charity money to cover his bets."

"I'm not." I casually stuck my hands in my pockets. "All I'm suggesting is that you have an obvious and immediate reason to have done it."

His mouth moved, not knowing what to say. Percy and Gideon watched him closely.

To ease Archie's mind, I said, "Before it happened, you and Percy rounded the dogleg. Either of you would've had to have made a beeline across the fairway when you were out of sight from the tee box to reach him in time to bang him over the head and trace the beeline back to where you were by the time Detective Moody and I came to check out the situation. You didn't seem out of breath when I first met you, and neither Percy nor Gideon saw you do that, so that makes it difficult in my mind to pin it on you."

His shoulders relaxed. "Whew."

I held up a finger. "That doesn't mean you're off the hook. Crazier things have happened."

"Thank you," Archie said.

I turned to Percy. "Same goes for you. Of course, all three of you could have been in cahoots."

This time, it was Percy and Gideon's turn to squirm. They started to protest, but Dame held out both hands. "Don't even start. Keep your cool. They'll get this sorted out." He turned to me. "Are you done questioning them for now?"

I squinted at the trio and thought about what Gomez might do for a moment, knowing that I had the police department's backing. To Dame, I said, "Take them back to the clubhouse and have them give you their clothes."

"Our clothes? *Why?*" Archie demanded.

"Yeah." Gideon pulled at the hem of his shirt. "These are all I have with me, mate."

"You got money," Dame countered. "Save yourself the embarrassment of leaving here in forensics gowns and buy yourself a nice Swaying Palms t-shirt and pair of shorts from the pro shop."

I stifled a laugh.

"Hey," Archie protested, "I have clothes in my locker I can change into."

"No, you don't," I said. "Everything in that locker is potential evidence now."

Archie's face turned redder.

Percy had a more level head and spoke for his friends. "No problem. We're happy to comply. I'm an attorney. I understand your reasoning."

"I don't understand the reasoning," Archie said to his friend.

"Because," I said, "I want to have your clothes tested for blood at the crime lab. If we find blood on any, you're going to have a lot of explaining to do."

CHAPTER
FIFTEEN

I INSTRUCTED DAME and O'Brien to take them back to the clubhouse. Officer Nichols listened, disappeared into the woods, and reappeared three minutes later with two crime scene technicians. One was Kevin who I vaguely remembered from Myrtle Beach State Park's beach the morning of Connor West's death. The other was a stranger to me. She had short, puffy red hair, tinted glasses, and introduced herself as Ann.

O'Brien would watch while they bought new clothes. Ann would bag the clothes they were now wearing while Kevin would confiscate their golf bags and hold them for evidence.

I had no clue how long I would have to remain at the golf course, so Tom volunteered to drive Bo back to our parents' place.

After Bo, Tom, and the suspects left, I was alone by the bunker on the 11th hole. Shouts and voices came through the trees from the direction of Zach's body. Clouds thickened in the sky. Birds chirped. The smell of fresh cut grass permeated the air.

If it weren't for the dead body, the muted voices of communication, and the crime scene tape, this might have been a peaceful moment enjoying the outdoors. There was something about being on a golf course that soothed the soul. I breathed it in and centered myself, trying to play out the scene in my mind.

From where Moody and I had been parked behind the tee box

up on the ridge, we'd had a decent view of this area of the 11th. I'd seen Zach's ball fly over the bunker and enter the trees. I scanned back from the tee to the tree line to my left and tried to pick out the approximate spot where Zach's ball left the course.

I stepped over to the area where I thought that might be. A line of tall grass three inches thick defined the boundary between the woods and course. Bushes dotted the spaces between the tree trunks. Zach and Gideon's push carts were parked nearby.

Archie's and Percy's remained in the fairway closer to the green. They must have left them there when they heard Gideon call out after finding the body. One was parked on the left side of the hole near the trees on this side, a hundred yards away from where I stood. The other cart rested in the center of the fairway, ten yards shy of a sand trap between the short grass and water separating an undulating green. I recalled that Archie had Chanticleer club head covers over his big clubs, likely hybrid irons and woods, which meant that the set of clubs near the bunker in the fairway was his.

If those were his, it was difficult to imagine him being able to run into the trees and whack Zach over the head and run back without anyone seeing him, as I had surmised earlier. Unless he had a partner. Percy, on the other hand, was a different story.

I headed in the direction of his clubs. There was something I needed to see. He could have gone into the woods on this side under the premise of looking for errant balls while he waited for Zach to make his shot. If he disappeared far enough from Archie's view while doing that, then it's possible to have run along the cart path on the other side of the trees, back to Zach, and done the deed. Percy looked like he was in excellent shape for a man pushing fifty, so I didn't discount the notion.

It didn't take long to close the distance. I glanced at the clubs in his bag and counted two with head covers. Likely a driver and 3-wood. Nowadays many golfers use those two big clubs, plus fatter hybrid irons or fairway woods. Those types of clubs combined the loft of an iron into the fatness of a big club, making lower numbered irons easier to hit. The new set of clubs Bo bought for me last night had three hybrids to go along with the driver and 3-wood. I had five clubs with head covers in my bag.

The clubs rested about ten feet from the edge of the trees. It was here where the pines ended, opening up the space around the green. Tall palmettos were strategically placed around the green. One stuck out of the fairway on the left-hand side of the bunker where Archie's clubs sat near, adding to the difficulty of the hole. As though the sharp dogleg off the tee wasn't enough, the ball of fronds at the top of the intrusive palmetto upped the ante. The hole design was downright evil.

But that was what made this such a popular course to play. The beauty of Swaying Palms and the challenge it provided intersected to give golfers a memorable time.

Today would certainly be a day etched in my memory — for all the wrong reasons.

Turning back to the edge of the woods near Percy's bag, I did, in fact, find a beaten down area of grass. Two as a matter of fact. He had entered the woods. One patch must have been where he entered the trees; the other one nearby would've had to have been where he exited.

The underbrush here was thick enough to trace his trail. I followed it between and around trees for several feet until the underbrush thinned out to the point where his trail disappeared in the grass. I stood close to the back of the tree line. From here it would have been a short distance to the outside cart path. Not only did the grass end, but his footprints also disappeared. If he would have been running, then the heavy footfalls should have left indentations in the dirt. Heavy rains had passed through Myrtle Beach overnight, so the ground here was soft.

I crouched down at the last place where I had traced his trail but didn't see any footprints between here and going in the direction of the cart path. I would have forensics come through here and try to find footprints. They were better at this than me.

I picked the trail leading back to the fairway, which I had to admit was close to where I'd lost the trail halfway through to begin with. Looking back in the direction of the fairway, I imagined that this might have been the limit to how far an errant ball might have made it through these trees. This would have been a good stopping point in Percy's quick search for free golf balls.

Or, Percy could have pushed farther in, reached the cart path, and ran back to Zach and murdered him.

CHAPTER
SIXTEEN

I PUSHED THROUGH the woods and returned to Moody and the crime scene via the outside cart path with the trees to my left and the waterfront homes to my right. The asphalt on the narrow road had a darker tone. There were few cracks or potholes in it, suggesting it was a newer addition to the course.

The first house I came to was the one with the immaculate back yard. As I passed by, I saw a woman standing on her back deck overlooking the inground pool. She was watching the crime scene techs scuttle back and forth from the trees to their carts to get supplies or stow items away.

She was tall, waspishly thin, and had short silver hair. A purple satin robe enclosed her. Matching purple framed eyeglasses perched atop a button nose. We were closing in on noon, but she appeared to have just gotten out of bed. She held a cup of coffee in one hand, the other plunged down the front pocket of her robe.

As she took a sip, she noticed me passing by. I raised a hand and called out, "Hello!"

She returned the gesture with a cautious wave but remained silent. Her head darted back to the crime scene and back to me. She didn't move.

I called across the length of the yard, "Can I ask you a few questions?"

She took another look at the technicians before stepping down onto the recently cut grass in her bare feet. Each step she took was measured. She couldn't keep her eyes off the scene playing out to the right of her back porch.

We met at the low fence. Besides a few well-defined crow's feet, her face was smooth. Long fingers embraced the handle of the coffee cup. I caught the aroma of Arabica beans coming from it and hoped she would invite me in for a cup. Her arms were thin, face gaunt. She appeared to have either just gotten over a battle with a long-fought illness or only ate once a week.

"What happened?" she asked.

I pointed in the direction of Zach's body. It wasn't visible from here, thank goodness. "A man was killed over there earlier."

She took the hand out of her robe pocket and held it to her mouth. "My goodness. Who was it?"

Again, my understanding of police protocol was unclear on this point. I recalled that they had to contact the family first before releasing the name of a murder victim. "Can't say at this point."

"Was it a man or woman?"

"A man."

Her head bobbed slowly, taking in the information. She had a shaky voice. It might be from nerves talking to me and learning that someone had died within feet of her back door.

Before she grew suspicious as to why I was passing by looking like any other golfer she would see daily, I said, "My name is Clark Thomas. I'm collaborating with the police on trying to figure out what happened here."

She eyed me up and down. "You look vaguely familiar."

I didn't want to say that she had perhaps seen me on TV or in the newspapers involved with murder investigations. I didn't want that kind of attention, but it came with the territory.

"You don't look familiar to me," I said. "Guess I have one of those faces."

Her eyes searched my face, trying to place where she had seen me before. When she couldn't, she said, "Must be. How can I help you?"

I wasn't sure what she might have seen from her house. If she saw anything. Nor was I sure how much time had passed since the murder. I glanced at the clock on my phone. I didn't wear a watch.

"Did you happen to be looking out your window half an hour ago?"

"No," she answered. "I just got out of bed. I worked overnight at the hospital as an ER doctor."

I scanned the backside of her house but didn't see what I was looking for. "Do you have any security cameras aimed at your backyard?"

"I have one on my doorbell that looks out on the front porch and into the road, but not back here. I think I will now."

"Good idea." I turned and commented on her yard, "I wish my backyard looked like this."

She gave a faint smile. "Thank you. Besides work, it's all I have to take care of."

"Ah," I said. I understood. She had a sad countenance, reminding me of how I must have appeared in the months following Autumn's death. Like, life moves on, but when you lose a close loved one, you have moments where you wish it didn't. You grab onto a fond memory and hold it there. She wore a wedding band on the hand holding the coffee mug.

I didn't want to intrude. I'd only just met her. Didn't even know her name. Speaking of which, "What is your name?"

"Genevieve."

She didn't offer to shake my hand, nor did I offer her mine.

"I'm a doctor at Grand Strand Medical Center," she said. "The big one up on the bypass. I worked overnight last night and got home sometime this morning. I had just stepped outside after pouring my first cup of coffee when you walked by."

"So, you wouldn't have seen anything? The man was killed after he entered the woods on this side of the golf course.

"Goodness," she said and somberly sipped from the mug. "It's a shame. I had to deal with a stabbing victim last night in the ER."

"Is the person going to be okay?"

She shook her head. "He didn't make it."

That might help to explain her overall sadness. I had trouble imagining having a job where you had to try to save someone's life in an emergency like that. I've watched the medical shows on TV, and while I know much of what happens on the operating room tables are over-dramatized for ratings, the emotions the doctors portray afterward when they can't save a patient must hit close to the mark.

"Sorry to hear that. Are you okay?"

Another wan smile. "Not the first one. Won't be the last. I save more than I lose in those cases, but it's the ones I can't save who take the biggest toll on me, you know?"

I didn't, but I could sympathize. "Thank you for what you do."

"It's what I chose to do in life," Genevieve said. This time she gave a hint of a genuine smile.

Before Genevieve made me too depressed, I asked, "Do you

ever see people from the golf course use the cart path on the other side of your fence?"

"Yes. The groundskeepers at the golf course use it to get their mowing and other equipment from one hole to the next while disrupting the golfers as little as possible."

"Do you play?"

"Some. I played in college at Oklahoma. My husband and I used to play regularly." She ran a hand over the wooden porch railing. "That's one of the reasons why we bought this home."

"How long has he been gone?"

She turned and faced me fully for the first time since I stepped onto her porch. "How did you know?"

I lifted my shoulder. "I notice things."

She seemed to take my explanation at face value. "You must be a great detective."

"Oh, I'm no detective. I own a bookstore on the Boardwalk."

One of her eyebrows arched while the other dipped. "You lost me. You said you were with the police?"

"I am…in a way."

She took a cautious step back. "In what way? I have to deal with the police from time to time as part of my job. I did just this morning, as a matter of fact. None of *those* work for the police department in a capacity like that."

"Those? Like what?"

"Like a bookstore owner, as you say."

I chuckled. "Oh, I'm sorry to confuse you. I was hired as a consultant on this case."

She cradled the coffee mug in both hands. "Now I'm really confused."

I set her straight by giving her an abbreviated version that led me to be standing in front of her.

"Oh," she said, "that's how I recognized you. I've seen you on TV before."

"Yeah, that's me." I didn't care for the attention that came after solving murder cases, but Gomez kept telling me that it's extra newsworthy when a civilian such as myself discovers killers. That is, when Gomez and I used to speak to each other.

"My husband passed, going on six years now," she said. "Died in a commuter plane crash going from here to Charlotte."

"I'm sorry to hear that," I said for the second time in our conversation. "I lost my wife three years ago to a heart attack."

"She must have been very young to have that happen."

"Autumn had had a heart condition that followed her from her childhood. We always knew it was a possibility."

"Such a shame," Genevieve said. "She must have been a lovely woman."

"That she was." Now I was sad and depressed from thinking about Autumn, learning about Genevieve's late husband, the death of the stabbing victim whom she tried so save, and from my fractured friendship with Gomez.

I wasn't sure what other useful information Genevieve might provide, and was about to wish her a good day, when I glanced at the unkempt yard next to hers behind the house next to the crime scene.

"What's the story with your neighbors?"

She huffed. "That's another shame. That place."

"How do you mean?"

She sipped the last of her coffee, and said, "A lovely couple used to live there. They sold the house when the husband retired and moved to God's Waiting Room."

Look at the tired, sad doctor cracking a joke in a serious moment. I had to adjust my initial impression of her. "You mean, Florida?"

"I do. Anyway, the company who bought the home turned it into a rental, but it hasn't been lived in for months. No one has even mowed the grass, much less trimmed the hedges. It's an eyesore."

We both regarded the property. "I agree."

"I've reported it to the homeowners' association numerous times, but nothing ever gets done about it."

"Interesting. Do you recall the name of the company who bought it?"

"I never learned it. I just wish that they'd resell it to someone who would take care of it."

It went to show you that even the nicest neighborhoods still had blights. I doubted most of these homeowners would roll up their sleeves and mow their lawns, but rather hire landscapers. Most rental property agencies would have someone take care of the lawns no matter if someone lived there or not. I was sure that the homeowners association wouldn't approve. Of course, I'd only seen the unkempt backyard. The front might be immaculate.

When there was no more to discuss, I stepped off Genevieve's porch and said, "Thank you for your time."

"Have a nice day," she returned.

It didn't turn out to be a nice day, and nothing she said seemed important at the time. Little did I know at that moment, but the owner of the rental property had something to do with who killed Autumn.

CHAPTER
SEVENTEEN

I RETURNED TO the crime scene, lifting the crime scene tape that marked the rear investigative area and ducking under it. None of the technicians gave me a second look. They were focused on the task at hand. For all they knew, I might have been a random golfer looking for his lost ball in the woods. It wasn't up to them to keep out interlopers. Officer Battles had cleared me through.

The area was a swarm of activity. One woman was going around marking potential spots of interest on the ground with small flags. The coroner had come and left with Zach's body. The area around where he fell to the ground had dozens of markers, including a scattered line of them near the top of where his body had been. They marked where blood had splashed on the ground after the murderer took a swing with the club and collapsed the side of his head.

Moody huddled with a tall man who had slicked back hair, a square jaw, and bulging muscles all over his body. A short sharp shock of distaste passed through me.

Lucien.

Gomez's fiancé.

The man who accepted Autumn's phone with the ominous text messages and then promptly had it "stolen." I put the word in mental air quotes after speaking to the former mafioso, Tony Bruno. He had his ear to the ground about what was really going on in

Myrtle Beach and warned me to trust no one. I met Lucien for the first time not long afterward.

Not only did he possess a devilish name, but as soon as he crushed my hand in his grip and glowered at me, I knew I couldn't trust him. His parents gave him the name, but he had control over not coming off like a slithery snake. If I had thought I might be working with Lucien, I may have declined Mayor Rosen's offer.

Then again, a small voice in the back of my head warned that my distrust of Gomez's beloved might have been rooted in a teensy-tiny bit of jealousy. It was a voice I squashed like a bug but kept the notion in my mind as I approached him and Moody.

They raised their heads as I came closer.

Lucien smiled a devil's grin. It might have been my imagination. "Moody tells me you're filling in for Gina on this."

Moody grunted.

Lucien held out his hand. I took it and tried not to let him crush mine. I was unsuccessful. He kept a neutral smile on his face as the pain shot up my wrist.

After I reclaimed my mangled hand, I said, "Yeah. Right person at the wrong place at the wrong time, I guess."

The crooked smile on his face hadn't ebbed. "That's how it goes sometimes. Thank you for doing this."

"No problem," I said, although it might become a big problem later. "Did you tag the random golf ball that was in the path Gideon said they took after entering the trees?"

"We did," Lucien answered. "A Srixon."

"That was it. Thanks," The sun was at its highest point in the sky somewhere above the tree canopy over our heads. Perspiration beaded on my forehead. "Have you discovered anything new?"

Lucien deferred to Moody, who answered, "Yeah. We did. Right over here."

He led me away from Lucien down a specific path in the other direction from the two homes on the waterway but still to the rear of the tree line. The cart path meandered in both directions where the trees and undergrowth ended.

There was a beaten down area of tall grass between two trees at the edge of the woods. He pointed at it. "Look down through here."

I tilted to the side and looked directly down where he gestured back toward where the body was found. Crime scene flags marked either side of the grassy indentation and dotted a trail disappearing into the trees. The marked path curved around several trees before it disappeared from our view. The path he had led me down to get here parallelled this suspicious trail so we wouldn't disturb any possible evidence.

"We believe this is where the killer entered the woods," he remarked.

"Ah," I said.

We walked back toward Lucien, following the flags. "The trail leads to a fat tree near the body. It seems like the killer hid there in wait for Zach."

I scratched my ear. "That confuses the matter more, doesn't it?"

"It does, but it gets more confusing from there," Lucien said.

"How so?" I asked.

"There are two sets of prints after the trail enters the woods," he answered, "but only one leading to them."

Moody squinted in concentration.

"Two people might have been involved," I suggested. "Maybe

two people were in the cart and followed each other from there to the woods and split up."

"Unless the prints came from one of the groundskeepers sometime during the morning. We'll ask if any were near here." Moody shook his head. "Unless one of those guys Zach was with outright confesses to it, this isn't going to be easy."

"It never is," I said.

He snorted. "With you, it isn't. Gomez and I are fortunate that most of the murders we work on are normally open-and-shut cases. It's just your luck that you end up involved in these twisty ones."

"Hurray for me." My tone was not celebratory.

"Try to follow the trails through the woods," Moody ordered Lucien.

"We'll do our best to track them."

I scanned the grassy area between the recently created path in the woods back to the outside cart path. A trail of footprint depressions lay in a straight line between the two.

"Did you see this?" I asked Moody, pointing at the faint trail.

He crouched down to get an angle closer to the ground. His eyes narrowed. "These must be the killers."

"Makes sense."

We followed the trail back to the paved cart path where it ended. A set of tire tracks marked where someone had driven off the path into the grass.

Moody and I scanned the marks in the grass. We were behind the second hole of the back nine at Swaying Palms. Trees separated us from the corner of the dogleg with the oversized sand trap. The 10th hole was back in the direction of the clubhouse. The clubhouse and groundskeeper shed wasn't too far away to our left, compared to if the driver headed in the other direction, toward the 12th hole. I said, "I wonder which direction the cart was headed."

He pointed at an area where both tread marks stretched. The tire marks didn't change over the distance of about three inches. "See there. Looks like that's where the cart came to a sudden halt and skidded."

We bent to get a closer angle. Where the stretchy marks ended before continuing in a more normal manner, the soft turf mounded. Like a giant had pinched the ground together in two places and the tire marks had rolled over them.

Moody stood and called into the trees, "Hey, Lucien! Come over here!"

I didn't know the grizzled detective's voice was capable of getting that loud. A moment later, Lucien emerged from the woods.

"Watch where you step," Moody warned him, pointing at the area we had discovered. "There's a trail of footprints in the grass between here and where the murderer entered the trees. They go back to these tire marks here."

Lucien squinted and moved cautiously away from the prints and stopped near us. He examined them from where he stood. "I'll have someone come mark them."

"Thanks," Moody said. "Look over here."

He showed him the tire marks, focusing on the skid marks. "The perp could have come along here on a cart and skidded to a halt."

Lucien turned away from the tire marks on the pavement and studied the trees, then the patch of green turf in between them. The pair of loblollies on the edge were tall. They didn't align in a perfect line with the cart path, causing the line of trees to curve at a sharp angle before straightening out farther down the path in the direction leading away from the clubhouse.

"This would have been a good place to temporarily ditch a golf cart," Lucien suggested and then scanned back along the path. "If a groundskeeper was coming from the clubhouse back there and driving past, they might not have seen the cart."

"Makes sense," Moody said. "They would have if they were coming in the other direction back toward the center of the course. I need to figure out which way the cart was headed."

Lucien kneeled by the skid marks and peered closely. His head turned in both directions and then nodded to himself. "Away from the clubhouse."

Moody accepted the answer. "Okay then."

"We'll do our thing to be sure," Lucien said, "but I would place odds on the cart coming from the direction of the clubhouse, stopping here, and then leaving in the same direction."

I listened to the exchange. Something Lucien said registered with me. "Is it possible that these tire marks and the path leading into the woods have come from a groundskeeper who came through here earlier and not be connected to the murder?"

Moody and Lucien shared a knowing look that suggested that one of them would have to condescend to answering a silly question from an untrained rookie. I was untrained, yes, but not a rookie.

"I'll give you the possibility of a groundskeeper," Moody answered. "That's a good idea, but with where the path in the woods ends near the body, it has to be related."

His logic made sense. At least he didn't laugh at my question completely. "Okay. Just throwing that idea out there."

"That's good," he said. "We need all the theories we can get right now. We're at the stage where we're trying to weed out the good ones from the bad."

I smirked. "And these marks being unrelated is one of the bad ones."

He studied the patch of ground in question. "You said it, kid." To Lucien, "Extend the tape back to here and mark it. Photos, everything."

"Will do," Lucien said and returned to the woods.

Moody and I stood in silence for a moment, assessing what this meant.

With Moody being Moody and me being me, I spoke our shared thought aloud first, "If these tracks belong to the killer, then that would rule out his three partners."

"Maybe," he grunted. "It wouldn't totally rule them out but, at the same time, open it up to everyone who worked here, people who live in the neighborhood, boaters cruising by on the Intracoastal, etc."

I rubbed the beaded sweat off the back of my neck. "I get it. We go from three suspects to an unknown quantity."

"It might make it easier, actually."

"How so?" I crossed my arms.

"Because the CCTV might have caught the killer zooming around on their cart."

My head did a slow up and down as I accepted this. It made sense. This corner of the course didn't have security coverage. That didn't mean other areas didn't. It seemed easy. Check the security footage and use the time signatures to backtrack and find the killer.

If only it were that easy. Checking the cameras only made matters worse.

CHAPTER
EIGHTEEN

GRAY CLOUDS GATHERED in the sky as Moody chauffeured me back to the clubhouse, leaving the crime scene technicians to do their jobs. The breeze intensified, signaling a coming storm. Afternoon pop-up thunderstorms were a common occurrence in Myrtle Beach and in the South as the atmosphere heated throughout the day and the blanket of humid air gathered in the skies.

I used the towel hanging off my club bag to wipe the sweat from my face and neck. Moody perspired profusely. His moisture-wicking golf shirt wicked about all the sweat it could. While the new technology in fabrics enabled people to wear cooler clothes that kept the sweat away from their bodies, one drawback was that the soaked up sweat caused shirts to stink much quicker. Moody emanated a funk that mingled sweat, grass, and the outdoors that I was sure came off me, too.

Gotta love soupy Myrtle Beach summers.

Moody had navigated our cart to an access space to join the outside cart path that would take us directly back to the clubhouse. We moved past the two homes on the edge of the waterway before turning inland back to the center of Swaying Palms. Genevieve watched the techs operate from her back porch, sipping from her mug. She gave me an unenthusiastic wave as Moody and I passed her property.

The stray golf ball troubled me.

The Srixon was a perfectly good ball, and it stood out in the path. If it was Zach's lost ball, why didn't one of them pick it up? If it wasn't, I for sure would have pocketed it for use later. Searching for lost golf balls in the brush and ponds was a common pastime for many men, for good reason. Most discovered balls were reused by the treasure seeker or sold secondhand for profit.

I asked Moody, "What do you think about the ball?"

"What ball?"

"The clean, fresh Srixon that was on the ground near where Zach was killed."

"Oh, that one." His heavy brow lowered.

How had he forgotten about it? He had more on his mind than only this investigation. How did Gomez keep him focused? *Did* she keep him focused?

After a moment, he said, "From the way it laid on the ground on top of the pine needles, I figured it was the ball he hit into the woods."

"Yeah, but if it was, why didn't he or Gideon pick it up?"

"Good question. Gideon said Zach only played Titleists, and that might be why he didn't pick it up. Like it was below his level of ball. It was on the path Zach took after he and Gideon parted. That might be why Gideon didn't take it."

"I can see that. It sat there plain as day. Surely Zach would have seen it, grabbed it, and returned to the course. What do you think made him plunge farther into the woods?"

The cart rounded a bend and hit a bump. I grabbed a handle on the edge of the cart's roof and held on for dear life.

Nonplussed by his erratic driving, Moody commented, "Gideon

said he heard Zach yell something, and then heard more yelling a minute later. Someone must have agitated him enough that he went deeper, almost to the other side."

"From the path through the woods we found at the back of the hole, it's like someone was waiting there for him. They may have yelled something at Zach that ticked him off."

"True, but Gideon didn't say anything about hearing another voice."

"Let's ask him."

"Good idea."

We bounced back to the clubhouse and arrived as the sky opened up and the rain began to pour.

CHAPTER
NINETEEN

ZACH'S FRIENDS SAT alone in the dining room of the clubhouse. Archie had a half-eaten burger on a plate, along with three remaining fries, in front of him. A glass of ice water oozed condensation onto the wood top table. Neither Percy nor Gideon had food, but both had hands wrapped around the handles of tall pint glasses filled with cold beer.

All were dressed in clean clothes complete with the Swaying Palms logo, fresh from the pro shop.

Officers Dame and Battles guarded them. Dame eyed Archie's burger with envy. Other uniformed officers and crime scene technicians moved about. All of the other golfers must have been sent home.

Moody conferred with the course superintendent, Warren, and clubhouse manager. The clubhouse manager was the same blonde we had seen on the practice range this morning. The one Bo had tried to flirt with.

Newly minted police chief, Sue Miller, joined them. If she was here, this must be serious.

I stared out the window at the verdant course, falling rain, and swaying palms while they talked business. The poor people who were caught out in the rain scurried for cover. I hoped the technicians had gotten what they needed from the crime scene or had covered it with a tarp. This rain might not last long, but it was enough to wash away potential evidence and reset footprints in the grass.

After finding where the killer had entered the woods after screeching to a halt in their golf cart, it made it difficult in my mind to link Archie, Gideon, or Percy to the slaying. No matter how many variations of what might have happened played through my head, I couldn't correlate one of them possibly being the killer knowing that someone had arrived at the scene on a cart.

Unless the tread marks from the cart and the murder occurred at separate times, which left all three men in play. That wasn't what Lucien suggested, but I wouldn't close the door on the idea. Gideon was in the woods with Zach, but they had split up trying to find his ball. The Kiwi said that Zach disappeared during their search.

Speaking of disappearing, both Percy and Archie had rounded the dogleg and vanished from our vantage point in the golf cart by the tee box. That seemed like forever ago, but it had been less than two hours.

My stomach growled despite having seen a man with his head caved in earlier. The clock on the wall read half past twelve. I wasn't sure when I would get a chance to eat. Apparently, the kitchen was still operating as evidenced by Archie's burger. As tempting as it was to go order one myself, I knew that this was no time for a break.

Moody and Miller broke away from Warren and the clubhouse manager and came to me by the window.

Miller was of average height, had brown hair that fell below her ears, and wore a blue buttoned-up shirt. She had a focused demeanor and stuck out a hand when she came close enough, which I shook.

"Clark, thank you for agreeing to help on this," she said. "I might be new in the position but was aware of you from my former station. Your record speaks for itself. If Mayor Rosen and Detectives Moody and Gomez say you can handle this, then I believe them."

"Thank you," I said, releasing her hand. Her statement indicated that not only had she spoken with Rosen and Moody about me but had also put in a call or exchanged text messages with Gomez too. "Glad to be of service."

Miller gave me a curt nod. "Good. Then I'll leave you and the detective here to it." She turned to Moody. "Let me know if you need anything."

"Will do, Chief," he said.

She exited the clubhouse without looking back.

I asked Moody, "What do you think of the new chief?"

He grumbled something.

"What's that?" I leaned closer. The sweat smell came off his shirt the same as it did mine.

He cleared his throat. "She's finding her way. Used to be the chief out in Loris. It's taking time getting used to the size of the job."

I held up my thumb and forefinger close together. "Myrtle Beach is just a teensy-weensy bit larger than Loris."

He imitated a sort of laugh. "Yeah. By a couple hundred more on staff. She and Rosen apparently go way back. He saw to her getting the position."

The mayor of Myrtle Beach had the power to hire and fire police chiefs as he or she saw fit. Same went for other members of the police department.

An uneasy moment passed. Moody mumbled something under his breath. like he was upset with himself for doing, or not doing, something.

I didn't comment. He would tell me what agitated him if he wanted. After an awkward few seconds, I asked, "Now what?"

Moody crossed his arms and grunted to himself. In my limited knowledge of Detective Moody's career, I wasn't aware of him being the lead investigator on any case. He seemed like more of a Cro-Magnon version of Dr. Watson, Sherlock Holmes's sidekick. A helpful person who kept investigations moving and did his part, even sometimes offering intuitive suggestions that helped lead to solving the case—in this case, with less dignified caveman-like mannerisms.

However, being the front person might be new territory for him. I waited for a moment while he digested the morning's events. Heavy rain pounded on the roof. Gusts caused sheets of water to pound the floor-to-ceiling windows. A nearby crack of thunder caused the building to vibrate.

Finally, he said, "Let's go talk to Dame, Battles, and Kevin. See what happened after they brought them here."

We exited the dining room and followed a passage lined with photos of celebrities and professional golfers who had played here in the past. An old black-and-white photo showed a picture of Bob Hope, Dean Martin, and Jerry Lewis kneeling down on the green looking up at a camera. Hope had a cigar dangling out of the right side of his mouth. Another showed Kevin Costner wearing sunglasses watching the flight of his ball. Greg Norman stood next to him, wearing his signature straw hat. Another photo was an old black-and-white of Steve McQueen standing in a sand trap waiting for someone to toss him a ball. The photos went all the way to the rear exit.

This who's who of the golfing world who had played at Swaying Palms lent another level of prestige to the course. Both the men's and women's changing rooms were located down this hallway near the rear of the clubhouse. Their placement made it convenient for golfers to change and head out the backdoor to their golf carts, or vice versa when they returned from the eighteenth hole. I didn't pass through here earlier. I came dressed to play and had no need of using the lockers.

The door to the men's room lay to the right down the hall. The women's room was on the opposite side of the hall. The door to the men's room was propped open. The *clang-clang* of metal came from within. Someone was beating something hard, and it sounded like a locker.

We entered to find Officer Nichols banging on a lock with a hammer hanging from a locker at the right rear side of the stuffy room. Kevin stood off to the side out of harms' way watching Nichols work.

"Hey!" Moody shouted.

Nichols stopped beating and turned to us. Sweat glistened on his forehead. "Kevin suggested a few hard whacks might open it."

After taking a licking, the lock wiggled on locker number 32 before coming to rest. It was a typical combination lock with a turn dial in the center and numbers engraved into a ring on its bezel.

Moody's face shriveled like he'd heard a three-year-old tell a lie about why the cookie jar was broken. "Don't you have bolt cutters for that?"

Kevin glanced at Nichols before answering. "Well, yeah, but I left mine back at the crime scene. I didn't think I would need it here."

"And you thought damaging potential evidence was the way to go?" Moody said, crossing his arms.

Kevin blubbered, "Uh, didn't think it would be that hard. A good solid whack with a hammer does the trick if you hit it right and hit it hard."

Nichols's muscles bulged under his uniform. I didn't think him not being able to hit the lock hard enough would be a reason for the lock not to open. He gave Kevin an annoyed look. "Hey man. I was just doing what you told me to do. It's not like I use a hammer every day."

Kevin gestured at the suspect lock. "I didn't know it would be so sturdy."

"Stop arguing," Moody said in a tone parents would use to calm two squabbling siblings. To Kevin, he said, "Better hope that lock's not damaged or Lucien will have your hide."

Kevin grimaced and bent to inspect the lock. "Looks like a new one to me. Don't see a scratch on it." He drew back from the imposing Nichols. "No offense."

"None taken," the Officer said with a tone making it obvious that he had taken offense.

"Where did the hammer come from?" I asked.

"I asked someone who works here for it," Kevin said. "They grabbed it from a cleaning closet down the hall."

Moody closed in on the lock. "Okay boys. If you're done arguing, can one of you explain why you were trying to break in?"

"After we got back here," Nichols said, "everything went fine. The other three had changed their clothes in here and placed them in evidence bags. Gideon picked out clean clothes and footwear from the pro shop and came in here to change. When we came in here, Archie was unable to get his lock to open."

"Was it a new lock, and he forgot the combination?" I asked.

"Negative," Nichols answered.

"Maybe the pressure and stress of the situation got to him, and he kept screwing it up," Moody mused.

"I don't think that was it," Kevin said.

Moody and I had the same inkling. Was Archie hiding evidence there?

"Go grab a cart and retrieve your bolt cutters," Moody ordered Kevin. "Pronto."

"Yes, sir," Kevin said and walked past us out of the locker room.

"Which lockers belonged to Zach and Percy?" I asked Nichols.

The lockers were arranged in a big U with a wide lacquered wood bench in the middle atop a gray tile floor for people to sit while changing and putting on shoes. Each locker was about six feet tall. Long enough to hang clothes in and have room for spare shoes, toiletries, etc. More photos of famous golfers and prestigious awards Swaying Palms had received decorated the walls over green wallpaper. The space carried the typical smells associated with a men's locker room: sweat, body wash, deodorant, and damp towels.

Nichols pointed at the locker to the right of Archie's. "Percy's is here. Number 43." He turned and pointed at the opposite wall. "Zach had locker 12. Gideon lives on the course. He doesn't have a locker."

Moody squished his lips with a thumb and forefinger. "Got it. Kevin will need the bolt cutters anyway to open Zach's locker."

Kevin returned ten minutes later with the bolt cutters in hand. It looked like an enormous pair of pliers, but made to cut, not to clasp. He offered it to Nichols, who accepted it.

"Now this, I can handle," he said and stepped beside Archie's locker.

He glanced at Moody for the go-ahead. The detective dipped his head in confirmation.

Nichols grasped both handles of the bolt cutters and placed the jaw around one side of the curved shank that held the lock in place. He grunted with effort as he squeezed the handles together. The shank broke with a loud *snap*!

Moody put on a pair of latex gloves as Nichols stepped aside. The detective handed the broken lock to Kevin, who placed it in an evidence bag.

"Let's see what we have here," Moody said to himself as he thumbed the locker open.

The door opened. I bent to the side to get a better look over Moody's shoulder. A shelf near the top created a cube-like area where Archie had stowed his car keys, a pack of cigarettes, a roll of cash, and deodorant. A work shirt and a pair of slacks hung from hooks below the shelf. At the bottom was a pair of uncomfortable-looking work boots. Something long and straight lay vertically behind the clothes at an angle.

"What's back there?" I asked.

Moody grunted and pulled the shirt aside to reveal a 3-wood. Moody didn't touch the club at first. The club grip was at the top of the locker. The shaft exposed itself where the length of the clothing ended. The clubhead lay at the bottom, tucked behind the shoes. The was the type of club that might have shattered Zach's skull.

At first glance, I would say there was a good chance this was the murder weapon.

A large dent contorted the back of the clubhead. It was haloed with flecks of blood.

CHAPTER
TWENTY

WE STARED AT the bloodied club for a minute, taking in its implications. We had found the murder weapon, but it didn't make any sense how it got here.

I turned to Nichols and Kevin. "Did Archie leave your sight after getting back here?"

The officer and crime scene technician glanced at each other before Nichols answered, "Yes. I lost sight of him for a few minutes while Gideon was in the pro shop picking out clothes."

"Where was Ann during all of this?"

"Also in the pro shop."

"What about you?" I asked Kevin.

He stroked his goatee. "I spoke to the course super, Warren, for a quick second while Archie came here to change and lost track of him."

"What did you ask him about?"

"I, uh." Kevin rubbed the back of his neck. "I, uh, asked him about coming back and playing a free round here sometime."

"In exchange for something?" Moody asked. If Kevin and Warren had struck up a deal, they might have considered it tampering.

"No, no," Kevin said. "It was more of him saying that if we needed anything to let him know and me adding that I'd like to play here sometime."

Moody gave Kevin a skeptical look. "If you say so. Where was Percy during all of this?"

"With me," Kevin answered. "He can corroborate my chat with Warren."

Moody batted a hand. "Bah. That's not important. What is important is losing sight of a suspect. You were supposed to have kept them together."

"Hey," Nichols said, "I did my piece and watched over Gideon while he picked out some clothes, like you told me to do."

"We'll assign blame later," Moody said, rubbing his face. "When did you see Archie again?"

"When we came in here," Nichols answered. "He was still trying to get his locker open."

"How long was he out of your sight?" I asked.

"Five, ten minutes tops," Kevin said.

I glanced at the open locker and back at the pair. "And he spent that entire time trying to open his locker?"

"That's what he said." Nichols was unrattled. He had a steely, cool demeanor that meant business.

Kevin was the opposite. Sweat had broken out on his face despite the air conditioning. His hands didn't stop moving. He ran a hand through his wavy hair and through his facial hair. He blinked more rapidly. Was he hiding something, or just not used to being questioned in this manner?

"He might've taken a leak," Kevin suggested.

I had surveyed where the walls met the ceiling in this locker room. There were no cameras. Nothing that would show us what Archie did for those five to ten minutes where he was out of everyone's sight.

I told Archie that everything in their lockers was considered evidence. Why would he still try to get into his? He didn't have the club we found with him. There was nowhere to hide it on his body.

Moody snapped his tongue and seemed satisfied with their answers. To Nichols, he said, "Go grab Archie and bring him back here."

"Roger," Nichols said and left the locker room.

"What about me?" Kevin asked.

"Go get what you need to mark this scene," Moody said, tilting his head toward where Zach was killed. "We should be clear of here by the time you come back."

"Gotcha," Kevin said, happy to no longer be under question.

He left the locker room, leaving Moody, myself, and the murder weapon alone.

"What do you think?" he asked me.

I met Moody and his counterpart, Gina Gomez, over a year ago. In the months that followed, when I ended up getting involved in the investigations into Connor West's and John Allen Howard's death, I wouldn't have expected such a question from the seasoned detective. The fact that he asked for my opinion told me he respected my judgment. A touch of pride warmed a spot in my chest.

I tilted my head toward the bloody club. "This complicates things."

"Agreed."

"We found Zach's broken 3-iron near his body. It appears to be the club used to hit him on the head, but seeing this makes more sense as being the murder weapon."

"Right. Because of the shape of his misshapen head. We'll let the ME figure it out, but the blade of an iron wouldn't have made that type of indention on someone's skull."

"That's what I was thinking," I said. "Here's another thing. Why is the back of the clubhead dented and not the front?"

"Good question."

My mind was spinning, and I was thinking aloud by asking questions. "Why are there two clubs that appear to have been used to kill Zach?"

"One to start the job and the other to finish it, I guess," Moody mused.

"Then why would Archie leave one club out there near the body and hide the murder weapon in here?"

"That's what we're going to ask him."

Nichols reentered the locker room with Archie in tow. "Here he is," the officer said.

Moody thanked Nichols and instructed him to go out where Dame and the other suspects sat in the dining room. He departed, leaving Archie with us.

He squinted past us at his open locker. "Oh, you got it open."

"You sound surprised," Moody said.

"No, I knew you could. Just didn't know how long it would take. Thanks."

"Why are you thanking us?" Moody asked.

One of Archie's eyebrows rose, causing the wrinkles in between the two to form. "Because you got it open."

"Why were you unable to open it?" I asked.

"Beats me," he said. "My combination wasn't working."

Moody held up the broken lock with a gloved hand. "How long have you had this?"

Archie scratched the back of his neck. "A couple years, I think."

"Long enough that you should know the combination by heart," I said.

"That's right," he confirmed. "Look. For whatever reason, it wouldn't open. I can't explain it."

"After you all got back here," I said, "Officer Nichols and the crime scene technician that was with you said you left their sight for five to ten minutes. Why didn't you stay with them?"

Archie directed his answer to Moody. "Because you told us to come back here and change our clothes. I didn't think I needed to be babysat to do it."

Moody breathed out slowly. "I should have given specific instructions to them to make sure the three of you didn't leave their sight."

"I don't know what to say," Archie said. "One of my close friends and clients just got murdered right near me. My stomach was upset, and I *really* had to use the bathroom. I was rattled and trying to help. I didn't think the officers would want to stand outside the stall while I destroyed it."

Moody's nose wrinkled at the imagined odor coming from Archie's stall. "We didn't ask for your help."

I held up a finger. "Wait. Zach was one of your clients?"

"He was."

"He was your client in what way?"

"My landscapers serviced his lawn."

"Did either of your other golf mates have business with Zach?"

"Uh, yeah." Archie's nerves were getting the best of him. He couldn't focus on us or anything. His eyes darted around the locker room. Perspiration gathered on his brow.

"I think Percy and him did business together."

"What sort of business?" I asked.

Archie gulped and then answered. "Percy is a divorce lawyer."

The plot thickened.

CHAPTER
TWENTY-ONE

ARCHIE MIGHT NOT have looked it, but was a fast thinker on his feet. At this point, he wanted to change the focus of the conversation.

"Why are you grilling me anyway?" Archie asked. "I thanked you for getting my locker open."

Little did he know that he was in a minefield, and he'd just stepped on a lump in the dirt.

I stepped aside to let Archie approach his locker. When he got close enough to it, he saw the club that had been hidden behind his clothes. "Ah, there it is."

"What do you mean, 'there it is'?" Moody asked.

Moody stopped Archie when he went to reach for the club. The golfer protested, "Hey, what gives?"

"What gives?" Moody asked. "I'll tell you what gives. There's a bloody club in your locker. That's what gives."

Archie blubbered, unsure of how to answer. He got it together after a moment. "I'm shocked, to tell you the truth. All I know is when I needed it, on the third hole, I think, it wasn't in my bag. I asked the others if they had seen it, but they hadn't."

Before Moody or I asked a follow-up question, Kevin and Ann returned with their gear, ready to process the locker room. They wore yellow rain slickers and were wet from head to toe.

"Let me know if you find anything in the lockers," Moody said to Kevin, not commenting on his soaked appearance.

"Will do," he answered, shoving back the hood covering his head, before going to work on Zach's locker.

Moody directed his attention back to Archie. "You say the others knew about your missing club?"

Archie blinked three times before answering. "They did."

"C'mon," Moody said, gesturing at the open door. "Let's go ask them."

I followed Archie and Moody out of the locker room and down the hall to the dining room. The detective had taken charge of the case since we returned to the club house. Now that he had time to get his wits about him and digest what transpired, his experience in investigating murders showed. He might not have been the lead on any of them, but he had observed Gomez and her predecessor, Ed Banner, enough to know what to do. I wondered what I would be able to contribute at this point. Since the rain started and we had returned to the dry safety of the clubhouse, I'd felt like a fly on the wall.

The thunderstorm still pounded outside as we made it back to the dining room. Water had started to pool in various dips on the grassy terrain beyond the expansive windows. Palmetto trees fluttered in the wind. Sheets of rain cascaded across the cart paths and concrete walkways. Not a soul was in sight outside.

My various devices had alerted me to the chance of rain this morning before Bo and I walked out of the house. The percentages had been small at that point in the day. As I've learned over the years, the coast wreaks havoc on weather forecasts. The meteorologists around here are right most of the time on their weather predictions, but there are atmospheric situations they can't predict. Sometimes, like today, what might have been a forecast of isolated showers after our round would have been finished had turned into a wide coverage downpour.

With this being a Saturday in the prime of travel season, a lot of people's outdoor plans would be ruined because of the rain. Not as ruined as Zach's, though.

When the three of us arrived at where Percy, Gideon, and Officers Dame and Nichols congregated at a table, Dame had said something that made everyone laugh.

Nichols had to wipe a tear away from his eye but stopped laughing when he saw us. He straightened his face and cleared his throat at Dame, gesturing with his head that we were standing behind him. Percy and Gideon stopped laughing as well.

"I don't even want to know what you told them," Moody said.

Dame batted a hand. "Ba. Just telling them about the guy who beat his wife up in Socastee and got away before I walked up on him the next morning sitting outside at The Bagel Factory on Farrow Parkway munching on a sausage, egg, and cheese bagel like any normal person would."

"I remember that," Moody said. "Easiest collar in the history of the department."

"Yup," Dame agreed. "Dude asked me to let him finish eating his bagel before I cuffed him. Complete moron."

Moody made a noise resembling a laugh, then said to Gideon and Percy, "Need to ask you a few questions."

Not that they had a choice in the matter. Moody and I pulled up chairs at the table in front of the suspects. Dame went to the bar and grabbed bottles of water for Moody and me while we got settled. Gideon, Percy, and Archie moved their chairs around to sit in a line across from us. Moody pulled out a small notepad and a short pencil he had used to keep score on the scorecard while we'd played golf. I pushed down a laugh. Leave it to the long-time detective to always keep the old-fashioned tools of the trade on him.

Gideon, with a poor choice of words considering the two armed police officers in the room, said, "Go ahead. Fire away."

"Did Archie make you aware that he was missing one of his golf clubs?"

Percy and Gideon looked at each other. Who would speak first?

The answer was Percy. "He did."

Gideon agreed. "He said he had used it on the driving range this morning, but it disappeared sometime between there and the first tee."

"That true?" Moody asked Archie.

His right eye spasmed. "It is."

The involuntary twitch might have been from pressure or nerves or both. Or he was lying to us.

"Did your clubs leave your sight at any time before teeing off?" I asked.

"They did," Percy answered. "The four of us all took a whiz before heading to the first hole. They told us at the desk that there might be a backup on the first tee."

"Which there was," I commented. "We were on the range when you left."

Gideon stared hard at Moody and I for a brief second. "That's right. I remember you blokes from the range."

His mention of the driving range brought a question to mind that would have to wait for a moment. I asked, "Where did you leave your clubs when you came inside to go to the restroom?"

"Out on the side of the cart path connecting the clubhouse to the first hole," Percy answered.

I glanced down the hallway leading to the locker rooms and to the outside where their bags would have sat unwatched. "And all of your clubs were grouped together?"

"They were," Archie answered.

"Did one of you stay back to watch them to make sure no one stole anything?" I asked.

Gideon smirked. "C'mon, mate. At this golf club, everyone has the best clubs. Who needs to steal someone else's? We're not exactly a den of thieves here."

"Good point," I conceded.

Moody grunted to me, "We'll see if there's a camera feed overlooking that area. It'll show if someone stole the club."

I've found that in the time I've gotten involved in murder investigations that video feeds weren't as foolproof as they were on TV. Views could be obstructed, or the recordings tampered with. "Hopefully."

I directed my attention to Gideon. "Did you enter the locker room this morning?"

"Yeah," he answered. "Chatted with the fellas and used the dunny."

I'd watched enough Bluey episodes with Libby to know that "dunny" is what people from Gideon's part of the world called a toilet.

"Who was the last person to leave the lockers?" Moody asked.

The three men made eye contact with each other. It might not have seemed important to them at the time, which was why the answer to the question wasn't immediately apparent.

"I think I was," Archie answered. "They left, and I shot off a quick message to one of my crew leaders. Didn't want to be bothered while we were playing."

I understood where Archie was coming from. The employees at my bookstore rarely bothered me anymore when I wasn't there. The store almost ran itself. However, when they did call or text me, it was almost always at the most inopportune time.

"Tell us about the betting on holes," Moody said, homing in on Archie.

Since Percy and Gideon weren't the ones gambling, the two men left the answering up to Archie. To his credit, he didn't deny the accusation. Would Percy, the lawyer, eventually jump to his friend's defense?

"Aww. You know how it is." Archie leaned forward, placing his elbows on the table. "We get out there. The competitive mojo gets working, and we place small bets from time to time."

"I get that," Moody said. "Not going to lie and say I haven't done it before. If I would have known Clark was as bad as he is, I would have tried to get some of his money, too."

"Hey!" I said. "I'm not that bad."

Moody turned to me. "How many balls did you lose in the first ten holes?"

I had stopped keeping track after losing the fourth. "Point taken."

Moving back to Archie, he said, "Betting fifty dollars here and there is small potatoes. Not worth our going out to every golf course and cracking down on it, but you and Zach were wagering in the thousands."

Archie held out his hands. "Look. I'm not going to plead that what we were doing was legal. I know that. Yes, I was a few thousand in the hole. That's nothing to Zach."

"What about to you?" I asked.

Percy and Gideon watched us like they were watching a tennis match. Their heads swung to and fro with every volleyed question. If they weren't being asked a direct question, they were content to stay quiet.

The corner of Archie's mouth twitched. "It was bigger to me, yes. Would it hurt to lose that sort of money? Yes."

Now Percy spoke, "We all bet money at some point. We play together every week. Sometimes the four of us do. Sometimes it's three. Today, it was just Zach and Archie playing for skins. Here's the other thing. We have a limit, don't we gents?"

Gideon and Archie bobbed their heads at this.

"Yeah. A thousand quid," Gideon said. "That was our cutoff. Anything else above that was for bragging rights and a free lunch paid for by the loser."

"That true?" I asked Archie.

He hesitated ever so slightly, "Y-yes."

Moody and I glanced at each other. I surmised that we were both thinking the same thing: These yuppies were full of it.

Here was another thing about Percy, Archie, and Gideon. They were close enough friends that each was aware of what the other was thinking, bluffing their way through a conversation while singing the same tune. They could cover for each other on the fly.

We might not get straight answers until we separated them. Moody was intelligent enough to be aware of the same fact.

Moody said to Percy, "Archie tells us he thinks you represent Zach. Was he getting a divorce?"

Percy pressed his lips together before answering. "Can't say. Client/attorney confidentiality and all."

"Yeah, but he's dead," I said.

"That type of relationship extends even after the death of a client," Moody informed me.

"Ah, okay." I stared at Percy for a beat, trying to think of a way around the confidentiality rule. My new partner might know from his years of experience.

Nothing came to me, so I asked a question I was interested in seeing how they managed as a group. It was the question that I had stuck in the back of my mind that related to us seeing each other on the driving range prior to the start of the round, a time which seemed like it had happened last week.

I scratched the top of the table and asked nonchalantly, "Tell me about the blonde who works in the pro shop that Zach was whistling at this morning."

CHAPTER
TWENTY-TWO

GIDEON LET OUT a low whistle. "Ah, you mean Zoe. She's a hottie." He paused for a moment and added, "And trouble too."

"What do you mean, trouble?" Moody asked.

"Now, Gideon. Don't be so harsh," Percy said and then to Moody and me, "She's good at her job. Not sure what my friend is getting at."

"What *are* you getting at?" I asked Gideon. The 'hottie' part was clear. She turned several heads this morning, including mine.

The New Zealander squirmed in his seat.

Before he answered, Archie came to his defense. "Just because she blew you off doesn't mean she's trouble." To us, he said, "Zoe has a reputation."

"What kind of reputation?" Moody inquired.

"That she was available," Percy answered.

"She turned *you* down, mate?" I asked Gideon.

He pressed his lips together and held up two fingers. "Twice."

As a group of men, we were all sympathetic to his pain.

"Happens to the best of us," Moody said.

"Not so much with Gideon," Archie said. "I mean, look at him."

Gideon sat back in his chair with a self-aware, confident look on his face. I had to admit, Gideon was a handsome man. The kind one envisioned gracing the covers of surfboard magazines back in the day. Women probably went cross-eyed over his accent. If he had made a move on Zoe, and she turned him down more than once, there had to be a good reason.

I took a sip of water. "How do you know she has a certain reputation?"

The three men exchanged glances.

"She's been known to sleep around with members of the club," Gideon answered.

I set the water bottle down. "Are these rumors or known facts?"

"A little of both," Percy answered. "She got busted a few years ago for sneaking around with a bank executive."

"What was the big deal about it?" Moody asked.

"The guy's wife was supposed to have been here playing a round with her girlfriends," Gideon said. "She came down with a stomach bug while playing, left early, went home, and caught her in bed with him."

"That'll do it," Moody commented.

"I was around Zach this morning. Even bumped into him right over there." I tilted my head toward the pickup counter. "He appeared drunk all morning, and let's be honest, he wasn't what many would consider to be a good-looking man."

Everyone at the table agreed with my assessment. I continued, "It seemed like he and Zoe were, at least, familiar with each other. Did she and Zach have a history?"

Gideon snickered. "Zach wished he had a history with her."

"He had liquid courage in him," Moody said. "Was that why he whistled at her?"

"That probably had something to do with it," Percy conceded.

"Did Paxton know he was trying to get with other women?"

Each person at the table stared at me with surprise.

We hadn't conducted a background check or anything on Zach. Moody was aware of this. He asked me, "Who is Paxton?"

"Zach's wife, apparently," I answered.

Moody's mouth hung open a smidge. "How did you know that?

I shrugged. "I was paying attention when we were at the driving range."

"You must have been paying more attention to them than your bucket of balls," Moody said. "That would explain why you couldn't hit straight except for one time."

Dame guffawed. The others snickered at the tension-easing comment from the straitlaced detective.

I twisted in my seat to face him. "No, that's not the explanation why I couldn't hit straight. The reason is that I flat out suck and haven't hardly picked up a golf club in years."

"Touche," the detective said. He turned his attention to the suspects. "What is it? Did his wife know her husband openly tried to hit on other women?"

Gideon turned his head to Percy. They made eye contact. Archie sat on the end to Percy's left. His bottom lip pooched out like this was news to him.

When they didn't answer, I said to Percy, "Ah. That's why he retained your services. They were getting a divorce."

Percy's mouth shriveled like he was sucking on a lemon wedge. "It's going to come out, but yes, they were getting divorced."

"Who filed for it?"

The attorney did a sharp intake of air before answering. "He was getting ready to."

Moody and I made eye contact. Our first motive.

"We'll need to speak to you privately later," Moody said to Percy.

"Sure thing," Percy said.

Moody continued with the line of questioning. "So, they were getting divorced. Meaning Zach might not have cared about openly coming on to other women. Was this a new behavior or part of his personality?"

"Both really," Archie answered. "He's been that way since we've known him. He was more low-key about it in the past, but recently made it known that he was on the market."

Zach might not have looked the part of a ladies' man, but his bank account would attract a certain type of woman. Of course, those accounts wouldn't be as fat after Paxton's lawyers were through with him. Unless there was something more to their divorce. A prenup perhaps? Percy would know. We'd ask him later. It wasn't any of Archie's or Gideon's business.

"Had Zach been successful in seeing other women?"

"Not that I'm aware of," Archie said.

"Me neither," Gideon added.

Percy didn't comment.

It was crazy and sad at the same time. The concept of divorce was almost foreign to me. Besides a first cousin of mine who lived in Cincinnati, there hadn't been any divorces in my family. I've lost track of how long my parents have been married. We had a quiet golden jubilee dinner for their fiftieth anniversary while Autumn was still alive. Bo didn't attend. He was too busy on the West Coast. The only reason I wasn't still married was because Autumn had been torn away from me. Here these people were treating the discarding of their significant others like yesterday's trash. It hadn't come up yet, and I doubted it would, but I wondered if these three had been through divorces.

"Okay then," Moody said. He backtracked and had them repeat where they were at the time of the murder, looking for one of them to change their story from earlier. What they recalled jived with what they attested to earlier.

When they were done, Moody gave me a look like he was satisfied with their answers and wanted to know if I had any follow ups. I didn't have a follow up, but I had one question not yet asked.

"Did any of you see a golf cart or anyone else moving in the trees between where Zach was killed and the tree line at the back of the course?"

"I was too far away," Archie said.

"Not that I recall," Percy answered.

Those two were the farthest away from where it happened. Them not seeing anything, or claiming not to, wasn't surprising. Percy said he had gone into the woods searching for lost balls while he waited for Zach and Gideon to catch up with them, which meant he lost sight of Archie, and vice versa. Anything might have happened when they were out of each other's sights. Gideon was by far the closest to the incident. If anything, we should focus on him. Of course, we did find a bloodied club in Archie's locker.

Gideon stroked his chin. "Reckon I saw a cart moving on the other side of the trees. I didn't regard it because I figured it was probably a landscaper."

"Was this before or after Zach cried out?" Moody asked.

"It was after," Gideon answered.

I set my water bottle on the table and leaned forward. "Did you hear anyone else's voice besides Zach's?"

Gideon glanced at the ceiling as he pondered the question. Percy and Archie hung on to his every word. As did I.

"You know what?" Gideon said. "I did. It was faint, but I heard it. I didn't think anything of it at the time because I didn't know what was about to happen."

"You heard this voice before he was killed?" Moody asked.

"I did."

Moody jotted a note. It may have been the insanity of the moment after the killing, but Gideon just now remembering this tidbit of information seemed suspicious. Was he trying to make us think SODDIT? Some Other Dude Did It?

Gideon laced his fingers together. "The words the other voice said weren't clear to me. Like I said, I thought it was a couple of landscapers talking to each other. Zach yelled and rushed in the other direction. He said something else. Then I heard the voice."

You could almost hear a pin drop in the room. The only noise came from the pounding deluge outside. I asked, "Did it say much?

Gideon tilted his head down. His eyes narrowed and lifted his head. "I don't think so."

"Then what happened?" Percy asked.

Gideon swallowed, reliving the moment. Tears formed at the corners of his eyes. He said, "I heard a thump and Zach called out. Like, 'Aaagh!' Then there was another thump, and that was it."

"Did you hear anyone running through the trees?" Moody asked.

"I don't think so." Gideon used his thumbs to wipe away the tears. His body shook. Percy put his arm around his shoulders.

"At that point," Gideon said, "I think the blood was thundering in my ears. I froze, not knowing what to do. Then I realized that someone might have attacked Zach, went to his defense, and rushed in that direction."

"That's when you discovered the body," I said.

"It was."

"Tell me," Moody said. "This voice. Was it a man's or woman's voice?"

Gideon took a deep breath. "A man's."

CHAPTER
TWENTY-THREE

AFTER GIDEON REVEALED that he'd heard a male voice nearby, and possibly arguing with Zach before his death, we weren't able to glean much more. Gideon told us that he was so rattled upon hearing Zach's scream that everything became a blur as he tried to come to his friend's aid. Albeit too late. It was completely understandable.

Percy reentered the golf course from the woods and rushed down the fairway to the corner of the 11th when he heard the commotion. Had he gone out the other side of the trees, he may have seen the attacker driving away on a golf cart—if that was the mode of transportation used to get to and from the attack site.

Archie ran from his spot by a green-fronting bunker in the middle of the fairway. He heard Gideon's anguished shout and ran back to them.

Their testimony set up a scene that closely resembled Swiss cheese. There were many holes to fill. The forested area where Gideon and Zach entered the woods wasn't dense with growth. That section didn't have any fat palmettos to hide behind. Instead, slim-trunked loblolly pines covered the area. It was possible to see from where Gideon said he stood when he heard Zach's initial yell before he trampled farther away toward whoever provoked him. Visibility grew more limited from where Gideon stood and where Zach was killed.

He may have seen his friend bolt off, but it was probably too far away for him to make out someone clubbing Zach over the head. In that case, if the attacker escaped from the woods on foot as fast as possible, then Gideon might have only had the impression of someone being there.

If the killer drove to the cart path from the direction leading away from the clubhouse, then Percy might have been deep enough into the woods to have seen the person pass.

We sent the three of them to the police station to give statements. Despite finding the bloodied club in Archie's locker, there wasn't enough evidence to hold any of them, although Moody would have been justified for booking Archie on suspicion of murder. The problem was the police didn't want to arrest someone later found innocent. Archie might have somehow ditched the club there when no one was looking. He had been in everyone's sight from the time Zach was killed to the time we sent him home. His clubs were taken as evidence before that.

Unless Archie was a magician, there was no way to have stowed the potential murder weapon in his locker, which meant someone had planted it there. There had to be a camera feed of everyone who entered and left the men's locker room. Since they will be providing their statements for the next few hours, any one of them might be locked up without trouble if we discover additional evidence during our investigation.

Moody and I were following the course superintendent, Warren, and their head of security to check the feeds. We walked behind them. The security guy was a bull of a Gulf War vet named Jeff with blue-green eyes and a goatee. How did I know he served having only just met him? It said so on his hat. He was all business and offered to help in any way possible.

He had conducted counterintelligence ops while in the military and had been the man responsible for Swaying Palms' current security setup.

Warren moved at a brisk pace, trying to keep up with Jeff. We navigated through less golf-inspired hallways behind the pro shop and restaurant moving toward the middle of the clubhouse. An "Employees Only" sign clung to the door leading to this labyrinth.

We made two more turns before arriving at the security station.

The hub filled a room not much larger than a janitor's closet. A bank of monitors sat above a desk that ran the length of the eight-foot-deep room. A desktop computer sat on the desk in the middle. The screensaver on the monitor flashed random, exquisite photos of the golf course in a slide show. Each had a Dave Gombka photographer signature logo in the bottom right-hand corner. A desk chair sat in front of the computer.

Each feed presented a different area of Swaying Palms. Most showed fixed live footage of the interior and exterior of the clubhouse. Those screens remained static. It made sense to have those locked. Those were the areas where theft most likely would happen. It might be someone shoplifting from the pro shop or grabbing money out of the register behind the bar at the restaurant. I hadn't spotted a feed from the pro shop yet, but that didn't mean it didn't exist.

Three screens displayed rain falling on various holes on the golf course. The pictures changed every few seconds to show another hole. As we entered the room, I scanned the screens, hoping to find a feed showing the exterior cart path bending around the perimeter of the 11th hole.

We bunched together in the room. Warren leaned against the

far wall and lowered an Appalachian State hat over his eyes. A Swaying Palms logo was embroidered on its side. Jeff stood beside him, then Moody, and me closest to the door.

Jeff had a walkie-talkie in his hand. He used the antenna on it to point at the screens. "Gentlemen, these are the eyes and ears of our security system. They capture real-time footage from various cameras placed around the property."

I figured Moody knew more about the ins and outs of security systems than I did. At the bookstore, I had one of those DIY security setups which I had upgraded after finding a dead body by the backdoor. It wasn't Fort Knox, but the coverage was much better after the upgrade. I'd been cheap and hadn't hired a professional security team to set up a system prior. I hoped my clientele were above petty shoplifting, although we did have books mysteriously disappear from our inventory when we updated the counts.

Based on my limited understanding of such systems, I said to Jeff, "That's a lot of cameras. How do you manage all that footage?"

"We've got a central monitoring system that processes and archives the video feeds," he explained. He pointed to a stack of servers behind Warren. "All of that gets stored in there. This allows us to review footage when needed and helps us watch everything happening on site."

"Efficient," I commented, expecting nothing less from this able security lead.

"Thank you," Jeff said. "I wasn't here this morning. This was my day off, but they called me to come in. No one was in this room when the incident occurred."

"Appreciate you coming in on your day off," Moody said.

"Yes. Thank you," Warren said.

Jeff ignored him and said to Moody and me, "No problem. Happy to fulfill my duty. This isn't what you would call a high-action job. The closest we get to action here is stopping the occasional forgetful golfer who tried on a new glove off the rack and forgot to take it off before leaving the pro shop."

"As you can understand," Warren said, "Swaying Palms' members aren't known for being petty thieves." He gestured with a pen at the bank of TVs. "The cameras are mostly to make our members feel secure."

"Ever had to have the police come here?" I asked.

Warren's lips curved, accompanied by a slight raise of one eyebrow. "Only as invited guests to play our course."

Got it. Swaying Palms was above suspicion, according to him.

I asked, "Do your golf carts have GPS trackers?"

Some golf courses have GPS trackers on golf carts to track the pace of play. If they find a group is playing slow, they can send a ranger out to move them along.

Warren shook his head. "We don't have them yet. We're looking into it. Because we're a private course, it's not difficult to keep track of who is falling behind the groups ahead. That's why we have a ranger out there when it's busy."

"Was there a ranger out this morning?" I asked.

"No sir," Warren answered. "He was just clocking in to start his day when we got the call about the incident. He was one of the ones we sent out to get everyone off the course. We usually don't have them work super early because the course doesn't start getting busy until 10:30 or so."

"That'd been nice," Moody said. "Does the ranger use the service cart path that runs around the outside of the course?"

"Sometimes," Warren answered.

I shifted my stance. "Anyone could have taken any cart and gone anywhere on this course at any time?"

He looked at the ceiling, trying to keep track of every part of what I asked. "Correct."

"Were any groundskeepers out at the time of the murder?"

"No, sir," Warren said. "We keep an early short-shift crew on the weekends. They come in before sunrise and start on the first hole and make their way through the course, watering and mowing the greens, raking the bunkers, and changing the hole locations. Then they make sure there aren't any fallen branches on the cart paths at sunup. Then they go home."

Jeff pulled out the chair and sat down in front of the computer. "What can I help you gentlemen find?"

"We're looking for two things," Moody said, moving to stand behind Jeff in his chair. "The victim's group stopped before teeing off on the first hole to use the restroom. They said they left their clubs in a group on the walkway leading to the tee box."

"Were they walking or riding?" Jeff asked.

"Walking," Moody said. "They each had pull carts."

"What time was this?" Jeff moved the mouse, and the screensaver disappeared. The home screen had five icons. I was too far away to see what they were. Jeff clicked on the top one on the left side of the screen.

As the security program loaded, Moody said, "Our tee time was at 7:50 this morning."

"We space out the tee times every seven minutes on the weekends," Warren said. "Fifteen during the week, when there aren't as many golfers. Their tee time was at 7:43."

"There was a backup on the 1st tee," I said. "They took their time getting there."

"Roger." Jeff clicked the mouse. "Let's see. Here it is."

A box on the computer monitor appeared, showing a live camera feed looking out from atop the doors near the locker rooms leading out to the course. A walkway made of red pavers in a herringbone pattern led the way to the gray asphalt cart path. Rain poured causing puddling. The focus was on the walkway. Where the men would have set their clubs to come into the restroom was far away from the camera's perspective.

What looked like a dimmer knob on a light switch for overhead lights sat on the desk to the left side of the keyboard, on the opposite side of the mouse. Jeff twisted the knob, and the feed moved in super speed backward through time. The rain and puddles disappeared as he went. When the rain faded away, golfers moved with exaggerated movements in and out of the clubhouse.

Right before Jeff stopped his time traveling, for the briefest moment, we saw Zach, Percy, Archie, and Gideon walk into the clubhouse together. The time in the corner of the display read "7:41:23."

"Here we are gentlemen," Jeff said like he was a taxi driver dropping us off at our destination.

The still image showed the four men standing at their golf bags, which they had pulled to the far side of the cart path from the camera's vantage point.

Moody grunted. We already had a problem.

CHAPTER
TWENTY-FOUR

THE PROBLEM WASN'T what was in the image. The problem was what would come after the video started moving.

The cart path was at the top of the screen in the distance. All that was visible to start with were the men's legs and the bottom half of their bags.

"That's not ideal," I said.

"I apologize, gentlemen," Jeff said. "That's the only camera we have on that spot."

"Okay," Moody said with a sigh. He motioned to Jeff with a finger. "Run it."

"Yes, sir." Jeff clicked the mouse, and the scene played out.

Zach, Gideon, Archie, and Percy left their bags and walked toward the camera to the door. I paid particular attention to Archie. He walked away from the next-to-last set in the line. The last set was Zach's to the right. Archie's were between his and Percy's. Gideon's were first on the left.

Zach already walked with a slight stagger from the alcohol. He opened the door and walked in, disappearing from view. Gideon held the door open for his other two mates.

Once they were inside, I trained my eyes on Archie's clubs at the top of the screen. It irritated me that the actual clubs weren't visible. During the time they were inside, two golf carts motored past and didn't slow when passing the clubs. Two sets of legs walked by, heading in the opposite direction from the first tee. The first set wore dark pants and moved at a brisk pace. The second set of legs weren't in a hurry and slowed as they went past the clubs before continuing at the same rate as before.

"Stop it there," Moody said.

Jeff paused the feed.

"Rewind it back a few seconds and freeze," Moody commanded.

Jeff did as he was instructed, leaving a shapely pair of legs frozen in time.

Moody looked over at Warren. "Any idea who those belong to?"

Warren didn't need to answer. Jeff did. "That's Zoe."

The superintendent confirmed Jeff's statement with a nod.

Moody jotted notes on a pad. "Continue, but only let it play until she walks up to the clubs and freeze it again."

"Roger." Jeff hit play.

Zoe moved from right to left across the top of the screen. Or her legs moved, that is. They hesitated ever so slightly when passing the clubs. Jeff paused during her pause. The feed displayed **7:43:06**. Moody noted it.

"Okay, let it play," Moody said.

Jeff clicked the mouse. The video moved forward. Zoe's legs walked out of view on the left side at the top of the screen. It was still early in the day during the video, and no one else entered the feed. Archie was the first player to return. He exited the door as Zoe disappeared. Zach was behind him, followed by Gideon and Percy.

They returned to their bags, grabbed the handle of the pushcarts, and pulled their clubs away to the first tee.

"Can't really tell anything from that," Moody commented.

Jeff turned in his chair to face us. "Didn't figure you would."

Moody grunted.

My eyebrows came together. "Can you go back to where she walked past the bags?"

"Yessir." Jeff twisted back to face the monitor and placed his hands on the mouse with one hand and the wheel with the other.

Moody rotated his shoulders toward me. "What are you looking for?"

I nodded at the screen. "I think the four of us focused on the legs during the first playthrough."

"Not that you can blame us," Jeff said absently as he rewound the feed.

The perfect pair of legs walked backward through time to a point before they walked past the grouping of clubs.

"Okay," I said. "Play it, first at normal speed and then again in slow motion. Try not to pay attention to her legs, but to Archie's bag."

Jeff complied and played the video twice, as I instructed. At normal speed, nothing seemed irregular besides the momentary pause as she walked past the bags. When he played it back in slow motion, I saw something different.

"Did you see that?" I asked.

"See what?" Moody answered.

"Archie's bag."

"What about it?"

"It appeared to wiggle the tiniest bit."

Moody squinted and leaned forward, instructing Jeff to replay it again at the same diminished speed. After Zoe crisscrossed the screen again at the slower pace, Moody said, "I don't see anything."

Jeff and Warren agreed. I was the odd man out.

I looked at Moody and pointed at the screen. "Would your forensics' team be able to tell?"

"Yeah. Probably. I'll have Jeff send this to us. You can do that, can't you?"

"Yessir," Jeff answered. "I can do that however you want in any format you want."

I figured Moody to be a guy who still had a working Betamax player stuffed in his attic. Did Jeff send it that way? I shook my head to clear away the offbeat thought.

"I'll have Lucien get with you," the detective said. "Do you have any cameras around the 11th hole?"

Jeff dipped his chin. "There's one on the tee. Because of the hole setup, with the homes on the other side and the 16th fairway being separated by trees on the right side of the hole, we couldn't get any other cameras back there."

"You got a perimeter cart path back there," I pointed out. "Why couldn't you have a camera there too?"

Jeff turned to Warren, whose face remained neutral and then back to us. This was Jeff's department. "I, I'm not sure the reason, to be honest. I guess I should have."

"Probably so," Moody said.

It struck me that Warren must have great trust in Jeff. That he had Jeff setup the camera arrangement and never went back to check to make sure all the bases were covered. We were still at the point in the investigation where I didn't trust anyone and there might have been a reason why Jeff didn't have that area covered. Or he could be inepter at his job than Warren or he let on.

We stood uncomfortably in the cramped room together while

Moody pondered what to do next. I was out of my element and left that decision to him.

At length, the detective said to Jeff, "I want you to search through and find every instance of the victim and his group on tape and send it to us."

"Yessir," Jeff said.

"What about Zoe?" I asked Moody. "Shouldn't we try to see where she was coming from and where she went after she passed the clubs?"

Moody said to Jeff. "Do that too."

"It'll take a while, but I'll pull it together and send it to you," Jeff said.

"Thanks," Moody responded. "I'll have Lucien get with you."

"I'll be looking out for him," Jeff said.

Moody, Warren, and I left Jeff in the security room and returned to the hallway.

"What now?" I asked.

Moody didn't have to think for long this time. "Let's go talk to the blonde."

CHAPTER
TWENTY-FIVE

ZOE HAD HER head down, leafing through a stack of what looked like sales reports behind the counter by the register. Her blonde ponytail fell around her left shoulder. Her hand moved up as she twirled a finger through the curl on the end. She wore a green athletic fit tank top with moisture-wicking fabric and the Swaying Palms logo on the left chest. I couldn't envision any amount of sweating would cause her to stink like Moody and I did.

The pro shop was empty except for her. Moody instructed Warren to vamoose while we questioned the potential witness. I personally wouldn't have allowed him to remain in the security room while Jeff showed us the camera feeds on the chance that he was in on Zach's murder. It was Detective Moody's case. I deferred to him on those matters, but perhaps I should speak up next time. After all, that's what the mayor was paying me the big buck to do.

She raised her head, cocking it to the side, when she sensed our presence, giving us a smile as she glanced at us. "Gentlemen, what can I do for you?"

"We were hoping to ask you a few questions," Moody said and introduced himself and me.

She gave me an appraising look with her vibrant blue eyes. She had an angular chin and high cheekbones. I wasn't sure why she would spurn Gideon, but I imagine that if they ever had a baby, it would be either the most beautiful girl or most handsome boy in the world.

"Hello there," she said to me. Her eyes glimmered and lips formed a slight curve.

I'd seen that look before from women, especially after Autumn died and more often after I lost much-needed weight. I'd packed on thirteen pounds following her loss, but I'd worked at losing it after meeting Gomez. I did it telling myself that I needed to take better care of myself, but in the back of my mind, I was aware I wanted to look good for Gomez.

Then she got engaged to Lucien and that went out the window. No matter. My new physique was closer to my baseball playing days and might have been what attracted Andrea, and that's who was important to me now. At least that's what I told myself. Meeting Andrea made me double my efforts at getting in better shape.

The look Zoe was now giving me not only set my heart racing, but my mind told me to *be careful*.

"How are you doing?" I asked.

She cocked her head to the other side and propped it up under a fist, her elbow resting on the counter. I kicked myself for asking such a stupid question, but in her presence, with that smile, it was the best I could come up with. No one will ever accuse me of being smooth with the ladies.

"Better now," she said, grinning and looking up at me, batting her eyelashes that seemed too long to be real.

Moody grunted and kicked off the questioning. "Is this your department?"

Zoe tore her eyes off me and shifted to the detective. "It is. I'm also a PGA certified instructor and give lessons."

"Are you the course pro?" he asked.

Her nose wrinkled ever so slightly. "No. That honor belongs to Ken Huff. I mostly instruct the women, although he takes a few of them on occasion."

Moody took out his notebook and jotted the name down.

"Mostly," Zoe said, "this is my domain."

"How long have you run this pro shop?" I asked.

She puckered out her bottom lip, pulling down on it with her forefinger. Bo would have melted at the sight had he been here. I might have gotten a little weak in the knees myself. It really was too cute. "Going on six years, I think. Right after I left the tour."

"You were on the LPGA Tour?" Moody asked, impressed. As was I. Talented too? She seemed to have it all.

"No," she said, the disappointment clear in her voice. "The Women's All Pro Tour. One notch down from the LPGA."

"Oh, nice," I said.

"It's the qualifying tour to make it to the LPGA circuit," Zoe explained. "I never quite made the cut. I chased that dream for several years after college before it became apparent that I didn't have what it took to reach that level."

I ran a finger over the edge of the counter. "Where did you go to college?"

"Clemson. Made All-ACC on their golf team."

Clemson University in the Upstate of South Carolina was a member of the Atlantic Coast Conference and competed at the highest collegiate levels. If she made the All-Conference team, she must have been good. She'd probably take most anyone who belonged to Swaying Palms to the cleaners, men included.

"Nice," Moody and I said simultaneously.

"I graduated with two degrees in business and had a golfing background," she said. "When I learned that this position was open and got the job, I traded in my tour card and moved here."

Finding someone born and raised in Myrtle Beach was akin to finding a unicorn on the moon. Most residents I've met moved here from other areas. The demographic skews older, so there are plentiful retirees in the Grand Strand. When I met someone as young as Zoe—I had her pegged as being a decade younger than myself—they often had the same story she just told. They were stuck in whatever job or role they had in life and found an opportunity to live here. Even if the pay was less, you still got to do what you love and live at the beach. Win-win.

"What qualifies Ken to be the club pro over you?" I asked. "If I had the ability to tout a former professional golfer giving lessons to members, I would put you ahead of anyone else."

I didn't add that if her face and body appeared in the brochures as the main golf instructor, they'd have men beating down the doors to hold a session with her.

She hefted a shoulder. "Thanks, but Ken's been here for years. Flirted with the PGA Tour in the eighties." She absentmindedly ran a hand down her ponytail, drawing our attention.

Moody had had enough small talk. "You heard about the murder."

Zoe lowered her chin. "It's a shame. Zach was a valued member here."

A bit of a dry response, but I understood from my limited time from being around the deceased how he might rub people the wrong way.

"We were on the practice range this morning," Moody said. "You were there in the first space, weren't you?"

"I was. I like to get in at least a small bucket before I open the shop."

"Thought so," Moody said.

"We were down from you, past Zach and his playing partners," I said.

Zoe crossed her arms. "Okay." She rolled her eyes as if that kind of detail would escape her.

"Zach whistled at you," I said. Her face remained unexpressive. "You didn't seem to notice."

"Oh, no," she said. "I noticed. I learned to ignore him long ago."

"Not the first time he'd done something like that?" Moody asked.

"Nope. He makes crude remarks to me, to the beverage cart girl, Grace, and even to ladies on the wait staff. He branded himself as a real Casanova."

"You don't seem upset at his death," Moody said.

"I'd be lying if I said I was." Her crossed arms tightened, inadvertently drawing attention to her chest, forcing me to look away. "Yeah, I'm aware he was this big real estate mogul and philanthropist, but that doesn't mean I had to like him. Doesn't mean I wanted him dead either if that's what you're getting at."

It took three minutes for Moody to get on Zoe's bad side. Maybe we were playing good cop/bad cop. Or that was just the detective's glowing personality. Either way, I played the good cop.

"I'm not sure that's what my partner is implying," I said. It occurred to me that referring to Moody as my "partner" was something I never imagined I would say. I shook the idea away. "You're making an observation, right, detective?"

Moody glared at me like he would shoot me if he had his gun

on him. After an uncomfortable moment, he said to Zoe, "Yes. That's all it is. An observation."

Her shoulders sagged in guarded relief. She was ready to get us out of her shop. "What else would you like to know?"

"Did you know the victim outside of the golf course?" Moody readied his pen over his notebook.

"No, I've only seen him here."

"Where were you at around 7:43 this morning?"

She tapped a finger on her left biceps, arms still crossed, defensive. "That's a specific time. Let's see. That was about fifteen minutes before I opened the shop. I'd finished hitting my bucket." She stared at the corner of the ceiling as her finger continued tapping on the well-toned muscle. "Oh, I'd gone and talked to the starter on the first hole."

Moody jotted a quick note. "What did you talk to him about?"

"His wife had been trying to get in with me for a lesson," she answered. "I'd gone over to let him know that I'd had a cancellation this afternoon if she wanted to come in."

That was something to confirm with the starter.

While Moody wrote on his notepad, I asked Zoe, "Did you see Zach or any of his partners as you were going to or from the starter?"

Another glance at the corner of the ceiling. More taps with her finger. A cute scrunching of her forehead. "Not that I recall. I had to rush back and get things ready for the beverage cart girl, Grace. She was running late. She's an actress playing a man in some all-girl comedy troupe and their performance went late last night. One of Zach's friends has a daughter in the same group."

"Which one?"

She puckered her lips. "I think it's the attorney guy."

"Percy?"

"Yeah, that's the one." Zoe tapped a finger on the counter. "Grace is also going to HGTC to be a paralegal. She's hinted that she might go to work for Percy after she graduates."

"Interesting," I said.

"Which direction did you come back into the clubhouse after speaking to him?" Moody asked.

"I came back in through the employee entrance at the front of the clubhouse."

The detective shifted his weight. "When you were walking out to speak with him, which direction did you take?"

"Around the back side."

"On the way to him, did you see a group of clubs near where golfers exit the locker rooms?" I asked.

"Maybe. Probably," she answered. "They're such a common sight that they blend in with everything else. I remember thinking about who else I might get to fill the hole in my afternoon if the starter's wife couldn't make it. I might not have noticed."

"Zach and his partner's clubs were left there where the cart path passes by the locker rooms while they tinkled before starting their round," I said. "Are you sure you didn't see them?"

"Am I sure? No," Zoe responded. "Like I said. I see a million golf clubs a day. I've seen you around on the news. You own a bookstore, right?"

"I do." I already saw where she was going with this.

"And you're there most every day?"

"Seems like it."

"And you probably have thousands of books in your store."

"I do."

"If I asked you about a specific book that you might have passed in the store early one morning before you opened, would you be able to tell me exactly where and what it was?"

It was a stretched metaphor, but I got her point. "Sometimes. It's easy for books to blend in with one another."

"Okay then," she said, like she'd made her point. "Do you have any other questions for me about this?"

We didn't. Moody informed her we might have more questions later.

She bit her thumbnail and stared at me with hungry eyes. To Moody, she said, "I'd be perfectly fine if you sent your partner to my house for a follow up later tonight."

Moody didn't know how to respond. Nor did I. My face caught fire. I never liked it on mystery shows when a potential suspect brushed off the investigators in such a way, like they had the authority to end an interview, particularly in this forward way. It always made me suspicious when they did that, but you realize at the end when it's revealed that the person was innocent all along. They were just busy and wanted the investigator out of their hair because they were jerks.

The question was, was Zoe a jerk, or did she know something she didn't want us to discover?

Zach's partners were absolutely correct. Zoe was trouble.

Also, I had that nagging suspicion that she'd said something during our conversation I should have paid more attention to, but I couldn't put my finger on it.

I hated it when that happened.

CHAPTER
TWENTY-SIX

"WHAT NOW?" I asked Moody as he led the way out of the clubhouse.

We stood on the landing at the top of the stairs leading down to the parking lot. Rain dripped off the overflowing gutter at the edge of the overhang along the front of the porch. The parking lot was still half full. Most of the vehicles were from the police department. A long, black Mercedes was double parked near the front. Two black vans with the words CRIME SCENE on their sides were parked up front in the fire lane. A mixture of civilian cars, trucks, and SUVs were parked at the rear of the lot. I assumed they belonged to the employees.

The drone of rain falling on the porch's roof calmed my nerves, bringing back memories of my early childhood in Southern Ohio. We had a sliding glass door that led out onto a concrete porch. When it rained like it was currently, I'd spread out my favorite blanket my grandma made for me and sit for hours watching the rain. I recalled several times when Mom would wake me up from a nap that I didn't know I was taking. For that reason, I loved a good, long rain shower.

However, having one happen today of all days hindered the investigation.

Moody stopped halfway between the front door and the edge of the porch and looked out. There was no sign of the rain letting up anytime soon. Gray clouds stretched to infinity in the sky.

"This isn't helping," he said.

I stood beside him. "Nope."

I waited for him to decide on our next course of action. The driving range lay off to our right. The first tee was in the opposite direction. A security camera was mounted above the front entrance behind us. Another camera hung on a light pole at the front of the parking lot between where we stood and the driving range to deter theft from the myriad of the members' luxury vehicles.

There weren't any cameras between us and the first hole. If Zoe was telling the truth, that was the direction she would have taken to come back inside after speaking to the starter. I couldn't tell if there was an employee entrance between here and the edge of the clubhouse in that direction. Perhaps there was. If so, there should be a camera there as well.

Moody had requisitioned a couple of clear heavy-duty rain ponchos from the crime scene crew for him and me to use. We put them on but still wore our golf clothing underneath. The thick plastic of the ponchos had "MBPD" stenciled on the back. At least that made us look official and not like victims being protected from the rain.

The rain had a calming effect on Moody as well. When it seemed like he was about to fall asleep on his feet, he echoed my impressions about Zoe's story. "Let's walk down that way," he said, pointing to our left.

I led the way, taking a hesitant step off the porch and into the storm. A million droplets of water at once began pitter-pattering on the plastic poncho. Moody grunted as he stepped out into the open beside me.

We walked with a brisk pace down the sidewalk, separating

the perfectly manicured flower beds that ran along the front of the clubhouse and the parking lot. The edge of the building was perhaps a hundred feet away from the front entrance. The overflowing gutters created a bevy of tiny waterfalls along its length.

A gap in the bushes halfway between the entrance and the building's edge led to a recessed alcove with an employee entrance.

It was my turn to grunt. "No camera."

We studied inside the alcove, outside the alcove, and at the parking lot directly across the sidewalk from the alcove. We didn't spot any security coverage for this door. *Fantastic.*

Despite the rain slickers, we still sought shelter from the rain and ducked into the alcove. Water dripped from the plastic covers we wore onto the dry cement. I sniffed. I recalled reading somewhere that the smell of rain was called "petrichor" and that the earthy aroma came from a form of actinobacteria. I loved that smell. It brought calmness.

We both ducked, although there was no reason for it, looking to spot any CCTV cameras in the parking lot pointing our way. I saw none, and judging from Moody's negative grunt, he didn't either.

"For a guy so confident in his security setup," I said, "You would think Jeff would have at least put eyes on the employee entrance."

"Common sense isn't all that common," Moody commented. "I want to go talk to Zach's wife, but there's a couple homes near the crime scene I'd like to visit first. See if anyone saw anything."

"I already spoke to the woman who owns one of the houses," I said. "Her name is Genevieve. She's an ER doctor at the hospital and worked overnight last night. Said she had just gotten out of bed and didn't see anything."

"What about the house next door?" Moody asked.

"It's a vacant rental house."

"How long has it been vacant?"

I couldn't quite remember what the good doctor said. "A few months, I think she said."

"Any cameras at either property?"

"Genevieve only has one of those doorbell cameras. Nothing on the back. Not sure about the other house."

Moody twisted his lips. "We'll check into it with whoever owns the rental."

"Genevieve said she sees people come and check the property occasionally."

"Did you ask what they looked like or if she knew their names?"

"I don't think she was aware of who currently owns the place but misses the couple who used to live there. But, no, I didn't get a description."

"Let's go do that."

CHAPTER
TWENTY-SEVEN

WE CHANGED OUT of our golf cleats and into street shoes so as not to destroy too much of the crime scene. Besides, my sneakers were much more comfortable than the golf shoes. Moody commandeered a golf cart and we splashed back out to the 11th using the outside cart path. Rain fell in buckets. The ride was much shorter than navigating the paths weaving around the holes.

We passed one of those small utility vehicles, a little larger than golf carts, coming in the opposite direction. It had a flatbed on the back of it, which was normally used to carry bags of mulch, plants, tools, and the like for the groundskeepers around the golf course. A Hispanic man drove the cart. He held up a peace sign with two fingers in passing.

The crime scene techs were folding tarps used to cover the evidence and wrapping up as we arrived. Moody checked in with Lucien. I kept my distance, trampling and splashing over to the golf course property boundary and then waited beside Genevieve's back gate. The good doctor had gone inside during the storm.

Moody walked back to me. "Lucien said there was nothing else to log, so they were wrapping up and taking any evidence back to the lab for processing. You can go there with me later. The body will be sent to Charleston for the autopsy."

I'd wanted to visit the crime lab ever since Autumn's phone

had been stolen to discern how that might have happened and who might have had access to it.

"Okay," I said without enthusiasm, much like Moody's normal tone. We turned to the large house in front of us. "Should we go through the gate or knock on her front door?"

The rental home stood to the left of Genevieve's. It was the last house on the street. The pavement ended near where a curve in the Intracoastal swung in toward the golf course boundary. A line of short grass lined the back fence of Genevieve's and the rental's property. The house on the other side of the doctor's didn't have a rear fence, but instead had a hedgerow defining the property line. Tall trees on the other side of the hedge blocked our view of that home.

From our vantage point, the grass running along the back fence swung around the corner where another line of loblolly pines marked the edge of the golf course. There appeared to be a gap between the trees and the fence.

I pointed. "Let's go that way and get around to the front."

Moody grunted and led the way.

We made it to the back corner of the fence. The gap between the pines and the fence was about ten feet wide. Far enough apart that if a tree fell along the edge, it might miss damaging the fence.

A four-foot-tall cast-iron fence with black pickets and pointy tops bordered the rental, offering open views of the backyard. It would have been a nice backyard to spend time in had it not been for the overgrown grass and unkempt foliage. A white gazebo that had seen better days surrounded by a weedy flower bed was nestled near the rear corner. A path composed of brick pavers wound its way through the yard to a back deck overlooking a modest, but empty, inground pool. A set of sliding glass doors led to the outside, where a white pergola leaning slightly to one side covered the rear porch.

The house itself was two-storied and made of brick. It appeared unremarkable from the rear of the home.

Moody and I splashed through standing water on our way around the front. Good thing we changed out of the golf shoes. I would have been clinging mud out of the cleats for days. We came to a street that ran along the Intracoastal with concrete barriers, keeping motorists from plunging over the bank and into the water. Five houses fronted the water along this street. They weren't quite waterfront, per se, and that diminished their value. Regardless, the property values on these homes were way above my price range.

"Decent place," Moody said as we rounded the corner and stepped onto a sidewalk.

The plainness of the rear of the home didn't give a hint as to what its front looked like. This colonial home had a front porch with white pillars that ran its length. An elegant white chandelier hung down from the top of the porch above a grand entrance. Two sidelights framed an aged set of white doors. An arched panel of stained glass depicting an egret in flight crowned the doors. A brick chimney stuck out on the side closest to Genevieve's house.

The home was stately and breathtaking when taken in at a distance. As we came around the corner and started up a brick-lined walkway leading to the front door, the home's neglected condition showed. The black shutters had paint peeling. The chandelier was lit, but half of the lights were dim and needed to be replaced. The rental owner must keep it lit to deter would-be thieves, although I wasn't sure how any would get to this home unless they already lived in the neighborhood or played the golf course. It seemed unlikely, but of course, that didn't mean it couldn't happen even in the most upscale of neighborhoods such as this one.

"Think anyone's home?" I asked.

Moody studied the light on the porch and grunted, "Maybe. They left the light on for us."

I doubted it since Genevieve had said the place was vacant, but you never know when the owners might happen to be here. A two-car garage was attached to the house on the left side. The door was down, but it was possible the owners had pulled in and closed it to keep their vehicle from getting soaked.

The rain abated as we stepped onto the porch. Our ponchos dripped onto the otherwise dry cement. The blinds in the windows were closed, offering us no view of the home's interior. Wood rails lined the porch. The paint on them was cracked and peeling.

The detective thumbed the doorbell. A bell *rang* an ominous sound inside. I half expected Lurch from the Addams Family to open the door.

"Such a shame," I said to myself. It was easy to understand why the house had no tenants. The rent was probably through the roof as it was, limiting the pool of would-be occupants. *If* I was the type of person who had the money to live here, the condition of the home would be below my standards.

We waited a solid two minutes before Moody said, "Nobody's home."

He looked to his left at Genevieve's home on the other side of the fence. "Let's go speak to her."

CHAPTER
TWENTY-EIGHT

WE STEPPED OFF the porch and back into the downpour. The Intracoastal streamed past the street, carrying a musky scent with it. Thunder vibrated in our ears through the plastic hoods. Moody held Genevieve's front gate open for me after stepping through first. Stately magnolia trees flanked either side of the walkway leading to her front porch. Well-kept flower beds ringed both trees. A mermaid statue blowing water from a conch shell had its own special space in front of the tree on our left. Each blade of grass in the yard was of the same exact height. Weeds were *non grata* here.

I rang the doorbell this time since I had met Genevieve earlier.

"Introduce us," Moody said. "Let me do the talking."

"If you say so."

He gave me a cross look but didn't respond.

Genevieve opened the door. She had ditched her purple satin robe for a black shirt that read "Icahn School of Medicine" across the front. I vaguely thought that it was from Mount Sinai Hospital in New York but wasn't positive. A pair of teal athletic pants clung to her long legs.

"Hello again," she said.

"Hi," I said. "Sorry to bother you, but Detective Moody here would like to ask you a few follow-up questions."

Moody stuck out a hand, which she took with a cautious touch.

"I'm Detective Phil Moody of the MBPD, and I'm the lead investigator of the incident which occurred behind your house this morning. I'd like to fill in some gaps in what Clark told me you said to him."

Her mouth opened and closed and subconsciously leaned away.

"Don't worry," I said. "You're not a suspect. We were looking for more information about the house next door."

Moody shot me another sour expression. I'd already violated the rule he set forth before she answered the door. Sometimes, I can't keep my mouth shut.

"We've met," she said to me.

"Yes," Moody said. "Didn't recognize you out of your doctor's coat."

Genevieve's shoulders relaxed. Her fingers twisted a thin silver necklace which hung around her neck. "Yes, I would be happy to tell you what I know."

She hadn't invited us into her home—which I would have been curious to see if the inside matched the perfection of the outside—nor had Moody asked to come in. Like most conversations with him, he likely expected this to be a short conversation. Rain droned on her porch roof.

He pulled out his notepad and readied the stubby pencil. "Clark says you don't recall the name of the people who purchased the house next door."

It wasn't a question, but Genevieve answered, "No, I do not. Never met them."

"No problem," he said. "Should be easy enough to do a property search."

If there were no cameras and no one lived there, I wasn't sure what the point of doing that would be.

"Have you ever seen them? The people who own it?"

"Yes. They pop in from time to time at all hours. I even see lights on in the place in the wee hours of the morning when I come home from the hospital."

"Maybe they forget to shut them off," Moody suggested.

Genevieve shrugged. "Don't know. It's possible, but it seems to happen a couple times a month."

"What about during the day?"

She rubbed a hand across the side of her face. "About the same frequency."

"Have you ever introduced yourself?"

"No, I haven't. When they come in the front, they park in the garage and close the door."

Moody made a note. The way she said that last part raised a question in my mind. Despite Moody's warning to keep my trap shut, I said, "You said when they come in the front. Have you seen them come in the back way?"

Moody didn't shoot laser beams out of his eyes at me on that one. Maybe he thought it was a good question. I did.

"I have," Genevieve answered.

"What do they look like?"

Her lips compressed and eyebrows came together. "Let's see. It was hard to tell because I always saw them from a distance. It was a man and woman. Never got a good look at his face. Same with the woman, although she seemed like she was pretty."

"What makes you say that?" Moody asked.

"I don't know," Genevieve said. "More of a feeling, really. I mean, she carried herself well, had long blonde hair, and seemed like she was in good shape. If they were a couple, I'd call her his trophy wife. Perhaps she worked for him."

"Again," Moody said, "what makes you say that?"

"He had the keys to the front and back door."

"Oh," Moody and I said together.

He asked, "You say you saw them come in the back door?"

"Yes. That was the only time I saw them. They would come from the golf course and go through the backyard."

Moody said to me. "Then he might be a member of Swaying Palms."

"That's what I was thinking," I said. To Genevieve, I asked, "Did you ever see them come in the front together?"

She rubbed her chin. "No. Like I said, when he came, he'd pull into the garage and shut the door behind him. I never knew if anyone was with him."

"What kind of car did he drive?"

"Some long, black Mercedes."

"How do you know it was him driving?" I asked.

She gave me a condescending look, like I had insulted her intelligence. "Because I saw him through the car windows."

"Ah. Makes sense." My cheeks warmed.

I glanced over at Moody who was trying to hide a smile. He cleared his throat. "When you would see them come off the golf course together and enter the house, how long would they stay?"

"Sometimes ten, fifteen minutes. Sometimes longer." She pointed a long finger toward the back of the house. "I would see them when I would be sitting out on the veranda reading."

"Did they ever see you?" Moody asked. His little hand moved at speeds I didn't think the detective was capable of as he made notes on his pad.

"Not that I could tell," she answered. "I usually sit in the shade on the covered veranda."

"Ever speak to them?"

"Never."

His pen made final notations before he closed the pad. "Thank you for your time. If you think of anything else that might be helpful, please give me a call." He handed her a card from his back pocket.

She accepted it and studied its text. "Thank you. I will. Have a good day."

We said our fond farewells and stepped off her porch and back into the rain. It continued to drench us as we made our way back to the clubhouse. I pondered the conversation with Genevieve. It didn't make sense why they would leave the golf course to check on the house if they were able to come through the front of the house during their business hours. Why waste time popping into one of their properties when playing golf?

The obvious answer hit me: the rental might have been a love nest.

Once back to the much drier clubhouse, Moody imparted instructions to Kevin and Lucien, who had joined us there, and then met with Warren one more time.

I didn't have much to say during those conversations, especially not to Lucien. On a superficial level, it was easy to see what Gomez saw in him. I'm secure enough in my masculinity to admit that he's a handsome man with a roguish appearance. If he wasn't wearing his work clothes, then I pictured him in a bright orange jumper with a prisoner number stenciled on the back. The tiny voice in the back of my mind wouldn't shut up.

It was interesting to watch Moody in action as the lead detective. After being around the man during the past year or so, I had him pegged as a stereotypical bumbling detective that you see on TV. What I saw today was the opposite. With Gomez away at a conference, he assumed command of the situation without hesitation. There were no missteps or goof ups that I could tell.

After we said our goodbyes to them, Moody and I stepped back out onto the porch. The rain showed no signs of letting up. My Jeep seemed like a long way away across the parking lot. I didn't look forward to crossing open territory to reach it.

Moody took a deep breath when he and I were alone. No one moved in the lot.

"Thanks for your help, Clark," he said.

"No problem. What now?"

"I'm going to go home, shower, and then head to the station. I suggest you at least go get dry. You can meet me there, and then we'll go speak with Zach's wife."

I would love nothing more than to get into dry clothes right now. If the pro shop wasn't closed, I would have gotten at least a pair of shorts and a t-shirt from there. Maybe talk to Zoe again.

"I can do that."

"I'm going to have to start a report when I get to the station, so you can take your time getting there. I'll send you a text and let you know when I'll be ready to go talk to Zach's wife."

"Would it be okay if I just met you at their place?"

He grunted. "Sure. I'll send you the address."

"Thanks."

He pulled his notepad from his back pocket and wrote something with his pencil on a blank page near the back. He ripped it out and handed it to me.

I looked at the paper. In barely legible print, it read:

horrycounty.org/apps/LandRecords.

"Horry County has a website where you can search property records," he said. "You can access that from any computer. While I'm doing the preliminary report, see if you can figure out who the rental belongs to. That's Investigating 101. Shouldn't be too difficult to find out and report back to me." He grinned. "Now you get to do some of the tedious work Gomez and I do while you have done all of the legwork in the cases you've solved."

I glanced down at the paper he gave me not knowing that this simple web address would start a cascade of events leading to figuring out who killed Autumn and why.

CHAPTER
TWENTY-NINE

ONE OF THE best feelings is when you finally take a much-needed shower. The one I took after getting home was one of the most cleansing showers of my life. Not just to wash off the stink, but to clear my mind. Tom had dropped Bo off at my parents' place after they grabbed lunch at the Kindbelly Café. Turned out that Tom was also a vegetarian, so Bo told me via text that it hit the spot.

I do my best thinking in two places: the car on long drives and the shower. The coffee bar idea in the bookstore came about on a road trip back from Destin while Autumn and I were discussing the possibility of opening Myrtle Beach Reads.

The scene that took place on the 11th hole played on repeat in my mind. From our viewpoint, the closest person to Zach at the time of his murder was Gideon. Gideon had said he was in a different area of the woods when he initially heard Zach call out. However, there were no witnesses to that. We had to take his word for it.

Yes, Moody and I saw the path in the woods where Gideon said he and Zach parted. It might have been fresh or an old deer trail. It's possible Gideon went the other way at first to establish the path and then circled back and hit Zach over the head with a club.

Percy was the second closest of the group to Zach. I'd crossed through a narrow patch in the woods to get to the perimeter cart path. It's possible that Percy entered the woods under the guise of searching for lost balls to pocket, but instead backtracked down the cart path to get to Zach. What nagged me about that was, how would he have known Zach would be in the woods long enough to kill him? Or was it a gamble? Gambling was a pastime these men enjoyed. It wasn't difficult to figure that carried over to his personality.

It was possible that Percy did it. If so, why? He was going to be Zach's attorney in divorce proceedings with his wife. Was Paxton aware that he was planning a divorce? Had she already asked for one? Either way, Percy would get paid for his efforts. It didn't make sense to murder a client who hadn't paid yet, and by all appearances, should have had the dough to cover Percy's fees.

Archie said he had been on the fringe of a sand trap by the green. Percy backed that up. I didn't see how he would have done the deed.

Moody and I were going to meet with Paxton later. She should know about her husband's death by now. It would be interesting to gauge her response to Zach's death if their marriage was, in fact, on the rocks. She likely was more familiar with him than anyone else and might tell us who held a grudge against her late husband.

Of course, if they were getting a divorce and she knew it, maybe he had ticked her off, and that was the final straw.

One factor I hadn't thought of was the trail leading from the perimeter cart path to the location where Zach was killed. It seemed like a fresh trail and could have been the killer who left that trail, but a landscaper could have also made it this morning.

If it was the murderer, the lack of cameras along that path would make it difficult to track people's comings and goings.

I finished rinsing the soap from my body and turned off the water. Once I had gotten dressed, I was famished. Wanting something quick, I took two slices of bread out to the bread box, some sliced turkey and muenster from the fridge, and put a generous dollop of Chick-fil-A sauce on it. That stuff tastes great on just about anything.

The covered back deck was calling my name. I grabbed my laptop, sandwich, and a beer from the fridge and sat at a picnic table in the middle of the deck overlooking the lake so the laptop wouldn't be in danger of getting wet. Rain dripped off the sides of the porch roof. Lake Vivian wasn't an enormous lake. It was more of a retaining pond for the defunct golf course that used to surround our neighborhood. With it long gone and the clubhouse torn down, home developers had come in and built cookie-cutter subdivisions on overgrown holes.

I wasn't sure how it got its name or why it got a name, but the deed on my property said my parcel of land had twenty-four feet of lakefront property along "Lake Vivian." Which reminded me of the reason I brought the laptop out here. I fired it up and bit into the sandwich. While the computer loaded, I twisted the cap off the beer and took a chug. A million drops of rain pitter-pattered the top of the lake.

Once I brought up the web browser, I entered the web address Moody gave me. The screen displayed a large map with a cream-colored background centered on Conway, the county seat. Squiggly lines across the screen denoted the larger roads. Faint blue lines depicted the rivers, streams, and lakes.

A search box in the top-left corner said that it accepted searches for Owners, PIN, TMS (whatever that was), Addresses, or Subdivisions. I punched in the rental property address at Swaying Palms from a note I'd taken on my phone and hit ENTER.

Another panel appeared below the search box with a pre-formatted version of the address I had entered. I clicked it. The map flashed and reappeared, zoomed in on the rental property from above. A pin with a blue flag marked the home's precise location. Clicking a box in the lower-right would have enabled me to get a satellite view of the house and the surrounding area, but I didn't see the need.

I clicked on the flag. The map highlighted the property lines in blue. An information box appeared on the left side of the screen. The top line read: **SWAYING PALMS SUBDIVSION; LOT 74**. The information below displayed the full address, year built, square footage, tax values, etc. My eyes widened upon seeing the tax value.

The listed owner was Summit Capital Holdings. I'd never heard of it. The name sounded like one of those generic names an investment company might use. That's where the information about Summit Capital ended. There was no way to click on their name and learn more.

I Googled the name in a new tab and found over a hundred thousand results. I rubbed my jaw. That was too many. The first page was for one company named Summit Capital Partners. That led to a website for a global investment business.

I clicked back and searched through the first two pages of listings. Nothing came close to any company who might have rental properties in Myrtle Beach. I added "Myrtle Beach" to the end of the search string and hit ENTER.

The screen refreshed and narrowed the search down to ten thousand results. I closed my eyes and took a deep breath. This was getting frustrating. Moody handed me this task because it was supposed to have been easy.

My phone buzzed with a text from Moody. In true Moody

fashion, it was succinct and to the point. The message contained an address and a time to meet him there. The home was on 47th Avenue N in Myrtle Beach. I had a premonition as I punched the address into the Maps app on my phone.

The map moved from atop my house and zoomed in on an oceanfront home three doors down from another house I was all too familiar with. John Allen Howard's former residence.

I was heading back to the Golden Mile.

CHAPTER
THIRTY

THE COLOSSAL HOME sat a short walk away from John Allen Howard's old estate. I drove past the place where I'd been a guest for dinner at the same time a tropical storm had passed through. A waterspout came onto land while we were waiting for dinner to start and threw everything into chaos. The composer was shot during the twister. We were stuck in the house for hours while fallen trees blocked the front gate on the road and the unexpected storm surge kept us from getting out via the beach. It was a night I will never forget.

After Howard's death, the estate went up for auction. I passed by the gate and saw children's toys in the front yard. A huge oceanfront estate would be a nice way to grow up. I grew up in a cul-de-sac in a small, hilly, tree-lined neighborhood in southern Ohio. My childhood was nice, but I wouldn't have complained if my parents raised me on this illustrious stretch of Myrtle Beach.

Moody's gray police-issued Ford Explorer sat on the grassy berm at the front of the address he had given me. I parked the Jeep behind him and got out, throwing a hood over my head from an L.L. Bean rain jacket I had grabbed from my closet. I checked to see if any cars were coming. There weren't. I hopped up on the sidewalk and jogged up next to Moody's car.

I waited in the pouring rain while he tapped on the keyboard of a laptop in the passenger's seat. He closed the screen and stared at me through the passenger's side window. The invitation I was hoping he would give to climb in the car never came, and I just kept getting wetter.

Another minute passed by before he opened his door and got out. I wondered if he left me waiting on purpose.

"You ready?" he said.

"Sure," I answered in a noncommittal tone. My normal response to that question was that I was born ready. As I looked up at this impressive home, I didn't feel the same confidence. Maybe it was because, going in to question a potential suspect, I was kinda sorta on the job. In the other times I'd done this, there wasn't any pressure. I was trying to solve cases out of pure curiosity (except for when Tony Bruno kinda sorta threatened my life). I had to admit, because Gomez wasn't here and Moody had me tag along, I was feeling the pressure. Sure I'd solved cases before, but not in any official capacity. Gomez had been alongside on those. The partner that I had worked so well with wasn't here, and that nagging voice in the back of my head whispered doubts as to whether I was capable of solving this one without her.

A car sloshed past us. Water streamed along the sides of the sidewalk, bound for a storm drain, or seeking an outlet to the ocean.

"Does she know?" I asked.

"About her husband? Yeah. Someone's been by."

I felt a sense of relief of not being present when Paxton learned of Zach's death. Another thing that made me relieved was the fact I didn't do this for a living. I never had to be the bearer of bad news in the other murders I'd solved.

We'd rather be anywhere else on this rainy Saturday afternoon than standing outside in this weather getting ready to speak to the widow of a man killed this morning.

A brick wall obscured our view of the house, except for a tall, terra-cotta tiled roof. We strode past the edge of the wall to an ornate gate with iron bars. The enormity of the estate came into view. It was breathtaking. While not as big as John Allen Howard's former residence, it was impressive. The sprawling architecture featured wrought-iron accents and an expansive terrace along the front. A well-manicured lawn and flower garden decorated the front of the home.

Moody pushed a black button on the call box next to the gate. It beeped. We waited. Rain cascaded off the hood of my jacket and off the brim of his gray trilby hat. He wore a tan trench coat that fell below his knees. Our shoes were soaked. The air smelled of rain. A salty breeze blew from right to left, causing the rain to come down at an angle.

The speaker on the call box crackled, and a smoky female voice said, "Enter" accompanied by the *creak* of the automatic gates opening. We walked through into the driveway once the gates stopped moving. They returned to their position as soon as we were inside.

A stone archway framed an all-glass double door. Marbled glass obscured the small person standing behind it, which had to be Paxton. The door opened before we rang the bell.

I was wrong. It wasn't Paxton standing behind the door. It was a little boy with a cherubic face framed by unruly, sandy-brown hair that fell in soft waves around his ears. He had wide, expressive eyes which were a striking shade of hazel. He had a slim build and delicate features, giving him an innocent and endearing appearance.

He had one hand on the doorknob and the other curled up into a loose fist, cradling his jaw. After initially looking at us upon opening the door, his gaze fell level and unfocused on something in the distance, maybe the rain smattering onto the pavement.

The swift switch in his attention told me this must be the autistic son for whom Zach established the charity. I saw why. I immediately adored him.

He created a soft spot in my surly partner too. Moody bent forward to get more on his level and said in a fatherly voice, "Hello. Is your mother here?"

The boy looked up at Moody but didn't speak. His eyes and expression conveyed a depth of emotion and intelligence. He turned and gazed off to the side.

"Who is it?" a female voice called.

The boy didn't answer but waited for his mom to arrive with his eyes averted and fist on chin.

Paxton came into view. As an able-bodied man, the first sight of a beautiful, captivating woman can leave me at a loss for words. I'd had this feeling twice. When I first met Autumn and, later, Andrea. My attraction to Gina Gomez grew quickly, but I didn't have this feeling the first time I met her. In her defense, I had just found Paige Whitaker's body behind the bookstore and was shaken for other reasons.

I stood straight and sucked in my gut. Paxton was of average height, but that was about all that was average. She had straight, black hair that came down below her shoulders, alabaster skin, and a trim figure. It was easy to see where her son got his angelic face. Paxton had a soft beauty that caused my heart to quicken. She wore a cream-colored tank top with a lacy pattern atop green and white striped short shorts.

"Who is it, Ethan?" she said. The smoky voice we heard through the call box now up close made my heart beat faster. The contrast of voice to cherubic face was a heady combo.

Moody said that someone had been by to break the news about her husband's death. Her present appearance suggested two things: either she was putting on a brave face for her son, or she didn't care. No red, puffy eyes. No tissue balled up in her hand. Nothing.

Despite meeting her for the first time, if I didn't know any better, I would think we'd caught her at home on a normal late Saturday afternoon.

The boy didn't answer.

Paxton put an arm around the boy's shoulders. "Thank you for opening the door." She tousled his hair and said to us, "You must be the detectives."

Moody introduced us. She didn't give him a second look. Her eyes lingered on me. I couldn't tell if she was trying to place me or liked what she saw. Maybe both.

"Hi," I said, sticking out my hand. "I'm sorry for your loss."

She shook my hand with a delicate grip and then placed her hands over Ethan's ears. "No need for condolences. Zach had it coming."

CHAPTER
THIRTY-ONE

I'M NOT A person who gets surprised easily. There have been occasions in my life where I was held speechless. One time was when Autumn and I went on our honeymoon to Hawaii. We'd made plans to go scuba diving, attend a luau, visit volcanoes on Maui, and, of course, relax on the beach.

Autumn had known about my love of coffee since I met her. I was literally drinking a cup when I met her at a tailgating party before a Coastal Carolina football game during our sophomore years. Our classmates were pounding beers. I was drinking coffee. She was sipping tea. We connected instantly.

During one afternoon on our honeymoon, my plan was to spend an afternoon on the beach. Autumn had different plans. She told me we were going out but didn't tell me where we were headed. She blindfolded me after we climbed into a waiting taxi outside our resort lobby.

I calmed down after my initial panic attack. She told the cab driver to go and held my hand all along the way. We rode in the cab for about half an hour. I trusted her. My ears popped at one point, so I knew we were going up in elevation into the mountains. I didn't know what to expect. Ideas flew through my mind of what Autumn might have planned, but what she had in store for me wasn't one of them.

When the taxi finally stopped, Autumn removed the blindfold. We sat in a narrow parking lot outside a nondescript gray building with palm trees flanking both sides and three flagpoles out front. There were no signs or any indication of where we were.

She paid the driver. We exited the cab. Wind blew against our faces. The air carried the best aroma known to man: roasting coffee.

I took a deep breath and asked Autumn what was going on. She had a huge smile plastered across her face. She told me we were going on a backstage tour of the Hilo Coffee Mill. I remember being speechless. That afternoon was one of the best experiences of my coffee-loving life.

It was almost as shocking as when I discovered the body of Paige Whitaker behind the backdoor of my bookstore.

Those two were the first things to pop in my mind when thinking of shocking, speechless moments. Hearing Paxton say that her husband "had it coming" would be added to the list.

We were dripping wet. Paxton didn't make any sign that she wanted us to come in and get comfortable, nor did I blame her. Upon glancing at the designer furniture in the house, I wouldn't want two soaked commoners like Moody and I sitting on my furniture either.

She excused herself and led Ethan away. He didn't make eye contact with us once, after opening the door. He kept his head down with a hand ever-present on his chin. His head bobbed constantly, as though he had a song he liked stuck in his head.

The open foyer led into a massive living room with expansive windows facing the ocean. We weren't invited to go any further than the foyer. Rain limited the view, but there were two brave souls out there walking on the beach. At least this rain system wasn't accompanied by strong winds.

Paxton hadn't brought us here to get comfortable. I wondered if family or a nanny were on their way to help with Ethan while Paxton dealt with the details of her husband's death.

She returned a moment later, without Ethan. "Sorry," she said. "Had to get him comfortable and occupied while we talked."

Paxton pulled out a phone from her back pocket and began messing around with the screen. Without looking up, she said, "What would you like to know?"

I wasn't well versed on proper decorum in a murder investigation interview, but I'd watched enough episodes of *Monk* to know that a potential witness/suspect/family member should be attentive during the conversation with police. My hope was that she was checking messages concerning her husband's death. I leaned forward to glance at her screen. I was taller than she was, so it wasn't difficult. She was scrolling through pictures in her Instagram feed. I'd let Moody handle telling her to put the phone away.

He didn't. Instead, he said, "Clark and I were in the group behind your late husband this morning."

She didn't look up. "Uh-huh."

"We saw the way he acted and treated others. He even had a brush-up with Clark in the grill while we were making the turn from the front 9 to the back."

She glanced at me briefly with a carnivorous eye before going back to Instagram. "That's not surprising."

Moody did most of the talking. He played it cool with her uncaring aloofness. I wanted to snatch the phone from her hand.

"How often did he play?"

"Once a week. Same time. Same place."

"How long had they been doing this?"

"Years."

"Have you been to that golf course before?"

"Yes. Zach was a member, and I was his dutiful wife. They had social occasions where he would have me attend."

"Did you ever play the course?"

"A few times."

She answered every question without taking her attention away from Instagram. My face warmed. I wanted to yell at her, but Moody took it in stride. He's had to speak with countless spouses of victims in his career and likely encountered every perceivable response to losing a loved one.

In this case, I had the sense Zach wasn't loved by Paxton. She might have loved his money, though.

"Then you know about the tricky 11th hole."

"The sharp dogleg with the big sand trap in the corner and water in front of the hole?"

"That's the one."

"Yeah. Challenging."

"Then you are aware of how the hole is shaped."

In a droll tone, she said, "Nothing gets past you."

For the first time, Moody got a little flustered, but kept his cool. I figured where he was going with this. Paxton's turn was coming.

Moody shifted. "If you know the course and that your late husband played there at the same time every week, you might get a sense of when Zach might play through that hole."

He let the comment dangle.

For the first time, Paxton took the bait. Her thumb froze in place. She looked at him. "Are you implying that I killed him?"

"I'm not implying anything," Moody said. "All I'm saying is, you might have a good idea of where he might be on the course at a given time."

She didn't lower the phone, nor did she lower her eyes back to the screen. Moody had made his point.

When her finger swiped the phone for the thousandth time, I got fed up. "Do you even care? Your husband, the one responsible for bringing you this way of living, is dead. And you just keep scrolling, scrolling, scrolling like it means nothing."

Moody placed a cautionary hand on my wrist. "Easy."

My neck was flushed. I took a deep breath. "Sorry."

She tucked the phone in her back pocket. "Sorry."

Moody pretended nothing happened.

"Look," she said, "I'll be the first to admit that I hated the guy. I'm not sure I ever loved him."

"You just loved his money, right?" I asked.

To her credit, she didn't get angry with me. "I'm not going to deny that's why I married him. I mean, I did like him, you know? He promised me the world, and I accepted."

"Did he?" I asked.

She held up two fingers. "Been around it twice."

Now that I had waded into the conversation, it was Moody who stepped back and let me help with the interview.

"He held up his end of the bargain," I said. "What did you do for him?"

She puckered her lips and put a hand on her hip, which she canted to the side suggestively. "What do you think I did for him?"

"Gotcha."

"Look, we got along okay for a long time," Paxton said. "Then he seemed to get bored with me and stopped paying me attention."

"What did you do?" I asked.

Hungry eyes bore into mine. "Found someone who *did* pay me attention."

I gulped, not knowing what to say. If Zach was planning on divorcing her, then that behavior might have been the cause. They had a son with special needs, but the sheer selfishness in this relationship made me feel for Ethan. He didn't deserve this.

Moody jumped in. "Did Zach know about this?"

"Yes, he found out."

"What was his reaction?"

She shrugged. "I didn't care."

"That doesn't answer the question."

She smirked. "He was upset, but we had an open relationship. He had it written into the prenup."

"Had what written?" I asked.

"That we were free to take on partners outside the marriage, and it wouldn't be held over our heads by the other in a divorce."

I took an involuntary step away from her. That explained why she mentioned in her previous comment about finding another man to satisfy her needs so casually. I already carried a sense of loathing toward these people, and we were just scratching the surface. "How often have you done that during your marriage?"

She held up a well-manicured finger. "Just the one time. We got along well for most of our marriage until recently. I'm not sure how often he strayed during the nine years we were married, nor did I ask, especially at the beginning."

"What happened?"

"We had Ethan."

Moody asked the question I wanted to ask, and I'm glad he did. "Is Ethan Zach's real son?"

She might have been offended, but after telling us about the open marriage, it was a fair question. "Yes, he was. I got pregnant three months after we got married, and he told me he'd stay faithful to me. Forget the prenup."

"What do you think changed that?" I asked.

For the first time, Paxton showed a hint of sadness. "I think he went back on his word."

"You mean," Moody said, "he started cheating on you?"

"I'm not positive, but there were clues."

I listened while Moody continued the questions, "Like what?"

"His shirts smelled like perfume I don't wear. Finding a cheap phone lying between pillows on his bed in the pool house."

"The pool house?"

"Yeah," Paxton said. "Zach moved in there last month."

"Why did he move out?"

"We were fighting. A lot. Like I said, he'd lost interest in me and Ethan."

I needed to apply some pressure, get her to react. "Did you know he had retained Percy's services?"

She glared at me. "No."

No indication from Moody that I was out of line, so I kept going. "Does that surprise you?"

Paxton crossed her arms, tapped a foot, and chewed on a manicured thumbnail. I was sure she had her nail technician on speed dial to repair it.

"Not really, to tell the truth. It was heading that way. We couldn't stand the sight of each other. He wasn't good to me."

"How about with the boy?" I asked.

"He was okay with Ethan. Are you aware of the charity foundation he has for autism awareness?"

"We are," Moody said.

"It was all a front to make him look like a decent human being. It was fake."

"You mean he kept the money the foundation raised?"

"Some of it," Paxton answered. "I mean, yeah, he gave a chunk to research. It's all documented, but after the annual galas, he'd take the cash donations and award himself with a new Rolex."

It's standard knowledge that when one person in a marriage gets killed, a large percentage of the time, it is the spouse who ends up committing the crime. Which meant that Paxton was near the top of our suspect list. Thus far, she'd been bluntly honest.

She just told us that her husband embezzled from his own charity. I'd come across that crime during the investigation into the death of John Allen Howard. His own daughter, DeeDee, had been caught for misappropriating funds in his charity and went to prison on federal charges.

Paxton's admission of her husband's guilt was no small thing and, I thought, volunteered too easily. However, there comes a time when questioning such a suspect that investigators have to wonder if they're being *too* honest. We had to consider if she said that to draw attention away from herself.

If so, what skeletons were hiding in *her* closet?

CHAPTER
THIRTY-TWO

I ALREADY HAD a poor picture of Zach before stepping onto Paxton's doorstep. That picture had changed to that of a disgusting human being. Autumn and I would never have had an open relationship the way Paxton said hers was with Zach. The thought of it made me feel . . . icky.

To each their own.

"You're talking about embezzlement and tax evasion," Moody said to Paxton.

The corner of her mouth quirked. "I had nothing to do with it. You'd have to talk to his attorney."

"You mean Percy?"

Her mouth opened, hesitated, and then said, "I mean his other lawyer."

"We'll get their information from you before we leave," Moody said.

"Gladly."

"Did anyone else know about this?" I asked.

"I'm not sure," she said. "I would imagine his friends serving on the foundation board might be able to tell you."

"Were you ever a part of the organization?"

"No," she said in a flat voice. "He never asked me to be a part."

Moody held up a finger. "Wait a sec. He started this big charity for autism awareness because of your son, and he never asked you to get involved? That doesn't smell right."

"Nothing gets past you, detective." This time, she made that statement without a hint of sarcasm.

I was ready to leave. Good looks can only get a person so far. I'd already determined Zach was a slimeball. Paxton may be the more attentive parent, but she had a deplorable attitude. It made me sick to think people like her and her late husband lived such an opulent life.

"Besides taking care of your son, do you do any work?" Moody asked.

She reached into her back pocket and held up the phone. "I'm an influencer on Instagram."

Moody's face looked like he'd sucked on a lemon wedge. "What does that mean?"

She gave a lengthy explanation that I didn't understand and made me glad I shied away from social media as much as possible. Being paid to promote brands, makeup, herbal supplements, or clothing through photos and videos of herself? Something told me she was likely popular through provocatively posed photos. It sounded like something an airhead Miss America contestant might say when asking how they would improve the world.

Paxton ended her explanation with, "At the end of the day, I just want to give people hope for what is imaginable."

"Uh-huh," Moody and I said at the same time.

Moody cleared his throat. "Look, we don't want to take any more of your time. I know this is difficult for you, and we might have to come back at a different time when we know more about the circumstances of your late husband's death."

She brushed the hair off her face with a hand and tucked it behind an elfish ear. "It's okay. Ask what you need."

It bothered me that she didn't seem to care about Zach's death or catching the person who did it.

"How well did you know the other members of the golf foursome or their families?" Moody asked.

Paxton pondered it for a moment. "Not too well, to be honest. Archie mows our lawn. I talk to him when he and his landscaping crew come to do their thing. His wife is pleasant, but a gold digger."

Look at the pot calling the kettle black, I wanted to say, but held my tongue.

She continued, "I had lunch with Percy's wife a couple of times. She told me he once had an autistic sister who passed away at an early age, so he had a soft spot for Ethan. They have a son about Ethan's age, and we would get them together for play dates. It's difficult because Ethan doesn't play like normal kids, but they get along okay."

"Are you around during these play dates?" I asked.

"Not normally," she answered. "It was a Zach and Percy thing. I let them handle it."

"Understood," Moody said. "What about Gideon? Know him well?"

She glanced away for a beat and tapped a fingernail against her phone. "I wouldn't say we were close. They played soccer together on a scholarship at Coastal Carolina. They liked to watch games together on weekends, mostly in the pool house."

"Is that more like a man cave?" I asked.

"Something like that," Paxton answered. "It was his area. I oversaw the decorating of the house but let him have his space. He chose the pool house."

Moody jotted a note on his pad. "How did you feel about Percy representing your husband in the divorce?"

She held his gaze for a moment, pondering her response. Her mouth opened then closed and then stared into nothingness. If it was possible, her forehead wrinkled as she found the words. "I hadn't considered it, but of all of Zach's friends, Percy was the closest to us. He and I got along all right. If anyone, I figured Zach would hire him. I feel a little betrayed."

I cocked my head to the side. "Why is that?"

"Because of his soft spot for Ethan," she replied. "I would be the one to gain custody of him. Percy knows I'm the better parent. I can't imagine why he would want Ethan to go with Zach."

"Where were you this morning?" Moody's pen was poised above his notebook. He'd ditched the scorecard pencil at some point.

"I dropped Ethan off at my mom's and got a facial at Dolce Lusso in Market Common."

The pen moved. "We'll confirm that."

Paxton tilted her head forward. "Go ahead."

"I know we're jumping around here," Moody said. "Did you know your husband gambled while playing golf?"

"Oh, ho. His gambling extended well beyond playing golf," she said. "He was a degenerate gambler. He placed bets on every sporting event possible."

"Did he ever lose large sums of money doing it?" I asked.

"Yeah," she said, "but I'll have to give him credit. He was good at it."

"Did he ever talk about playing for money while golfing?"

Moody asked.

"Yeah. It was mostly between him and Archie. Zach always looked down on Archie for whatever reason and tried to make things miserable for him out on the course."

"What about off the course?" I asked.

"They were friends," she answered. "I don't know what it was when they stepped onto a golf course—testosterone or ego."

"Or both," Moody suggested.

"Yeah, or that," Paxton agreed. "Zach used to laugh in private at the things he said about Archie. Of the three, Archie and Zach weren't really friends, but connected by friendships with Percy and Gideon."

"Do you know if Zach ever won large sums of money off Archie?"

She bit the bottom corner of her lip. "Seems like it went both ways sometimes."

"What about recently?" Moody said.

She turned to the detective. "Yeah. Zach came home after the last time they played, bragging that he'd won four thousand dollars off Archie that day." She stopped speaking for a moment and then said, "I don't know about you, but if someone spent years laughing at my expense, taking my money through bets, and making fun of me every time we were around each other, I'd want to kill them too."

Moody and I communicated the same thought to each other with a look: There was a motive for Archie to have done it.

Before we asked another question, Ethan appeared. He had one hand placed on his chin. The other carried a tablet. His eyes were cast on his feet.

Paxton stroked his hair. "What is it, buddy?"

He held up the tablet for Paxton. He'd written something on the screen. I craned my neck and saw it. It read: **want my dad.**

CHAPTER
THIRTY-THREE

WE STEPPED OUTSIDE into the rain. The mother-in-law suite where Zach had taken up residence was behind the house by the pool. Paxton didn't offer to let us traipse through her immaculate home in our dripping clothes and wet shoes to get to the rear.

Moody and I made our way around the corner of the home. He had the key to the pool house grasped in his right hand. We walked along the side of the house on a brick paved walkway between a wall and a tall fence.

Moody said, "Look, I know the way she was acting affected you, but sometimes you gotta take a step back and watch. I didn't say anything about her fixation on the phone because I was watching her body language."

"Right, because when a husband gets killed, most of the time it's the wife who did it. I get it."

"Exactly. That woman's a cool character. Eventually she broke, but now I don't know if it was because you called her out on it and it was time to act like she cared, or if it was genuine."

"And now we won't know for sure which way it was."

"Exactly."

"I'm sorry."

He gave me a silent nod. "Don't apologize."

We passed the back edge of the house. My breath caught. The

pool was shapeless and curvy. One side had a built-up waterfall complete with torches burning like the Olympic eternal flame despite the rain. A covered pergola with a stone kitchen and flat screen TV on the wall lay on the other side. A dozen lounge chairs were scattered on the stone deck. One "corner" of the pool curved into a three-quarter circle of hot tubs.

I figured Zach's backyard setup had to cost more than my home. The annex lay on the left side in the rear corner of the property. Sea oats wafted in the soft ocean breeze. High tide pounded the beach. Rain pounded on our heads.

"They lied to us about the betting," Moody said. "About the max."

"Yeah, I caught that. Gideon said they had a limit, but we also learned that Archie was thousands of dollars in the hole. Surely, they wouldn't let him continue racking up debt like that."

"You would figure so," Moody said, "but then again, we're talking about the Myrtle Beach elite here and a group of friends who go way back. We don't know how they operate."

"I think we're getting an idea."

"Agreed," Moody grunted.

They built the pool house out like a studio apartment. We stepped inside and out of the rain.

"Hold up," Moody said, reaching into his coat pocket. "Put these on before you touch anything."

He handed me a pair of latex gloves, which I snapped over my hands. He put his on and flipped on the light switch.

The pool house echoed the aesthetic of the main house. It had hardwood flooring. The small kitchen had granite countertops. The lights overhead were high spec. There was a massive flat screen television mounted on one wall and a leather seating set that dominated the middle of the space.

An unmade bed lay in the corner beside a chest of drawers. Two of the five drawers weren't shut all the way. Crushed beer cans were everywhere. Even though he was apparently filthy rich, I took Zach to be like one of the meathead frat boys who chugged Natty Light and then crushed the can against the side of his head before belting out a guttural howl of manliness.

Moody echoed my thinking. "Looks like a college kid lives here."

"Maybe that's why the house was so neat," I said. "He moved out here and Paxton didn't have to go around cleaning up after Zach."

"Guarantee Paxton has a cleaner that comes in for that."

"True," I said. "What are we looking for?"

Moody twisted his lips. "Anything that might point to someone wanting to kill him."

"Okay then." His comment seemed like the obvious thing to do, but I just wanted to check. "What if I started over there?"

He grunted and took the bedroom corner. I drifted over to the living room.

The coffee table was a mess. I used my gloved hands to push around various manilla folders with client files and magazines with scantily clad and unclad women. An oversized manilla envelope containing divorce papers he had yet to serve to Paxton lay on top of everything.

I sat on the leather sofa and picked up a stack of envelopes. I tried not to touch the nudie mags. The first envelope showed a contract to sell a home valued at $1.5 million in Grand Cayman. The second was to purchase a tract of land in Guadeloupe for apparent development. Zach was going to shell out a meager $1.25 million for thirty acres. The company name listed on the selling contract was **Lawson Luxury International**. The purchase agreement had a different name: **Salty Sands Holdings.** Zach's signature was at the bottom of both contracts. Maybe Salty Sands Holdings was a development venture he was involved in.

After placing them back in the pile, I picked up the divorce petition. With hesitation, I opened it. I wasn't sure what the protocol was for looking at private files in the attorney/client grand scheme of things. If I got yelled at, I'd plead ignorance. I just wanted a peek.

The petition was written in legalese. There were two copies of it. One for him. One for her. It had Paxton's and Zach's names at the top. He filed the divorce for "Irreconcilable Differences," which I took to mean that they had grown to hate each other. The paper laid out that the prenuptial agreement was to be followed under the Division of Assets and Debts section.

The next section stopped me cold. Zach asked for full custody of Ethan. Paxton wouldn't like that. His reasoning was that it would be in the best interests of Ethan. Zach provided a stable and nurturing environment for the child, including emotional, educational, and financial support. The financial and educational support I understood. Perhaps Zach was a better dad than I gave him credit for. Ethan had the message on the tablet that he missed his dad.

The decree said that Zach would cover all legal fees for both parties. Their current living arrangements would remain in place until he found somewhere new to stay. That shouldn't be a problem for someone like Zach.

I read the rest of the petition and placed it back in the envelope. We'll never know when Zach had planned to give it to Paxton.

The rest of the living room held little to note.

"Check this out," Moody called to me from across the pool house.

I navigated around the furniture back to where Moody stood in front of the walnut dresser. A bottle of whiskey, two joints, four cell phones, three passports, and a stack of photos lay on top of it. He spread out the photos in a line.

"What do you make of those? Spicy, huh?"

The photos looked like they'd been shot from outside a bedroom window, looking through the slats between a mini-blind. A quick glance showed three different rooms, but six different people. They were taking part in similar activities. Things couples do behind closed doors.

One set showed the blonde from the pro shop, Zoe, canoodling with Archie.

The other showed Paxton and Gideon in bed together. They were not taking a nap, if you know what I mean.

The last set depicted Zach with a mystery woman with blonde hair and green eyes we had yet to come across in our investigation.

CHAPTER
THIRTY-FOUR

MOODY CALLED LUCIEN and told him to send a crew to tackle the pool house. Moody selected one picture from each spread and placed them in his coat pocket. I didn't know if he was saving those for himself or when going to interview suspects.

All the figures in the pictures went to the top of my suspect list. The photos of Paxton and Gideon made that reason obvious. They were having an affair and may have wanted to bump off Zach before any divorce proceedings. As for the pictures of Archie, Zoe, Zach, and the Mystery Woman, the only conclusion that came to mind was blackmail. The reason behind the blackmail wasn't apparent to me at this point. That domino might fall into place if we discovered the identity of Mystery Woman.

We stepped out of the pool house. Moody locked the door behind us. We stood under an overhang where water fell like a waterfall. The rain showed no signs of letting up. I figured that the famous local meteorologists Ed Piotrowski and Frank Johnson should have been on top of this. Nobody's perfect.

"You thinking what I'm thinking?" I asked the detective.

"Yep. Blackmail." He tilted his head toward the main house. "Need to go back and ask Paxton about the photos."

Ethan stood behind a window on the back of the house, looking down on us. Paxton came up and pulled him away. The boy didn't give any resistance.

"When we were talking to her earlier," I said, "Paxton said she didn't know Gideon very well."

"That's a lie if the pictures of her and him are any sign."

"I wonder if she knows about the existence of these photos?"

He smacked his lips and headed into the rain. "Only one way to find out."

I pulled my hood over my head and set off after Moody. We sloshed our way back to the front door. Moody rang the doorbell. I sensed his agitation at being lied to. What else had Paxton lied about or withheld?

This time, Paxton answered the door. She held out her hand. "Finished? Can I have my keys back?"

Moody made no move to grant her request. "Afraid not. We're going to have to process it first."

She put her hand down and arched a well-formed eyebrow. "Process it? Was Zach hiding something?"

I know Moody had told me to keep my yapper shut as much as possible, but I am who I am. "Was *Zach* hiding something? What about *you*?"

Paxton gave me a look of disgust. Like, how dare I, a common plebeian, have the nerve to insult her "honesty."

"What about me? I told you the truth about everything."

I nodded toward Moody's jacket pocket.

When he pulled out the stack of photos, Paxton gasped. "What are those?"

"They appear to be pictures of Zach, you, and some of his friends."

She held out her hand again. "Let me see?"

Moody didn't budge. "I think I'll hold onto them for safekeeping." He flipped through the stack, pulled out one, and showed it to her. "You said you didn't know Gideon very well."

I love that look a person gets when they're dumbfounded as Paxton was now. Her mouth opened. She had no words.

"Care to explain this to us?" Moody said.

Paxton closed her mouth and turned to see if Ethan was nearby. He wasn't. Just in case, she took a step closer to us and lowered her voice. "Don't guess I can deny it, so yes, I was sleeping with Gideon."

Moody asked most of the questions. "How long has this been going on?"

"A few months."

"Was this around the same time Zach moved into the pool house?"

She reached a hand up to her mouth and nibbled on a fingernail. "A little before."

"You said you had been faithful to him?"

"That's . . . false."

"Were there any other men?"

"No, Gideon was the only one."

"How did Zach find out?"

"He asked me if I was sleeping with someone. I told him that I'd started sleeping with Gideon. We had an open marriage, after all. He wasn't supposed to get upset."

"But he did, right?"

"Oh, yeah."

"Because Gideon was his friend?"

"Correct."

Something was bugging me that I had to get off my chest. "Let me get this straight. You and Zach had an open relationship. That's not uncommon. Did he marry you basically to be his trophy wife? You don't seem like you had much in common."

"Perhaps," she answered. "I came from a poor family. When I met him and he offered me the world, I wasn't going to turn him or it down."

"Did you love him?"

She exhaled. Her eyes watered. "Not at first, but I came to."

"Before or after Ethan?"

She sniffled and wiped away a tear. "After. I think it was the same with him toward me. Like I was his arm candy at first. Then we had Ethan. He drew us close for a time."

"And you went from being friends with benefits and a joint checking account to a family with a boy who needed special attention," I said.

By now, the tears streamed freely down her face. She had stopped trying to wipe them away. Paxton tried to say something but choked up. She nodded an affirmation.

"Why Gideon?" Moody asked.

"Beyond his obvious looks," I added.

Paxton looked away. "I thought Zach had gotten bored with me. He's spent so much time working on the autism charity and traveling around the lower Caribbean doing business that he hadn't spent any time here. When he was here, he was wrapped up in business."

I didn't know what to say to that. Moody didn't either.

"Okay then," he said. "Let's backtrack. He found out you were sleeping with Gideon. Then what happened?"

"We had a big fight, and he moved into the pool house."

At this point, I didn't know if we should mention the divorce papers in the pool house to Paxton. This was Moody's department.

He clicked his tongue. "Let's say you did get divorced. Hypothetically, if he asked for full custody of Ethan, how would you have responded?"

Her mouth fell open. She shook with rage and bit out, "He better not. It wouldn't have happened. He would have had to have pried him from my dead, lifeless fingers first."

Moody and I glanced at each other. There was another hard motive on top of the affair with Gideon. He had left finding the divorce papers out of the conversation, leaving it hypothetical.

"What would be his reason for the divorce?"

"Irreconcilable differences or something."

"Have you hired a lawyer?"

"Not yet. I've spoken to a few. I would have hired Percy, but he was on Zach's side."

Moody showed her another picture. "Recognize those two?"

Paxton leaned forward and examined the racy photo. She placed a hand over her mouth and almost gagged. "Ugh. Yes. The pro shop girl and Zach's friend Archie. Thanks, that's a sight of him I never wanted to see."

"Me neither," I said. "Wish I could unsee it."

Moody shot me a scornful look. I didn't care. I hoped the comment would show Paxton that we were on the same team on this one. It might make her open up a little more.

Moody put the frightening image away. "Did you know they were seeing each other?"

"No," Paxton answered. "I don't know either of them very well. I've seen her."

"Zoe," I said.

"Yeah, Zoe. Zach didn't care for her. Said she liked to sleep with married men and runs a loan sharking service to members of the club."

That was a loaded statement. We had two things to unpack. We were already aware of the first part. The second was a surprise.

Moody covered the necessary ground before tackling the second part. "Do you know if she and Zach ever hooked up?"

"Not that I'm aware of. Doesn't mean he didn't try."

"Gotcha." Moody pretended to make a note. "Tell me what you know about this loan sharking service."

"Almost every member at that place gambled," Paxton explained. "On holes. Poker in the dining room after hours. Fantasy football leagues. You name it. They were high rollers. Sometimes, a member would get deep in the hole, not want their spouses to know about it, and go to Zoe to help cover the debt."

"How do you know this?"

"Zach told me."

"Did he ever use her for that?"

"He didn't need to. Zach was a good golfer and a keen poker player. He rarely lost money. When he did, he could afford to pay for his losses."

"Did she charge inflated interest fees?"

"Oh. Sometimes. Other times she wouldn't have them pay interest, but have them work it off in other ways, if you know what I mean."

Moody squinted. "What *do* you mean?"

"She would force them to sleep with her, and then use that power she now had over them for extortion and other sordid schemes. Zach was not a fan."

His behavior on the golf course toward Zoe this morning suggested otherwise.

Her phone chirped in her pocket. She ignored it. I wanted to give her a golf clap for her willpower.

She glanced over our shoulders. I turned to see a blue mid-2000s Honda Accord with faded paint waiting at the gate to be let in. Paxton leaned out the door for a better view. "It's my mom. That must've been what the phone beeped for."

She withdrew the phone from her pocket and tapped the screen. The gate opened and the car slowly drove through.

Paxton's shoulders sagged in relief. Mom was here to help.

Moody understood the situation. "We'll have to talk to you again about this affair with Gideon."

"I understand."

Moody reached back into his pocket and pulled out the photos. He leafed through them and presented one of them to Paxton. "Who is this with your husband?"

She screamed.

CHAPTER
THIRTY-FIVE

"*I WONDER IF* Archie knows?" I asked Moody as I buckled my seatbelt.

"If he does, there's his motive," Moody said as he put the police issue gray Ford Explorer into gear.

When we left Paxton's estate, I followed Moody in my Jeep to the parking lot in front of The Fresh Market and Back Again Book Shop off 79th Ave. I left my vehicle in an empty area near the end of the lot. On a Saturday evening, most people weren't grocery shopping or book browsing. I'd passed by the darkened windows at Back Again and saw their shop cats, Caramel and Midnight, looking out a window, like sentinels watching over their domain.

Margaret and Winona had begged me to get a kitty for our store. I told them I would think about it. Winona said she was going to have one at the Garden City location once it opened, whether I liked it or not. Work was coming along with the new store.

When Moody told me to meet him here and hop in his police vehicle, his ride wasn't what I expected. I figured they would deck the interior out with various buttons, sirens, lights, and a metal cage separating the front seat from the back. It wasn't that way at all. The only difference between his SUV and one you might pick up at Beach Ford was a police radio.

I was disappointed.

He pulled from the lot and sped to Archie's house. We met

where we did because Archie's address wasn't far from there. He lived north of the Golden Mile, in between it and the Dunes Golf & Beach Club. The golf course Swaying Palms competed with to get a PGA Tournament brought to Myrtle Beach.

Having a home in the middle of two areas of prestige meant that Archie was also in a high-rent district. The homes in his neighborhood reminded me of the row homes found in Market Common, but up on stilts since they were so close to the ocean.

As we approached his home on Monarch Drive, I said, "Do we need to discuss what we learned back at Zach's place before talking to Archie?"

"What's there to say? Zach had his wife tailed and discovered she was having an affair with his friend. He also had pictures taken of Zoe and Archie."

"Both of which could be used as blackmail."

"Right."

"What about the pictures Zach had taken of himself?"

"To me, it means he was one of those scorched Earth guys. If he was going to do it, he was going to burn the entire thing to the ground." The detective attempted a sardonic smile. "He probably wanted the whole lot of them in his pocket. That way, if they knew he had those pictures, they'd keep quiet about his misbehavior and would owe him something. Money, favors, whatever."

"They surprised Paxton."

"They did, and they're sure to surprise Archie. All of them."

"What about the alleged loan sharking scheme with Zoe?"

"Loan sharking is illegal. It's something else we're going to have to investigate. We'll haul her in for questioning."

With Detective Gomez still out of town, I wondered how thin

the investigative arm of the MBPD was stretched.

LED landscape lighting lit the front of Archie's home. It was a two-story house with periwinkle siding and a balcony. The two-car garage under the house had been bumped out to make space for three vehicles. The equipment Archie used for his landscaping business must be elsewhere. A big RAM truck with an extended cab and dual wheels sat in front of the bump-out garage door. The side of the truck advertised the name for his landscaping business: Myrtle Beach Palms & Pines Landscaping.

Moody parked on the street, blocking the driveway. Everything was wet. From outside the Explorer to inside the Explorer where we dripped all over the interior. We climbed from the SUV and splashed our way up to the front door. I rang the doorbell this time.

It opened a moment later to reveal the other person in the steamy pictures with Zach: Archie's wife.

* * *

HER BLONDE HAIR sat on top of her head in a sloppy updo. Like she'd done it to get it out of her way for the evening. The thump of small receding footsteps came from within.

Her eyes were tired. It seemed like it had been a long day for Archie's wife, Cricket. Paxton told us her name before we left.

It was about to get longer.

She studied us with caution. She knew who we were and why we were here. That is, she was aware of part of the reason we were here. She didn't know she was now part of this investigation. How long would it be until she was made aware of the photos? As with the other rounds of questioning, Moody took the lead. I was here to add my two cents when necessary.

She puffed a stray strand of hair off her forehead. "Hey, sorry. You must be from the police department. Archie is trying to get the girls corralled into their bedroom."

She didn't offer to let us in. We were soaking wet. The overhang on the porch offered us refuge from the rain. A glimpse of the interior revealed a house that looked like two little girls destroyed it during a pink glitter party.

Moody didn't ask to be let in. "Can you tell your husband we need to speak with him? We don't want to get everything in your house wet."

"Pfft. Not that it would matter. The house is a wreck." She turned and called to the interior, "Archie, the police detectives are here for you!"

We heard a muffled and stressed, "Be there in a minute!" come from the bowels of the house.

She turned back to us. "He'll be with you in a moment."

"Thank you," Moody said.

Cricket started to walk away, leaving the door open. Moody caught her first. "Mrs. Bristol."

She stopped in her tracks.

"Yes?"

"We need to ask you about something. Questions that you might be more open to answering without your husband present."

"Okay." She crossed her arms and leaned against the doorway. "I'm not sure how I can help, but glad to."

She wasn't glad after the tactful Detective Moody unloaded with the first question. "How long had you and Zach been having an affair?"

CHAPTER
THIRTY-SIX

CRICKET'S EYES WIDENED and jaw dropped, but she didn't answer right away. She turned her head to see if Archie was within earshot. He was still busy with the girls.

She closed the door behind her and stepped onto the porch with us. In a whisper, she asked, "How do you know that?"

Moody pulled the incriminating photo of her and Zach from his jacket and showed them to her.

She gasped and held a hand to her mouth to keep from screaming the way Paxton did when we showed her the photo. Cricket stared at it and called Zach several names in three different languages.

"Did you know these existed?"

She got herself together and fixed the detective with a firm stare. "No. I did not."

"Do you deny what they are showing?"

"How can I? That's obviously me and him."

"Does your husband know?"

Before she was able to answer, Archie opened the door and stepped onto the porch beside Cricket. She drew in on herself slightly when he put an arm around her waist.

"Hello again," he said. "How can I help you?"

He apparently didn't hear our conversation with Cricket. Her answer could have meant Archie might have wanted revenge on

Zach for sleeping with his wife. However, he wrapped his arm around her without hesitation, leading me to believe he was ignorant of the affair. If I were in his shoes, I wouldn't want to be near my wife if I learned she'd slept with my friend.

Moody grunted. His eyes lingered on Cricket for a moment before moving to Archie. "We're following up on matters. We learned you weren't being truthful with us about the gambling."

The detective didn't ask a question but opened a door for Archie to explain. The landscaper played smart and didn't deny it. "Yeah, so I lost more than I won."

"You also fell farther in the hole than what you said. Wasn't there a thousand-dollar cap on the wagering?"

"There was supposed to be," he answered. "Sometimes, Zach and I would get so competitive that we'd break the rule."

"You didn't tell me you bet on golf?" Cricket said. This time she distanced herself from her husband, removing his arm from around her.

He showed his teeth with a smile. "Uh. What happens on the course, stays on the course."

I felt the urge to grab a tub of popcorn and an easy chair. This unfolding drama might be fun to watch.

"Wrong answer," Cricket said. "How dare you bet our money!"

Archie glanced behind him to the home's interior. "Shh. I just got the girls put down for bed."

Cricket's face was beet red, and the volume stayed at 10. "And you can put them right back down! How could you do that? You know things are tight."

Archie cleared his throat and tried to remain calm. Just wait until we bring up the photos to him.

"I know. I know," he said. "I was just trying to get extra money from Zach. You know he was good for it."

"Yeah. *He* was." She poked a finger in his chest. "*You're* not. Where do you get off?"

"I'm sorry," Archie said, holding up his hands to his shoulders. "I got in over my head. Once I started, I couldn't stop."

"Where did you get the money to pay off Zach?" Moody asked.

The knot on Archie's throat bobbed up and down. "I dug it up from various places."

If Moody and I weren't present, Cricket might have punched her husband in the face. Her fists were balled tight. I wouldn't have blamed her.

"From Zoe?" Moody interjected.

Cricket turned to the detective. "What does that flirt have to do with this?"

"She runs a loan service out of the pro shop," Moody explained. "Apparently, gambling is rampant at Swaying Palms. Zoe offers loans to cover bets to members. We don't know much about it yet, so that's all I'm going to comment on."

Cricket digested this and turned to Archie. "You're canceling your membership tomorrow."

Her husband started to protest, but knew the battle was over before it began. "Yes, dear."

"How much did she loan you?" Cricket asked.

We had a new partner in Cricket. It might be a good thing because we had already caught Archie in one lie and might not want to dig a deeper hole if his wife were asking the questions.

He scratched the side of his face. "About three thousand dollars."

Cricket exploded. "Three thousand dollars! What type of interest did she charge you?"

Archie braced himself. In a quiet voice, he answered, "Two hundred percent."

This time, Cricket grabbed Archie by the ear and twisted. Hard. She was a little woman but packed a big wallop. Archie howled.

"Hey! Hey!" Moody shouted. "We'll have none of that."

Cricket let go of Archie with one last twist for good measure.

"Ah!" He grabbed the side of his head with both hands and checked for blood. There was none.

Cricket turned to Moody, breathing deeply, her face red. "I'm not apologizing."

"I don't expect you to," Moody said. "But do it again, and I'll have to arrest you for domestic violence."

Cricket crossed her arms tightly and stepped away from Archie.

In Archie's defense, he had no defense. He rubbed his ear and whimpered, "I'm so sorry, Cricket."

"Did you pay off the loan?" I asked.

"I'm working on it," Archie said through clenched teeth.

"Wanna go get some ice for that?" Moody asked Archie.

"Y-yeah," he said and disappeared inside the home. By the end of this, Archie might be sleeping in a hotel.

"While he's gone," Moody said.

Cricket spat out, "Yeah?"

"Did Archie know about you sleeping with Zach?"

Cricket was seething. Her life had crumbled around her over the course of ten minutes. First, discovering that someone was aware of her affair with Zach, and second, that Archie had lost money they didn't even have. "Not that I'm aware of."

I wondered if Moody would add to the issue by revealing both had cheated.

"What are you going to do?" I asked.

"What kind of question is that?" she said to me.

My face flushed.

She continued, "I just found out about all this. I haven't had time to process it enough to make any life-altering decisions, you dope."

"Hey," Moody said, putting up a hand. "I know you're hurt emotionally and physically, but there will not be any name calling. Be respectful. Clark didn't do anything to you."

"I'm sorry," Cricket said through her own clenched teeth.

"Apology accepted," I said. It embarrassed me to ask that question. Another rookie mistake.

Archie came back with a bag of ice in a Ziplock bag, and a kitchen towel pressed against the side of his head.

I figured Moody would lead with the pictures when resuming his questions for Archie, but he held that ace up his sleeve.

Moody asked, "If you and Zach didn't get along very well, how come you still played golf with him, much less engaged in illegal gambling activities?"

"It was more to be around Gideon and Percy," Archie said. It was the first thing he said that I believed outright. "I never cared for Zach, dating all the way back to college, but always enjoyed being around the other two."

"Makes sense to me," I said.

"Zach always held the fact that he had more money than me over my head," Archie said. "He was born with a silver spoon in his mouth and treated people on a lower tax scale as peasants. To tell the truth, being around him and his attitude made me want to have the biggest landscaping service in the Grand Strand."

"Is it?" I asked.

"Not quite, but we have some big contracts out there that make us close."

"You should be proud of what you built," Cricket begrudgingly said.

Archie puffed out his chest. "I am."

It seemed like members of Archie's foursome and everyone around them slept around like there were no consequences for their actions. I tried to figure out in my head a delicate way to ask a question surrounding the subject.

Moody beat me to the punch in his usual manner. "Did you know that Paxton and Gideon were boinking?"

It was there for the briefest of moments on both of their faces. It might have been the situation or Moody's use of terminology. A hint of a smile.

"Yes," Archie said. "We were aware of it."

"How did you learn of it?" Moody asked.

"We mow both of their lawns," Archie explained. "There have been times recently when we've known Paxton was at Gideon's house, or vice versa. Always during the day when Ethan was at school and Zach was in the office or out of town."

"Were they doing business together?" I asked.

"Depends on the type of business you're referring to," Archie said. "Gideon runs a surfboard company from his home and Paxton tries to earn money using Instagram. Not sure what type of business they would do together if it were above board."

"We know the nature of hers and Zach's marriage," Cricket added. "They lived the upside-down pineapple lifestyle, if you know what I mean."

"Got it," Moody said.

I must have worn a quizzical expression because Archie said to me, "That means they were swingers."

"Oh, right," I said. All this conversation was well and good, but it was late, and I wanted Moody to get to the meat on the bone.

"You know, I've been thinking about what happened to Zach this afternoon." Archie scratched the back of his head and glanced at his wife before saying to us, "I hate to say this — that of us three, Gideon seemed the most likely to have done it."

"Explain," Moody said.

"It seems obvious to me," Archie said. "Gideon was sleeping with Zach's wife. If he wanted her to himself, then maybe he planned on killing him when he had the opportunity. He was the closest person to Zach at the time of the murder, you know?"

"We're well aware of that," Moody said, leaving out the possibility of a person hiding behind a tree near the body. "I'll take that under advisement."

I turned to the detective. "Are you going to ask him about it already?"

Moody looked at me and grunted. Figurative steam escaped his ears. "Yes, I was getting ready to, as a matter of fact." He turned to Archie. "Mr. Bristol, we have learned that you had an affair with Zoe."

Cricket turned to Archie, screeching, "Excuse me?"

Two sleepy-eyed girls had emerged from the bedroom and were standing in the living room watching. Archie and Cricket didn't see them. If Moody did, he didn't say anything. I didn't have kids, but if I were a parent, this potentially traumatizing conversation between the four of us was the last thing I would want them to see or hear. But it was too late. The train was already plunging down the track.

The color drained from his face. He gave us a look of indignation and said to his wife, "That's crazy. Whoever told you that is lying."

"No one had to tell us anything," I said.

Archie wheeled on me. "What is that supposed to mean?"

If I were lying and trying to cover up an affair, I would not use the confrontational attitude Archie was assuming now. I'd blow off the accusations like they were absurd.

If he wanted to play it that way, I could too. I turned to Moody and gestured at his jacket pocket. "Show him detective."

"With pleasure," Moody grunted.

He pulled the stack of photos from his pocket and thumbed through them before showing a specific one to Archie and Cricket.

A tragic scene followed which I will not recount in detail here. We didn't know Cricket would react the way she did when we showed her a photo of her husband and Zoe. Archie never got a chance to react or respond before Cricket cold-cocked him. Let's just say that the girls ended up staying at their grandparents' place for a week. An ambulance had to come pick up Archie, and Cricket received a ride to the police station in the back of a squad car.

CHAPTER
THIRTY-SEVEN

WE FOLLOWED THE patrol car with Cricket cuffed in the back seat to the station. It disappeared around the side of the building. Moody parked in the front lot.

The last time I was here, I was with Andrea to speak to Gomez and Moody about Stanley Griffin's deceptive practices as the HOA president of his condo.

This time, Moody didn't need to flash his badge at the desk attendant inside the door. It was the same bored woman with thick glasses as the other time I was here. She sat behind a desk with an oversized Styrofoam cup from McDonalds near her hand.

"Detective," she said as she averted her eyes from a computer screen.

"Marge," Moody grunted. "I'll be late."

We didn't break stride as he moved past her desk and down a hallway. The detective was aware of precisely where we were heading. "You must come here a lot if you're on a first-name basis with the unit secretary," I remarked.

"I should be on a first name basis with her."

"Because you're here a lot?"

He grunted. "No. Marge is my wife."

I stopped in my tracks. Moody kept walking like a freight train.

"That's interesting," I mumbled to myself as he receded down the long hall.

While they booked Cricket for domestic battery, Moody had me wait in the bullpen, an area in the middle of the station where officers drafted reports and waited to get called out. The investigative unit took up one corner of the bullpen. I sipped a cup of stale coffee and reflected on the day. I stood against a wall, watching the four or five officers and support staff on duty go about their business. A plastic chair beckoned me, but if I sat down, I might not get back up.

Moody and I actually engaged in small talk from Archie's house to the station. The investigative unit of the MBPD operated twenty-four hours a day. Detectives Moody and Gomez worked in the Violent Crimes unit. I'd heard about them from investigating murders from past and present experience. He explained to me that his cases often involved robbery and kidnapping, among others. Domestic violence also fell under their purview, which was how he dealt with Cricket swiftly.

I had asked him about how the crime scene unit worked. He explained they had their lab and evidence storage in an annex behind the police station. Their space used to be on the other end of Oak Street but were brought closer together during the plans the Myrtle Beach Downtown Development Corporation conducted to revitalize downtown. One goal of the reshuffle was not only to bring the police divisions closer together, but also government operations.

Each crime scene technician was a "generalist," meaning they were trained in multiple forensic disciplines. The crime scene unit included seven technicians, of which Lucien was the unit leader.

This was the first occasion since the murder that I'd had time to collect my thoughts and, for some reason, they started with the previous murder I'd helped to solve. The last case I engaged in at Tidal Creek Brewhouse ended up having half a dozen suspects who might have murdered Emilie Smith and Stanley Griffin. Everyone we spoke to today about Zach, except for his son, Ethan, seemed to have a motive to want him dead. Zach was not a nice man. Period. He lorded his wealth over others. He slept with his friend's wife. I found it difficult to grasp all the different threads that might have led to his death.

Zach's wife was sleeping with his college buddy, and he had the pictures to prove it. He also had pictures of himself with Cricket and Zoe with Archie. Did he obtain those for his own amusement or, more in fitting with his personality, using them for extortion? If so, there were four people with motives. Archie had a double motive with the Zoe pics and losing bets in a big way.

Paxton pointed at Archie. Archie pointed at Gideon. It didn't appear that either knew Zoe well enough to cast her as the killer.

That left another question: who took the photos? I didn't envision Zach having the time or be able to hide his big, pudgy body well enough to remain hidden.

The motives were one thing. Being able to do it was another. Who had the means and opportunity? The bloody 3-wood was found in Archie's locker, a locker he had trouble opening for whatever reason. I didn't see how he may have killed Zach and hidden the club with no one seeing him. After the death, Archie wasn't walking around with a dented 3-wood in his hand. That specific murder weapon would be impossible to hide for that long. Maybe Archie didn't hide the club in his locker. There was the possibility that someone tried to frame him or hid it there for him with the hope that the police wouldn't check his locker. I'd already chalked Archie up to having a limited mental capacity, but surely he wasn't that ignorant of how a murder investigation works.

However, Archie's wife was having an affair with Zach. Cricket had turned into Rocky Balboa before we could have a conversation about it, but Archie might have learned of it and conspired with someone else for the murder. If so, who? Make that three motives for Archie.

Speaking of Percy, what was his motive? Of everyone, he seemed to have the most to lose if Zach died. I didn't know what kind of legal fees he might have charged Zach in the divorce with Paxton, but I can't imagine they were insubstantial. Had he racked up gambling debts to Zach too?

Then there was the video showing the four men's golf bags sitting alone by the cart path while they were taking a leak before teeing off. Zoe came walking by, and Archie's bag might have wiggled during her passing. That may have been when the club was stolen. If it was stolen. Archie had mentioned several times during the round that his club was missing. He might have been lying to plant the belief in his mates that it was missing. I had to take his claims at face value.

Moody came by, and without stopping, said to me, "Follow me."

Feeling fatigued, I drained the last of my coffee, and crushed the cup in my hand before tossing it into a nearby garbage bin. Moody led me through a warren of dimly lit hallways. It was after ten and a skeleton staff was on-hand. No one paid me any attention, for which I was grateful.

He led me through a rear door and across a short alley to a nondescript governmental building. A door stood by itself in the middle of the front of the building. There were no windows facing the alley. The city simply labeled the structure as "Investigations" in white lettering beside the door.

"In here," Moody said, pushing open the entryway leading beyond the plain exterior and into a hub of forensic expertise. A desk faced the doorway where a gatekeeper normally would have guarded the facility. That wasn't the case this late on a Saturday evening.

The scent of chemicals mixed with the aroma of freshly brewed coffee from a corner of the room. It mingled with the faint whir of machinery.

As I took in the maze of cutting-edge technology and meticulously organized workspaces, Moody grunted, "If anyone asks, you were never here."

I didn't know what to say, so I kept quiet. To myself, I muttered a very Keanu Reeves-like, "Whoa."

The main area of the lab was expansive. A high ceiling adorned with harsh fluorescent lighting cast a clinical glow over the room. Seven individual workstations were neatly arranged along the side walls, giving the techs plenty of elbow room to work. Each workstation was equipped with ultramodern analytical instruments and high-resolution computer screens. A pair of technicians clad in white lab coats wore focused expressions. They moved with purposeful precision and spoke in hushed whispers, as something deeply engrossed them in their work. It wasn't apparent what they were working on.

At the rear of the room stood rows of tall stainless-steel cabinets. Each was labeled and organized to store an array of chemicals, forensic tools, and biological samples. Shelves upon shelves of reference materials lined the walls. Each shelf held thick forensic textbooks and journals.

A glass partition separated a smaller section of the lab. High-tech equipment lay behind it, leading me to believe that space was dedicated to delicate procedures, such as DNA sequencing, toxicology screenings, and ballistics analysis.

The ambiance was controlled chaos. The occasional beep of a machine or the hum of a ventilation system punctuated the otherwise focused silence. Commendations and awards, acknowledging the lab's contributions to solving complex cases adorned the walls.

In the center of the room, a large, imposing conference table dominated the space. Case files, photographs, and forensic reports were strewn across its surface. Lucien sat at the table's head, poring over a stack of reports. Stray locks of his normally flawless hair fell over his eyes. A steaming cup of tea sat close by on the Formica tabletop. He appeared as tired as I felt.

Moody led me to where he sat.

Lucien said to the detective, "Good. You're here. Have a seat. You too, Clark."

He gestured at a row of empty chairs on the side of the table closest to us. Moody plopped down in a chair closest to Lucien. I kept my distance and kept a chair in between Moody and myself.

"Find anything?" the detective asked.

The corners of Lucien's eyebrows lifted. "Not much yet. Fingerprints from each of the foursome were on the club found in Archie's locker."

"Makes sense if they played together regularly," I said.

"Not really," Moody said. "Think about it. When I play golf, normally the only time I touch someone else's club is if I'm handing it to them on the green after they finish putting or holding the flag. Most of the time, it's a putter or wedge because they're what's used on and around the green. A 3-wood is used off the tee or on second shots farther away from the hole."

"Right," Lucien said. "You grab your 3-wood out of the bag, use it, and then put it back. No one else should end up touching it."

"Makes sense," I said. "Was it a new club that Archie was showing off and the others handled it?"

Lucien said, "The club wasn't old, but it had been used. There were marks on the club showing that."

"Gotcha," I said. Then something occurred to me. "I'm still confused about why the back of the club head was dented and not the front."

"That's baffling us too," Lucien admitted.

"Was anything else found in the lockers?" Moody asked Lucien.

"Nothing of interest. The usual items one would associate with being in a locker."

Moody grunted. "What about the trail coming from the perimeter cart path? Find anything with that?"

Lucien shuffled papers in front of him and studied one for a moment. "Nothing that tells us who it was. All we can tell is that someone drove a cart coming from the 12th hole, heading in the direction of the clubhouse. They parked their cart, got out, and hid near where the body was found. Another trail left showed them coming back to the cart."

"Footprints?"

"Yes. Looks like a size 9 or 10 golf shoe from the cleat marks. Can't tell what brand."

"Did any of the others wear that size shoe?"

Lucien consulted his notes. "All of them did."

"They all wear the same size shoe?" I asked. They were different sized men, but that didn't mean their feet couldn't have been of similar size.

"Correct," Lucien answered in a tone conveying annoyance at me for asking the question.

"What else?" Moody asked.

"We're still gathering evidence from his pool house," Lucien answered. "Kevin and Ann are there now bagging and taking photos."

"Speaking of which," Moody said and pulled the stack of steamy photos from his jacket. "We found these in the dresser."

He tossed the photos on the table in front of Lucien. He picked them up and leafed through them. He whistled. "Nice."

"Any way of figuring out where they came from?"

Lucien took one photo and flipped it over. "Hmm. It's possible. We can try to get geolocation data off 'em."

"How do you do that?" I asked.

He held up the photo and shook it. In the image, Zach's fleshy body flopped back and forth in a manner I would never unsee. "This is a good quality photo printed on good quality paper. Probably from an upscale printer. Nowadays, these good printers embed metadata on printed documents, especially if it's connected to a network. This metadata will have the printer's unique ID number, which might be linked to a specific location."

"That's nifty," I said.

"*Nifty* doesn't begin to cover what we can do," Lucien countered.

The man was either arrogant or didn't like me. Both?

"How long will it take to figure that out?" Moody asked.

Lucien lingered on the images. "Shouldn't take long to pull the metadata. If there's a network key, then that might take a couple days to figure out where exactly it is."

"So, by Tuesday?" the detective prompted.

"If not before."

"What about the lock?" I asked.

"What about it?" Lucien said.

"Did you get fingerprints off it?"

"Why? It was Archie's lock. His should have been the only prints on it."

"He supposedly couldn't open it. What if someone tampered with it and cracked the combination lock?" I asked.

Lucien sat back in his chair and crossed his arms. "We have it. I'll get it checked."

"Good idea," Moody grunted.

"What about the golf ball?" I asked. "Get anything from that?"

"The Srixon? Not much," Lucien answered. "There were no prints nor marks from where it had been hit. Besides pine needle residue, it was as though it had been taken out of its packaging for the first time."

"I wonder how it got there and how Gideon and Zach didn't see it when they first walked into the trees." I scratched my arm. "I mean, if I find a fresh ball in the woods, I'm pocketing it."

Moody agreed. "I would too. It's a good brand." To Lucien, he asked, "Find any blood on their clothing?"

Lucien shook his head. "Nada."

"Hmm." Moody turned to me. "Anything else you can think of?"

I shook my head. "Nothing comes to mind."

"Okay then," Moody said and pushed his chair back.

Lucien did the same, thinking that the conversation was over.

I wasn't done. This was my one certain chance to be in this facility. The case might lead Moody and I back here, but I wanted to take advantage of my one shot.

To Lucien, I said, "Gomez told me she gave you Autumn's phone to check out. What happened to it?"

CHAPTER
THIRTY-EIGHT

MOODY AND LUCIEN froze and looked at each other. Hair prickled on the back of my neck. Why do that if there was nothing to hide? I had already judged Lucien to be slimy. Nothing he had said or done since we met at the commendation ceremony, following the death at Tidal Creek case, had altered my judgment.

If a Hollywood casting director was looking for an actor to play a crooked cop, Moody was the perfect specimen. The beard and scraggly gray hair falling out from his trilby hat lent him an air of suspicion. Until this moment, nothing about him suggested he was anything other than an honest, if not bumbling, detective.

However, the glance he and Lucien shared hinted that Moody was aware of more than he disclosed.

I was suddenly fully aware of the fact that I was almost alone with these two men, late on a Saturday night in a building that housed chemicals capable of melting bodies.

"What?" I prompted.

Moody didn't jump at my question.

Lucien gestured for me to get up and follow him to the back of the room. "Come on. I'll show you what happened."

Moody remained at the table.

I got up from my chair and followed him through the workstations to the rear wall where the filing cabinets stood. Each metal cabinet was about five feet tall. There were eleven lined up together. A large, stainless-steel refrigerator sat at the end of the line. Each cabinet had a sign on top to identify its use. Each drawer had a label to organize the contents held within. Two cabinets for Evidence Storage, and one each for Chemicals, Forensic Tools, Reference Materials, Case Files, Photographs and Visual Evidence, Equipment Manuals, Quality Control Records, Digital Data, and Administrative Documents. The fridge had a "Cold Storage" sign on the left-side door.

He led me to the Equipment Manuals cabinet and put his hand on top of it.

"Since the phone Gina gave me of your wife's wasn't for a real case, I had to find somewhere to stash it until I could get to it," he said.

"So, you put it in the least used cabinet," I observed.

"That's right. Third drawer down in the back."

He pulled out a key and popped the drawer open for me to see for myself.

"There are manuals in here for tech we haven't had since the nineties," he said.

"This building is newer than that."

"It is, but when we moved everything from our old facility, we loaded these babies up on dollies and wheeled them onto a moving truck."

"Got it. No spring cleaning in the process, then?"

"Nope. We had work to do."

Lucien held the drawer open, giving me a good look at the back of it. Thick and thin instruction manuals were scattered about with no particular order. "I put the phone in an unmarked evidence envelope and stashed it here, under another manual so no one would be able to find it."

I straightened and held a finger over my lips. "But someone did."

"Appears so."

"Did you tell anyone about the phone? Who it belonged to?"

"Not a soul." The way Lucien said it made me want to believe him. I didn't want to question his integrity now because I wanted him to keep talking.

"Okay, then," I said. "Thanks."

"No problem."

I regarded the walls and ceiling. "There are cameras everywhere. Wouldn't they have picked up whoever stole the phone out of the cabinet?"

"Yeah, probably," he answered. "There was no way for me to check them though."

"Why not?"

His neck turned red. "Because surveillance of this place is above my pay grade. There's someone watching us to make sure we're not tampering with evidence."

"Okay." I said the word in a way that may have been taken for disbelief. He didn't care for my tone.

"Besides, who am I going to tell that there's a stolen phone that was never entered into evidence and shouldn't have been here to begin with? I was doing you and Gina a favor, man. Back off."

Veins popped in his arms as he squared his shoulders to me. I wasn't looking for a fight. I'd defend myself if I had to, but I had no desire to challenge a man trained to take down criminals for a living.

A flurry of questions to ask popped into my head about how anyone besides himself would have known about the phone. At this point, I didn't see how any more prodding would get me anything but a punch in the face. Lucien had thin skin, despite his confident appearance. He didn't like being questioned.

Before saying more, Moody walked up behind us and cleared his throat. We turned.

"Excuse me boys," he said. "If you're done posturing against each other, can we let Lucien get back to work?"

Lucien and I hugged it out and made up before we left the crime lab. Just kidding.

We had nothing left to say to each other. He gave me a hard stare I returned as we left. That little nagging voice in the back of my head kept asking if the animosity between Lucien and I had more to do with Gomez, his fiancée, and less to do with the murder case and lost phone. Maybe he was jealous of the time Gomez and I spent together in close quarters. That was his problem. If he only knew how close we got in the close quarters of her car.

CHAPTER
THIRTY-NINE

We HOPPED IN Moody's Explorer and went through the drive-thru at a Cook Out on Kings Highway. Nothing like finishing the day with a greasy double cheeseburger, fries, hushpuppies, and sweet tea, but I was famished. Moody ordered a chicken sandwich combo plus an extra hamburger. I've seen the man put away large amounts of food before. He had heart problems, and I hoped he didn't have a heart attack while driving me back to my Jeep.

The heavy rain had slacked off. It was still steady, but not like it had been throughout the afternoon. Traffic wasn't too bad for this time of night on a Saturday during the travel season when tourists would be strolling the Boardwalk or Broadway at the Beach, or dining at the many restaurants Myrtle Beach had to offer.

Cook Out wouldn't have been my first choice, but the good detective was driving and paying for my meal, so it worked in a pinch. I loved their sweet tea.

He dropped me off at my Jeep in the Fresh Market parking lot and said he'd touch base with me tomorrow morning. He thanked me for helping with the case today and told me to get some much-deserved rest. It was a side of the detective that I had only had rare glimpses of. Part seasoned detective, part fatherly advice. I didn't know how to feel about that.

After climbing into the Jeep and cranking the engine, I called

Andrea. I'd sent her a message earlier in the day to let her know that I'd gotten mixed up in another murder investigation. She had told me to be careful.

The phone rang three times. I sipped my tea. Just when I thought the call was going to go to voicemail, she answered, "Clark. Are you okay?"

Now that I was off the clock, the weight of the day began to set in. The surge of adrenaline I'd had since hearing Gideon scream ebbed. I either needed a strong cup of coffee or my comfy bed.

"Yeah. I'm good," I answered. "How's Libby?"

"Snoozing away," Andrea said. "I had the day off. LaDonna watched the store. She said it wasn't busy with the rain. I took Libby to EdVenture in Market Common to play."

"How long were you there for?"

"Four hours. She kept going from station to station to station and back again."

EdVenture was on the corner across from Barnes & Noble in Market Common. Andrea loved taking Libby there because they had various STEM related activities. She particularly loved being a cashier at the miniature Publix grocery store inside. It had plastic food and empty boxes that looked like the real thing. It was like a modern grocery store for Snow White's seven dwarves, complete with a bakery.

Windshield wipers whisked away rain as it fell on the windshield. "On a day like today, I can believe that. I haven't checked in with Karen, but I figure my store was about the same."

An app on my phone would allow me to check the sales figures when I got home. Sales were strong throughout the summer. Word had gotten out that the owner of the bookstore — me — had solved murders, and tourists and locals alike wanted to come check out the shop. Free publicity. A slow Saturday wouldn't hurt matters. Karen and Humphrey closed today. Humphrey probably twiddled his thumbs while Karen watched Turkish soap operas on her phone.

We had expanded the mystery section in the store because mystery readers wanted to meet me. I used to hide in my office to write, but now I typically sat near the coffee bar with a laptop and a steaming mug on the table. It slowed my work, but the first mystery book I released in the spring was the store's bestseller. It helped that they were all autographed.

"Probably so," Andrea said. Her voice sounded tired. I would be too after a busy day of playing with Libby.

"I feel the way you sound." I gave her the Readers' Digest condensed version of my equally long day as I turned left onto the Bypass off 79th Ave N.

"Sounds horrible, Clark."

"It is."

"Who do you think did it?"

My mouth opened to answer, but something told me to hold my tongue. "I'm still working it out. There's a lot we don't know yet. The body is en route to MUSC in Charleston for the autopsy. That should be done in the morning, and we'll get the results by noon."

"Okay."

The disappointment that I didn't answer her question with a name was evident in her voice. I understood her point of view. The truth was, I had a theory, but we still needed to talk to at least three people and await word from the medical examiner to see if it played out correctly. However, as I've learned from other cases, there's always a monkey wrench or two that gets thrown into the works.

"What are you going to do now?" she asked.

My bed called me, but I had a brother to grab first from my parents, which reminded me that Mom should be my next call.

"I've gotta swing by my parents' house and pick up Bo. They're probably watching the Braves game."

"Oh." The line went quiet. Then, "Libby is sound asleep. You could sneak in here, and she would never know."

My hands gripped the steering wheel as hormones I'd seldom had in over two years slapped me in the face and woke me up. That type of late-night intimacy wasn't something Andrea and I had discussed yet. Sure, we'd kissed a few times when Libby wasn't watching, but the physicality hadn't gone beyond that. I figured that if *it* were to happen, *it* would happen naturally.

Here, she offered an open invitation to spend the night and all the fun and games that went along with it. After seeing the pictures that we discovered at Zach's pool house, late-night gymnastics were present in my mind.

There was no doubt I found Andrea attractive, sweet, and easy to be around. I've never been the type of guy to rush into things, and that put off girls in the past, pre-Autumn. Yes, it's been a long time since *it* happened, and as a man in his prime, *it* was something I thought about.

Two months from now, if things progressed as well as they have to this point, hers was an invitation that I might not be able to refuse.

However, two things were rebelling against the pull to drive to her place and sweep her into my arms. One, I was dead tired and still needed to pick up Bo. Two, I had an early morning planned with Moody. As much as I hated to say it, I needed my sleep.

The next words out of my mouth were some of the most difficult ones I've ever had to say.

"Thank you for the invitation, but I need to pick up Bo from my parents' house and meet with Moody early in the morning."

"Bummer."

"Yeah. Otherwise, I'd definitely be inclined to take you up on it."

"I understand," Andrea said. Then she said something I hadn't expected. Or maybe I misunderstood her offer all along. Maybe she realized the way her offer might have come off. "I was going to let you sleep on the sofa. It has a pull-out that my mom says is quite comfy. I would have made you coffee and served you breakfast in bed. Libby might have liked jumping on you to wake you up in the morning, too."

She painted the ideal picture of family life that I had always wanted. It was so difficult to say no.

A never-ending stream of billboards streamed past as I crossed over the Farrow Parkway exit heading to Surfside. I felt like a bad boyfriend, but I did have valid reasons not to spend the night with Andrea. After her husband died in a car accident, maybe she wasn't in too much of a hurry to jump in bed with someone either.

I hung up and exhaled. There might have been a third reason I went home instead of going to Andrea's. When she suggested sleeping at her place, an image of Gomez in the green dress she wore to the fashion gala at the Chapin Art Museum flashed in my brain.

It concerned me that I couldn't help it.

CHAPTER
FORTY

THE BRAVES DOWNED the Nationals 3-1 in a pitchers' duel. Dad was happy despite Bo disappointing him with the news that he was now a San Francisco Giants fan. He lived half an hour from their stadium, and the Uber people used to set him up with box seats at games. He hadn't gone to a game since he sold his stake in the business for an egregious sum.

Bo hadn't worked a day in almost two years. The logical part of me wondered how long he could do that no matter how much money he had in the bank. I would get bored of not having a purpose, a reason to get out of bed in the morning. He lived an extravagant lifestyle, traveled to the ends of the Earth, and owned a mansion on one of the most famous golf courses in the world. He must have invested well.

I picked him up near midnight from Mom and Dad's. Mom wanted me to fill her in on all the details, but I begged off, saying that I needed to get to bed.

It was five minutes from their house to mine. Bo asked a million questions during the brief drive. I answered as many as possible. At this point, it was all a blur. I needed to rest and let my brain sort it out while the rest of my body was shut down.

Before retiring to our separate bedrooms, Bo informed me that he was thinking about sticking around for an extra day or two. He missed being around Mom and Dad and seeing me. Besides, he said, he wanted to watch me try to solve a murder. The entire process fascinated him. I told him the guest bedroom was his as long as he wanted. He said Mom and Dad offered to let him crash upstairs. The house had four bedrooms and only one was occupied. Mom and Dad slept in the master bedroom downstairs. It was like he'd have half the house to himself.

"Besides," he said with a wink and a nudge, "you never know when your girlfriend might want to have a sleepover. I wouldn't want to intrude."

I went to bed that night thinking about the day and what might have been had I taken Andrea up on her offer.

It was a fitful night of sleep.

* * *

Bo WAS STILL on West Coast time. His snores blasted through the bedroom door on Sunday morning as I stepped out the front door. I had told him before bed that I was set to meet with Detective Moody early this morning. He said not to worry. Mom and Dad's house was within walking distance, or an Uber was a few taps away to take him to breakfast with his free rides for life deal.

I had a tall travel mug of coffee in my hand as I climbed into the Jeep. I had a sense of déjà vu about taking the same route at about the same time of morning back to Swaying Palms.

The rain moved offshore overnight, leaving behind a marvelous post-sunrise cloudscape with splashes of oranges and fuchsias. Another thing the storm system did was bring in cooler, drier air behind it. It was almost a hint that fall was coming. The forecast called for a typical, sticky August afternoon ahead of us, but I would take the weather this morning all year long.

During the night, I tried to make sense of what I saw and learned yesterday. Gideon heard a male voice call out to Zach, but that was it. Percy would have been the next closest. Had he pushed through the trees, he would have come out to the cart path used by the maintenance team. From there, he could run back where Zach was at the bend in the dogleg, kill him, and then scamper back to his previous position. It was possible but didn't seem likely. Archie was the farthest away from the killing site. Of the three survivors, he was the one in the worst shape physically. He spent a good deal of time outside because of the landscaping company. As the boss, he issued more orders than getting his hands dirty. Yard work was a difficult job, and Archie might not have done much of it. My dad taught me about RHIP from his time in the Marines: Rank Has Its Privileges. As the owner, Archie might delegate all the dirty work to his employees.

At first, we figured it had to be one of those three men who killed Zach; then we learned every member seemed to be sleeping around with someone else, except for Percy. There was also the gambling aspect. If the pro shop manager, Zoe, ran a loan sharking service, maybe Zach would have held that knowledge and the picture of her and Archie to keep her in his pocket. Maybe she wanted to get rid of those threats hanging over her head.

Zach had found out about the affair his wife, Paxton, was having with Gideon. Reflecting on yesterday, I didn't sense any animosity between Zach and Gideon. Zach and Paxton's marriage was an open one. They may have wanted Zach gone before he filed for divorce and Paxton would only get half of his money.

There was also the factoid that Zach planned to get sole custody of their son, Ethan. If she had caught wind of Zach's demands before he delivered the divorce papers, did the potential of that outrage Paxton so much that she would have killed him? If she wanted to get away with it, it would have been better to kill her husband outside of their property. She might have slayed him in the pool house, but after seeing their security set up, it would be almost impossible for her to do it and get away with it.

The coffee from Benjamin's Bakery hit the spot as I pulled into the lot next to Moody's Explorer. We were parked in front of Blueberry's Grill beside the Publix off 79th Ave N in Myrtle Beach. I climbed from the Jeep and met Moody on the sidewalk in front of his vehicle.

Moody, never being one for "Good mornings" or "how did you sleep" cut to the chase. "The medical examiner came back with an initial report on the autopsy."

"Yeah? What did it say?"

"She found a round welt on his back that she couldn't explain. Said it was ante mortem, fresh, meaning moments before his death."

"Interesting."

"He was struck twice. Once at the base of his skull. That blow broke his neck."

"Eww. Was that what killed him?"

"She didn't think so. You can get your neck broken and possibly still live. The blow from the 3-wood was what did him in. The hit ruptured his temporal artery, causing massive bleeding on the inside of his skull. That kept him from suffering a great deal before dying."

"How can you break your neck and still live?" This was news to me.

"Depends on where the break occurs," he explained. "The lucky ones black out right after it's done and lose use of their limbs while surviving. The unlucky ones get the connection of the nerves between your body and brain disconnected. The unfortunate ones retain consciousness as their heart stops beating and their lungs stop breathing. The victim will have seconds, maybe as many as two minutes of consciousness, as they start to suffocate and panic before everything shuts down and goes black."

It was a chilling insight into what the last few moments of Zach's life might have held.

Before I replied, he said, "Gomez should be back later today."

"That's good." I wondered if that meant that I would be relieved of duty. Yes, my natural curiosity wanted to find the truth behind who killed Zach, but the truth was, this case, the victim, and the suspects involved were darker than the other murders I'd helped to solve. We were already aware of the tomfoolery that went on between members of the group and their families. Finding the scandalous pictures knowing that Zach might have been using them for blackmail put me off. I already had a negative opinion of Zach before his murder. Nothing we had uncovered had changed that. Every new bit of information made it worse.

Moody turned and regarded the entrance to the restaurant where a family was currently walking in. "Percy said he wanted to meet before church. Didn't want his kids to see him being questioned by the police."

"I can understand that. Did you tell him that you would interview him whenever and wherever you wanted to?"

"No, but I get breakfast out of this on the department dime. So do you. Come on."

We entered the restaurant and found Percy seated at a table in the back corner. He had his back to the dining room. A black hat was perched upon his head. He wore a plain T-shirt and dark glasses. It was as incognito as possible. Must have changed out of the dress shirt he would have worn to church, otherwise, it was his undershirt.

I had the impulse to come up behind him and shout, "Hey Percy!" at the top of my lungs, but sensibility kept me from doing so. That, and I liked to keep a low profile too.

He studied a thick breakfast menu as we sat across from him at the wood-topped table.

"Morning gents," he said without looking up.

A coffee and glass of water sat in front of him. He'd been here long enough to at least receive those.

"The chorizo benedict is sounding good to me," he said, like we were here paying him a social visit and not conducting a murder inquiry.

A waitress came and took our drink orders. While we waited for our beverages to arrive, I perused the menu. Everything looked good. The *clink* of silverware on plates and muffled breakfast conversation filled my ears. Aromas of sausage, coffee, maple syrup, and pancakes intermingled to fill the air.

She returned and set a coffee mug in front of me and tea in front of Moody. We ordered. Chorizo benedict for Percy, the Breakfast of Champions for me, and to my surprise, Moody ordered off the healthy menu. A Chicken Kale Omelet.

He patted a hand to his chest. "Doctor told me to take care of the old ticker."

I didn't say it, but he wasn't thinking about the "old ticker" when he ordered from Cook Out last night.

The waitress departed. Percy said to us, "Can you believe that rain that fell yesterday? It was a soaker. Supposed to be a beautiful day today. Might take the boat out for a cruise with the fam. What about you all?"

"Investigatin' a murder," Moody replied.

"Oh," Percy said and stopped stirring his coffee. He picked it up, sipped, and then asked, "What can I answer for you? Keep in mind that I can't discuss specifics of Zach's divorce. Attorney/Client privilege and all."

"We're well aware of that," Moody said.

Percy held the cup between both hands. "Okay then."

"How well did you know Paxton?"

"Paxton? I knew her okay, I guess."

"What about Ethan?"

A smile crossed his lips. "Love that little boy. Such a sweet kid. Reminds me of my sister."

I gripped my coffee mug. "She had autism too, right?"

"Yeah, she did." Percy's shoulders sagged. "Lost her a couple years ago. She was the best."

I hadn't been around too many people with autism, but in my limited exposure, I was aware that every case was different.

"I feel sorry for Ethan," he said.

"Why is that?" I asked.

"Because Paxton is all he has left." He leaned forward. "She's, uh, not the most engaged parent."

"She doesn't seem like the most engaged human being," I said.

I sensed Moody's eyes burning a hole in me. I didn't turn to meet his gaze.

Percy chuckled. "No, she's not. Thinks she is some sort of social media influencer. Can't stay off her phone."

"Like many people nowadays," I said.

"You're right there," Percy agreed. "All I have to say about her is, good luck doing that with all the looks in the world and no personality to go with it. She's gorgeous, but about as shallow as one of the water puddles out there in the parking lot. I've gotta go see her later, and I'm not looking forward to it. The divorce didn't happen, but I signed off on their wills. We need to discuss that."

His evaluation of Paxton restated my first impression of her.

"Noted," Moody said diplomatically.

"Here's the thing." Percy held out a level hand in front of him. "If you want to look at it this way. And I'm not supposed to go into too many details, but if they were together at the time of his death, then she'd be a made woman. If not, she'd be almost penniless."

The hair on the back of my neck stood on end.

"Understood." Moody said. He had out his trusty notebook and was busy scribbling notes. I glimpsed over, half expecting to see a sketch of a kitty cat.

Percy switched gears away from Paxton. I don't know if it was from nervousness or what, but we were getting an unfiltered version of Percy. "I didn't care for how Zach used Ethan as a prop to make him look better in the community."

"How so?" Moody asked.

"Come on." He looked at me. "You had a run-in with him. Both of you saw the way he acted toward Archie. Zach wasn't exactly the most pleasant person."

"But you were friends?" My tone was soaked in irony.

"Yeah. You experience things as an adult for the first time sharing the same dorm room. I was on the track team. He played soccer. We go way back and helped each other grow our careers. He might have been a clown, but he was *our* clown. You had to take Zach at face value."

"Noted," Moody said. "How did he and Paxton get together?"

"She was a waitress at Angelo's," he answered. "Zach met her there and kept going back for the steaks and all-you-can-eat Italian buffet. He was as skinny as a rail before that. His youthful metabolism must have changed during that time because he packed on the pounds. She's ten years younger than him."

"Interesting," Moody said. "Let's go over it again. What happened right before and right after Zach's death."

Before he started speaking, our food came. We dug in and he told us the same story as the day before, almost verbatim. Moody and I tried to poke holes in it, but as a trained attorney, he was too smooth to change anything.

We finished our meals. He wiped his mouth with a napkin and asked, "Am I a suspect?"

"You are," Moody answered.

Percy set the napkin on the table. "Okay, then. Let me know if I can help you make me not a suspect."

Moody blinked. "Are you trying to bribe us?"

"Nope. Not at all. All I'm saying is, if I can provide you with any information to clear my name, let me know."

"Alright," I said. "Even if it means rolling over on your friends?"

"I'm a sworn officer of the court." He held up a fist. "It's my duty."

We paid our bills and left a few minutes later. Next stop: Gideon's.

As I trailed Moody's Explorer in my Jeep, I thought about Percy.

Of the other two group partners, he seemed to be the least likely to have anything to gain from Zach's death. In fact, he'd lose business because of it. As I've come to learn, sometimes it's the least likely suspect that ends up being the murderer.

However, Percy said a few things about Paxton and Zach that I stuck in a corner of my brain that weren't relevant then but became so later.

CHAPTER
FORTY-ONE

I PULLED INTO Gideon's driveway beside the waiting Detective Moody. Inside the vehicle, he sipped from a mug that had to hold tea. The detective wasn't a coffee fan. I didn't hold that against him because Autumn was the same way with her tea addiction, except she preferred loose leaf teas. I wasn't sure about how Moody brewed his tea at home. He usually asked for Earl Gray when he came into the bookstore.

Gideon owned an imposing brick home as most were on this golf course. The driveway was wide enough for six cars to park beside and in front of each other. A black BMW SUV sat in the spot farthest to the right beside the corner of the garage. A shiny Alfa Romeo two-seater sat next to it. There were no other cars in the driveway besides mine and Moody's police Explorer.

Apparently, Gideon ran his business out of his garage. A modern office. The door was open, allowing us to peak in and see surfboards lining the walls. A desk with two glowing computer screens sat against the back wall. Utility shelving holding various boxes, parts, and wood slabs filled both back corners.

A pair of sawhorses sat in the middle of the garage. Gideon, wearing a pair of safety goggles, tank top, and a pair of board shorts, was using a wood planer to carve out ribbons of wood shavings from an eight-foot-long block of cedar. The project was half complete.

I had no doubt that the finished product would be exquisite and expensive.

Moody and I met in front of our vehicles and greeted each other. Gideon didn't seem to notice us.

We stepped into the garage side-by-side. Pop music from Lorde played through a Bluetooth speaker on the desk. I was vaguely aware of her being from New Zealand. I was surprised he wasn't listening to Keith Urban. Perhaps the country singer was on deck. That was the extent of my knowledge of the music scene down under.

Gideon made one more stroke with the planer to round out one edge of the side of the surfboard. He took off his safety goggles and set them on the half-completed board.

"G'day," he said and pulled out his phone. "One sec."

He tapped the screen and the music thankfully stopped. Lorde was not on my playlist.

"Morning," Moody said. "Need to circle back with a few questions."

Gideon placed the phone in his pocket. "No worries. You want any coffee? Tea?"

The detective abstained as he brought his mug with him, but I accepted another cup of coffee.

We moved the conversation to his back patio where I cradled a steaming mug in my hands. A flower garden that I wouldn't have pictured a bachelor like Gideon having lined all three sides of the back yard. It overlooked a fairway at Swaying Palms. The asphalt of the utility cart path created the boundary between his property and the golf course.

He told us his house bordered the 14th hole. We didn't quite make it that far yesterday.

This time, Moody hadn't told me to let him take the lead. He might have assumed that I would accept the role of second fiddle. That was fine yesterday. This was today, and we'd already spoken to Gideon more than once yesterday.

I didn't want Moody to come out firing with questions that might put Gideon on edge and on the defense. I hadn't gone to Investigate Discourse 101 or whatever type of training police detectives received, but I believed it might be easier if a friendly chat took place. Not an adversarial one.

"You said you were from New Zealand, right?" I asked Gideon.

Moody sipped from his mug and didn't shoot me a dirty look.

"That's right," Gideon answered.

"How did you end up here?"

"I was a pretty good swimmer along with playing soccer. Grew up a stone's throw away from Piha Beach west of Auckland. Familiar with it?"

"Can't say I am."

"No worries. It's one of our most famous surfing destinations. Let me tell ya, it's stunning. Black sand. Lush scenery. The works. My mates and I used to climb to the top of Lion Rock all the time to take in the sunrise over the Tasman Sea. Then we'd go out and surf until the sun went down over the Waitakere Ranges." He stopped for a moment to savor the memory. "Anyway, I took a job here in Myrtle one winter near the end of secondary school."

"Why take a job in the winter?" Moody asked.

"I think he means the winter there," I said.

Gideon chortled. "Correct. It'd be summer here, mate."

Moody nodded.

The Kiwi continued, "Came over. Spent three months. The best ones of my life at the time. Came back here, enrolled at Coastal, graduated, and became a citizen three years later."

"How did the surfboard business come about?" I asked.

He smiled. "My dad taught me how to carve a surfboard when I was an ankle biter. I could do it with my eyes shut by the time I became a teenager. He passed, leaving my mum to take care of seven kids." He laughed. "We were a handful, I'll say. Mum had her work cut out for her, but she did her best."

"That's good," I said.

"Still call her every week," he said. "The rellies and I share a group chat too. We're close, even though they're on the opposite side of the globe."

What he said reminded me of Bo and I not being in close contact over the last ten years. It wasn't like it was difficult these days to stay close with friends and family despite being separated by vast distances. The internet has shrunk the world.

"Look," Moody said, "we see you're busy."

Gideon waved a dismissive hand. "No worries. Anything I can do to help."

Moody took out his pen and a notepad. "What did you know about Zoe, loan sharking, and gambling among members of Swaying Palms?"

"Ah." Gideon smiled. "Get right to the point, don't ya, mate?"

"Answer the question," Moody grunted.

The grin faded. "That sheila is a smooth customer."

"How so?"

"I'm not sure how it started," he said. "I'm not even sure if she's the originator of the loan service."

"Describe the loan service. How did it go along with the betting?"

"Swaying Palms doesn't have a huge membership." Gideon scratched his chin. "But it's elite, mind you. We all know each other from various social events within the club, tourneys, or just getting paired up together. Members are ninety-percent men. Their missus and kids can play too. But it's mostly the blokes who play. Zach had asked me to join him for a round before I became a member. I was still living in a 'owse over Market Common at the time. We got paired up with another realtor and a dental surgeon. Right off the bat on the first hole, they wanted to play for skins."

"Playing for skins" is golf lingo for betting on holes. Players determine how much each hole is worth. If they tie on a hole, the "skin" from that hole is carried over to the next.

"I'd never done that before," Gideon said. "Zach said it was all right. Everyone here did it."

"How does Zoe tie into it?" I asked.

"If you lost, you were expected to pay up then and there. Sometimes, guys wouldn't have enough money to cover their debts and they didn't want to go home, grab the money, and possibly explain why to the missus. That's where Zoe came into play."

Moody made a note. "How were these transactions conducted?"

Gideon held up a pair of fingers. "Two ways. If you trusted your mate who owed you money and they didn't have it, they'd walk into the pro shop and ask her for it when no one was watching."

"Hmm," Moody grunted. "Going to have to check the cameras there."

"Good luck with that," Gideon said. "There are no cameras on the desk in the club house."

I turned to my partner. "Jeff said that the most action he gets is stopping people from stealing golf gloves they had tried on in the clubhouse."

Moody grunted. "Doesn't mean there are cameras in there."

"Hmm. If what Gideon says is true, that suggests the people who run Swaying Palms know about what Zoe does."

"Not necessarily," Moody said. "Just might be Jeff since he's the security guy. He and her could have an arrangement."

"Did you ever borrow money from her?" I asked.

"Yeah nah." Gideon answered.

Moody and I looked at each other confused.

"Never," Gideon amended. Of course, the manners of people down under frowned upon sounding too assertive which did not help while being questioned by the police.

He was indeed one cool customer. I asked, "Did you always have enough money on you?"

"Who needed money? I never lost."

Percy and Archie had suggested Gideon was better than them on the course. His answer wasn't smug, just a matter of fact.

"What about when the others lost to you? Were you around when they conducted business with Zoe?" Moody asked.

"Yeah nah, not in the clubhouse. I was never there when they approached Zoe in the shop."

"Was there another way to get money from her?" I asked.

"Nah yeah. She had a delivery service."

I was getting the hang of his double responses, taking stock of the second word only. "How did that work?"

Gideon wiggled his head. "Let's say we're coming to the end of the back nine and one mate is going to owe another money. We'd text Zoe with how much, and either she or the cart girl, Grace, would meet us on the eighteenth green. They used the beverage cart and would stash cash under lock and key inside the cooler on the back of it."

"Sneaky," I said.

"Too right," Gideon agreed.

"We haven't met Grace yet," I said to Moody.

He puckered out his bottom lip. "No, but we will after we leave here."

"You're in for a treat," Gideon said.

"Why's that?" I responded.

"She's not a stunner, I'll tell you that much. You'll see."

While I pondered what Gideon meant by the statement, Moody scrawled notes. "Okay. Got that. We'll follow up. Moving on. Were you sleeping with Paxton?"

Gideon didn't blink. "Nah, yeah. I might've copped a root now and then."

CHAPTER
FORTY-TWO

THE DETECTIVE GLANCED at me with a look suggesting he was simultaneously surprised and delighted at the honesty of the suspect. The man seemed honest, helpful, and open. I wanted to believe he was a genuinely good person. Except, I reminded myself, he might also be a killer who thwacked his friend upside the head with a 3-wood.

By him openly admitting to the affair, Moody didn't need to show him the photos, nor did we need to mention that Archie had seen them together.

"Did Zach know about it?" I asked.

He scratched his arm. "Not that I'm aware of, mate."

I would let Moody take over the questioning. Gideon's response signaled that he didn't know about the photos. He didn't know that we learned that Zach had known, if you follow me. I sipped my coffee. Moody took a contemplative drink of tea.

"What would you say," Moody said, "if I told you that Zach had pictures of you and his wife together?"

"You mean, like, at a restaurant or something?"

"Did you go out to eat together?"

"We didn't."

"Then, no, I don't mean pictures in a public place."

"Ah." Gideon rubbed the side of his face. "Caught us in the

sack, did he?"

"Correct," Moody said. "We found pictures in the pool house."

"Why the pool house?"

"Because that's where Zach was staying," Moody said. "He and Paxton got in a fight, and he moved in there."

"Can't say I'm surprised."

"We found pictures of some of your other friends, too," I added.

"Not surprising."

"Do you know of him blackmailing anyone?" I asked.

"Not that I'm aware of. He didn't me. I can only imagine if he tried to do that to Percy."

"Why do you say that?" Moody asked.

Gideon chuckled. "I can picture Percy now. Giving Zach extortion money in exchange for pictures or documents or something. He'd go home and shred those suckers right away ASAP like a bent solicitor."

"Is Percy a shyster lawyer?" I asked.

"No, mate. Percy is legit."

Moody grunted. "Do you know why Zach was filing for divorce?"

Gideon's jaw worked back and forth before answering. He drank from his mug, letting the question sink in. "Was it because of Paxton and me?"

"Not sure," Moody said. "His reason was for irreconcilable differences."

"Hmm. I was aware that they had an open marriage," he said. "Which was how Paxton convinced me to jump in the sack with her."

The actions of these people made me want to cringe. I felt icky for being involved, but there was no backing out now.

"Let's play a thought game for a moment," Moody said. "Let's pretend something."

"Alright," Gideon said. "I'm game."

Moody grunted. "Let's say you learned from Percy, Paxton, or Zach that a divorce was in the works."

"But I didn't."

"Right," Moody said. "Remember, we're playing a game here. Let's say you knew about it."

"I'm with you," Gideon said.

"Great." Moody opened his hands. "So, you and Paxton are sneaking around when you catch wind of this. She would know from the prenup that she would get half of Zach's assets."

"Which would still be a substantial amount," Gideon commented.

"That's true, from what I gather," Moody said. "We haven't had time to dig into his finances yet."

"Have fun with that, mate" Gideon said.

I raised my eyebrows. "What do you mean?"

"Zach used to brag about all these offshore shell corporations he had conducted business through. Gonna be a nightmare to sort that out."

Moody rubbed a hand over his face and sighed. "Good grief. Great. Now we'll have to call in the FBI, SEC, and maybe FinCEN."

"What's FinCEN?" I asked.

"Yeah," Gideon agreed. "Never heard of that one."

"They're a part of the Treasury Department," Moody explained. "They focus on money laundering."

"Ah," Gideon and I said at the same time.

Moody pulled out his phone and sent someone a message. "Just gave a heads up to Chief Miller. She'll love this."

A heron flew over our heads. We watched its majestic flight until it disappeared beyond the trees. I asked, "Do you know anything specific he did with these shell corporations?"

"Yeah nah. It was something complex set up through his solicitors," Gideon answered. "Zach said he didn't know half of it. They told him ignorance is bliss, in this case."

"Know who these lawyers are?" Moody asked.

"I don't."

"Don't worry. We'll figure it out in due time." Moody scribbled down a note on his notepad. "Back to the game. Let's say you were aware of the impending divorce and Paxton getting half of Zach's assets."

"I'm with you," Gideon said. "And you want to know if Paxton hatched a plan with me to murder her husband before he filed for divorce?"

"Read my mind," Moody said.

Gideon crossed his arms. "Yeah. We discussed it."

CHAPTER
FORTY-THREE

I LEANED FORWARD in my chair, pulse racing.

"But you said you didn't know about the divorce," I said.

"Correct," Gideon said. "I didn't."

"But you talked about killing him with Paxton?"

Gideon placed a hand on his chest. "I didn't. She did."

"How so?" I asked.

He fixed me in his sights. "Paxton is a whinger. Moans and groans about everything. It's annoying to tell you the truth."

"Are you still sleeping with her?" Moody asked.

"I am."

"If she's so annoying, why continue?"

"She's gifted in that department."

It made me feel dirty for even being around these people.

Moody ignored the salacious comment. "In what context did she discuss murdering Zach?"

Gideon pinched his lips. "There wasn't any planning involved, if that's what you're getting at. It was more of, he did this or that, she hated it, and said she'd kill him, almost like she was joking."

"Mentioning murder of anyone for any reason is no joke," I said.

"I agree with you there, mate."

Moody readied his pen over the pad. "But she said it?"

"Correct."

"Recently?"

Gideon looked up into the swaying palms and took a deep breath. "Yeah."

"How recent?"

"This past Wednesday."

"How did it come up?"

"Uh." Gideon's cool façade cracked. The kind of cracking a person does when they realize they've been caught in a lie and had to figure out how to wiggle out of it on the fly. The coffee mug shook in his hand. His face flushed. "Uh."

Moody closed the pad and leaned toward Gideon. In a stern tone, he asked, "How did it come up?"

"Alright, I lied," Gideon admitted.

"About what?" I asked.

"About the divorce," he answered. "She said Zach came in that morning before going to the office and said he'd divorce her and take Ethan with him."

Blood thundered in my ears. "What did she say about it?"

Gideon turned to me and gulped. "That she was going to kill him for real."

CHAPTER
FORTY-FOUR

AT OUR CURRENT position in gathering evidence and interviewing witnesses, Gideon's statement wasn't enough for Moody to put in a call to arrest Paxton. Gideon went on to tell us that while she said she wanted to kill him, she didn't mention specifics or any sort of plan. Beyond her statement, it was the last Gideon heard of Paxton issuing a verbal threat.

Moody tied up a few odds and ends and told Gideon not to leave town.

I backed out of his driveway as the garage door lowered. The surfboard shaping work might be done for the day. Moody had told me to follow him to the Swaying Palms parking lot, and said he had a call to make on the way to the clubhouse.

I trailed his Explorer in my Jeep as we twisted through the neighborhood surrounding the golf course. Spanish moss hanging from majestic oaks bordering the lane wafted in a soft breeze. My elbow was propped up on an open window to enjoy the morning temps as the air blew across my skin.

Despite his seemingly honest nature, Gideon had lied to us about the divorce. My mind tried to sift through what we'd learned to try to figure out why he would do that. He lied and then told us the truth at the point where Moody's scenario in the thought puzzle circled back to suggesting Gideon might have been in on it. He had to know we were going to follow up with Paxton about it. The only way to know what she had said about murdering her husband would only come from Gideon. What did that mean for their relationship? Was it all physical, or was there more to it?

If Gideon murdered Zach, it was possible that his reason for doing it had nothing to do with Paxton. Gideon, Zach, Archie, and Percy had a long history of friendship. Throughout the two-plus decades since they met in college, lives change, intertwine, and can move in different directions.

They were fortunate. I counted on two fingers the number of classmates I kept in contact with, and they didn't live anywhere near Myrtle Beach. I had to admit to myself that part of the reason I'd lost contact with my friends was because I'd shunned social media for so long. The only reason I had it was because of my books and bookstore. Even then, Winona managed most of the lifting on the various platforms for me.

All three might have been in on it. The only problem with that was, if Percy was an attorney familiar with the ins and outs of law, why would they stash the club in Archie's locker? That didn't make sense to me. It was possible that Percy and Gideon conspired together to frame Archie. I wasn't sure at this point why they would do that to their friend, but I wouldn't be surprised if we uncovered new evidence pointing to that conclusion.

My mind ran through different scenarios as to how that might have taken shape as we rounded a long curve past two stately homes bordering the course. Other, less grandiose estates lay on the left side of the road. Gideon was aware of the loan sharking service Zoe supplied but hadn't needed to use it. Archie had found himself in the hole and had. We would wait to ask him if the penalty for not paying back the money was having to "pay up" with Zoe in the bedroom, but since we were heading to the clubhouse and pro shop, I hoped we'd find direct answers there. If sleeping with Zoe was the "penalty," then the only conclusion I came to was that she did it as a way of controlling men. She only slept with married men. The reason being was to hang evidence of the affairs over her clients' heads. Pay up or she'd tell the wifey about the birthmark her husband had that only his wife, mom, and doctor would know about. I may as well call her the "Black Widow." Lure the men in with her beauty, wrap them up in their sins, and toy with them until she strikes or sets them free.

I know why she didn't sleep with Gideon. He was single. Zach was married and seemed like her type. Affluent and not afraid of keeping secrets. He may have told her about his open marriage. If so, then to her, it might seem like he was practically single. No repercussions for having an affair, so not worth her time.

After navigating through the neighborhood, we came to a roundabout. To the left lay the 17 Bypass. Straight ahead was the other half of the housing development. To the right was the long, palm lined avenue to Swaying Palms.

We took the first exit off the roundabout and headed to the clubhouse, passing a white Cadillac SUV and a Lexus sedan heading in the opposite direction. Birds twittered in a palm tree as I drove underneath it.

The weight of the world had settled on Moody's shoulders when Gideon mentioned Zach's offshore accounts. It sounded like it might be a tangled mess that would take months for the federal agencies to sort through. Despite his death, law enforcement might step in and freeze his assets during the investigation. Whatever Paxton was set to get from his passing, minus the government taking their cut, would have to wait. If she was aware of how he conducted business, she had to have an inkling that his deeds might surface and there was a chance she got nothing. In that light, she might prefer to take a clean divorce. The courts would take whatever they decided of Zach's money, he'd go to jail, and she'd get Ethan no matter what. Win, win.

Flipping the mental page, if everything we'd been told about Zoe and the loan service were true, how would the authorities handle it?

I didn't have to wait long for the answer.

* * *

THE PARKING LOT was more than half full when Moody and I arrived. Puddles from yesterday's soaking rain held on for dear life along the edges of the pavement. People on golf carts maneuvered through the rows of vehicles, loading and unloading sets of clubs. A half-dozen duffers made use of the driving range.

This scene repeated itself at any of the dozens of golf courses in the Grand Strand right now.

Moody picked a clear row at the back of the lot near the alley leading back out to 17 for us to park. We backed in, side-by-side, facing the clubhouse. He exited his Explorer and walked around the front of it to my Jeep, speaking on his cell phone.

I climbed from my Jeep and overheard his side of the conversation.

"Yep. Just parked." He listened and grunted, pacing around my vehicle to get a clear look down the tree-lined entry road. "Here they come now. Thanks. I'll be in touch shortly."

He ended the call and stuck the phone and his hands in his pockets.

"What's happening?" I asked.

He tilted his head at the drive. I turned to look in the direction he indicated.

Two large, armored vehicles thundered toward us. The smaller one, and that's relatively speaking, was a flat faced personnel carrier with a camouflage paint job. The other was what Moody would later tell me was called an "MRAP." That is, Mine Resistant Ambush Protected. It was a bulky, desert gray vehicle that looked like it would withstand a missile attack.

I couldn't believe my eyes. "You called in the SWAT team?"

"Yep," Moody grunted like it happened every week. "Put the fear of God into these fat cats."

The vehicles zoomed into the lot. Every wealthy golfer stopped in their tracks or cart and stared, openly gawking. Eight SWAT team members poured out of the personnel carrier and marched briskly up the front stairs to stand by the door. A pair of golfers opened the door to exit the clubhouse, saw the soldiers, dropped their clubs, and staggered back inside. They didn't want a piece of this.

"Freeze!" the lead woman in uniform shouted at the pair. They raised their hands in unison and turned around to face the troops. The officers stood at attention with automatic weapons in their hands. She gestured using the barrel of hers. "Over there. Hands on top of your head."

The two middle-aged, well-dressed men in golf apparel complied.

After the unit commander exited the MRAP, he issued orders. Four police cruisers came in behind the SWAT vehicles. Two cars blocked the exit.

As expected, there wasn't any resistance. Chief Miller arrived and shut the course down, pending a deep investigation. The names, addresses, and phone numbers of each golfer were taken down. They were told to expect a visit from a member of law enforcement with questions about the activities that took place at Swaying Palms.

Moody had arranged beforehand for them to round up certain employees and to place them in a conference room: course superintendent, Warren, security guy, Jeff, Zoe, and the cart girl Grace.

I was a spectator of the police department's activities. They were organized and efficient. Someone handed me a laminated ID card with a lanyard, so I didn't get sent away. Had my face on it and everything. It was my driver's license photo and not the most flattering, but I would hang on to it as a memento.

The starter from yesterday walked by me. There was a point about Zoe's comings and goings yesterday that were unclear, and he was the man to shed a light on it. I asked him if Zoe had come by asking if his wife would like a lesson.

"She did," he responded. "I called my wife, and she got all excited. She'd been dying to get another lesson." He held a hand over his mouth. "My apologies. Poor choice of words."

A while later, Moody, Chief Miller, Officers Dame and Battles, and I entered the conference room where four of the members of the Swaying Palms staff awaited.

Warren stood in a corner. He tapped a foot, chewed a thumbnail, and his gaze was cast on the floor. Jeff was calm, cool, and collected. He sat at a chair with a coffee mug in front of him, reading a newspaper. Zoe sat two seats from Jeff with her arms crossed.

Her assistant, Grace, stood next to her. Gideon warned us, but

I had seen her before. Her face defied description. If I included her in one of my books, the story might fit into the horror category. Let's just say her best attributes were from the neck down.

Warren had already been briefed on why the police shut down the golf course. I didn't know who owned the golf course, but my assumption was that Warren was about to lose his job, if not go to jail—depending on how much he knew.

Moody informed me before we entered the room that our job was to get to the bottom of the murder. Someone else would investigate the loan sharking.

This would be quick.

I didn't know then, but my part in what was about to take place would be cut short.

CHAPTER
FORTY-FIVE

I CLOSED THE door behind us. A panoramic window on the opposite side of the room showed an empty, wet golf course. The air was stuffy.

Moody grunted and said, "I'm sure you're aware of why you're here. The Feds are on their way to speak to you."

That caused a stir in the room. Jeff set down the paper. "I don't know why I'm here."

Moody was blunt with the security manager. "You should have known what was going on. From what we've gathered, this was done out in the open. There may not have been other members around when money exchanged hands, but it should have been on video. If gambling was as rampant as it has been let on, it had to happen almost every day. I refuse to believe *you* didn't see anything from your security room. Maybe that's why there are large gaps in coverage around the perimeter of the course."

No one flinched at the word "gambling."

I said to Moody, "I'd like to make a little wager of my own."

"What's that?"

My arms were crossed. I raised a finger off my elbow and pointed it between Jeff and Warren. "I'll bet that Jeff was paid to look the other way, and I suspect that Warren not only had awareness of it but was the one who instructed Zoe to do it when she was hired.

Pardon the pun, but I bet this has been going on for longer than she has been here."

"That's what I'm thinking, too," Moody said and turned to our now captive audience.

Zoe hadn't moved a muscle since we entered. Grace shifted nervously on her heels. Like Warren, she chewed on her fingernails in an absent-minded manner. While watching her, something tingled in the back of my mind, but I couldn't place a finger on it.

"Zoe," Moody said.

Zoe's reply was cold as ice. "Yes?"

Moody stepped forward and placed both hands on the back of an empty chair across from her in an intimidating stance. "How close is Clark's wager? Was this happening when you got here?"

She turned, scowled at Warren who wouldn't meet her face, and came back to us. "Correct."

If she continued to cooperate, this was a way to lessen the consequences of her actions. She seemed like the vindictive type. Like Zach. If she were going down, everyone would be dragged along into the depths with her.

She explained how she wasn't told about it when interviewing for the job. Once she accepted it and came on board, Warren took her out to an expensive dinner at Heirloom Bistro. It was there they told her about the scheme. It was there they promised her a cut under the table. A way to pay off her student debt in less than a year.

Warren didn't deny it. When Moody asked him about it, he said he'd wait for his attorney. Same with Jeff. That was fine with us. We'd let the Feds handle it.

The murder was our top priority.

Moody swung to face Zoe, leading to an abrupt change of subject and tone in the conversation. "Did you force anyone to sleep with you to pay off debts?"

If possible, her arms tightened. "I did."

"Mmm hmm," Moody grunted. "And Grace."

She snapped to attention. "Yes?"

"How did you fall into this? Were you aware of it when you were hired?"

Grace spoke with a sweet voice. "N-no. Zoe told me about it on my second day. She took a phone call, got into a safe under the counter, and gave me a bag of cash."

"What did she tell you to do with it?"

"To go out to the 18th green with the beverage cart, hide the money in the cooler, and meet up with a guy and give him the money."

"Who was it?"

Her eyebrows knitted together. "Frank Ludlum."

Warren groaned.

"Frank Ludlum?" I said. "You mean City Councilman, Frank Ludlum?"

"I think that's him," Grace answered.

Heavy hitters in Myrtle Beach played at this course. If this gambit started taking down members of local government, then this story might end up with nationwide exposure. *Great.* I hoped they would keep my name out of it.

"Thanks, we'll ask him about it," Moody said.

I asked, "Did you ever give money to Zach, Gideon, Percy, or Archie?"

"Mmm hmm," Grace replied. "Just Archie. I didn't care for Zach.

He was a loathsome brute, always trying to pinch my butt when I walked away."

Her comment didn't surprise me. To Zoe, I asked, "Did you have an intimate relationship with any of that group?"

Moody and I knew at least one of those answers.

"Not with Percy," Zoe said. "He never came to me for money."

I leaned forward, focusing on her. "What about the others?"

"Gideon didn't come to me for a loan either, but he has asked me out several times." She examined her fingernails like she didn't have a care in the world.

"Did you turn him down?"

"Yes."

"Why? He's a very handsome guy. You'd make a good-looking couple."

She *tsked*. "It's simple. I only go for married guys. No messy feelings."

I was unable to bite my tongue anymore. "You're disgusting. Was one of your life's goals to be a homewrecker?"

Moody placed a cautioning hand on my wrist. I backed down.

"I'm disgusting?" Zoe placed a hand on her chest, adding melodrama to the situation. "I'm disgusting? What about all these men who come in here leering at me? I'm not the one who makes the decision to cheat on my spouse. I'm more of an opportunist."

"That doesn't make it any less egregious," I said. "You use men to achieve your goals."

She cocked her head to the side and gave me a predatory look even with the other people in the room. "Too bad you aren't married. You're just my type."

Her comment brought my figurative kettle to a boil. Before I flung myself across the table at her, Battles grabbed me by the arm and held me in place. "Easy there."

Chief Miller had Battles escort me from the room.

CHAPTER
FORTY-SIX

OFFICER BATTLES CLOSED the door behind us.

I took a step to the middle of the hallway, bent over, and put my hands on my thighs. Everything was blurry around me. I took four deep breaths. Breathed in. Breathed out. Breathed in. Breathed out.

Battles came over and placed a thick hand on the middle of my back. "Got tense in there, didn't it?"

After a deep exhale, I stood and looked him in the eye. "I shouldn't have let her get to me."

"Look," he said, this time putting a paw on my shoulder. "This isn't your job. I know this. For a dude off the street, you do some cool things. Conflict management is something we're taught. I wasn't expecting her to say something like that to you."

"Me neither," I said. The tone of his voice and comforting hand gently squeezing my shoulder made the blood thundering in my ears subside. "I just haven't been around people as vile and nauseating as Zoe."

"Hey, we deal with people like her daily. They just don't always come in that type of package."

"Can't judge a book by its cover, can you?"

Half a smile formed on his face. "No, sir. That is absolutely true. What was it that sent you over?"

Breathe in. Breathe out. "Her saying that if I were married, I might be her type."

He clicked his tongue. "Because of your wife, right?"

"Yeah. I'm not single by choice."

Battles wore a gold wedding band on his left hand. Absent-mindedly, he twisted it. "I read ya. I grew up with a single mom. My pops passed when I was young. I don't know how you feel, but I feel you, know what I mean?"

"I do." Breathe out. "Thanks man."

He squeezed my shoulder.

Chief Miller and Moody exited the conference room, leaving Officer Dame to guard over the accused.

With all the players on the course told to get their clubs and scram and most of the employees being held in the dining room, the hallway in which we stood was quiet. The sun shone through a window at the end of the hallway. Dust motes floated in the stream of light. Quite a contrast to the dimness of yesterday afternoon.

Miller tilted her head at the door and said to Battles, "Go help Dame watch over them for a few minutes."

"Yes, ma'am," Battles said.

He and I exchanged a knowing look. For as big as he was, he had a calm demeanor that was just what I'd needed a moment ago. He'd never have to pay for coffee at the bookstore again.

After he closed the door behind him, Miller said to me, "Look, Clark, we appreciate your help, but you can't antagonize a potential suspect."

"I'm sorry," I said. "She got under my skin."

Moody came to my defense. "Maybe he's been watching too much TV with all that good cop/bad cop nonsense."

Miller eyed me. "Clark doesn't strike me as the bad cop type."

"I'm not," I said, holding my hands palms-out. "She said something that I took as a slight at my wife, my *dead* wife."

"She'd started to get under your skin before that," Miller said.

"I won't deny it. You're right. It won't happen again."

Her gaze lingered on me. "It won't happen again. I'm taking you off this case."

Moody started to come to my defense, but I waved him off. "Wait a second. I've been on this from the very beginning."

"You did this because the mayor asked you to. I didn't," Miller said. "You were here at the start. I'm aware of your history with the department, so I let it slide. The fact is, this is official police business, and you are not an official member of the force. I'll deal with Rosen."

After what happened in the conference room with Zoe and now this, I wanted to scream. My ears turned red. My face grew hot.

I remembered what Officer Battles suggested to calm my nerves. Breathe in. Breathe out.

She continued, "Detective Gomez will be back later this evening. Detective Moody will get her up to speed. We will contact you *if* we have any questions. Thank you for your time."

I took that as an immediate dismissal. Fine. Her gaze held firm. I tipped my head at Moody. He showed no emotion either way.

"Detective, pleasure working with you again," I said and left the clubhouse.

CHAPTER
FORTY-SEVEN

I FOUND MYSELF sitting behind the wheel of my Jeep with no memory of walking through the parking lot to get there. I tried ridiculously hard to never let my emotions get the best of me. I lived by Epictetus's reminder that I had no control over the events that happened around me, but I could control my reaction to them. There's always a moment between provocation and response. I'd trained myself to use that moment, no matter how small, to decide not to respond with anger.

That didn't happen in this case. I cursed myself for letting Zoe get to me. What I needed to remind myself was that she wasn't worth my time—especially now that I was off the case.

Most vehicles had left the parking lot. Several remained. The buzz of activity preceding our entry into the clubhouse had subsided. The SWAT team had left. Their armored vehicles were no longer parked in front of the door. They were replaced by a pair of police cruisers and a dark Suburban.

My thumb tapped the steering wheel as I pondered my next move. I was full of adrenaline and wanted to get as far away from this case as possible. I put the car in gear and hopped on the Bypass heading toward Surfside Beach and Garden City.

I cranked the radio up high to drown out my thoughts as I passed by the King Kong climbing to the top of the Hollywood Wax Museum beside the Roman Coliseum recreation used by the Gladiator Games Dinner Theatre. They weren't the most played musicians in my library, but right now, Metallica hit the spot. 80s Metallica, that is.

As it was still early on a Sunday, traffic wasn't bad. I took the 501 exit and headed toward the Boardwalk. The bookstore was about to open. A strong cup of coffee was just what the doctor ordered.

* * *

SUNDAYS WEREN'T THAT busy at the store, which was why we opened at noon. It was the day when vacationers checked out of their hotels and left the Grand Strand en masse. Check-in time was around four o'clock for most places around the Boardwalk. Books weren't at the forefront of travelers' minds after completing long trips and getting to their rooms.

Still, the store made enough money during the busy season that it was worth it to open on Sundays. In October, we'd change to offseason hours and stay closed on this day. Andrea's Coastal Décor was closed every Sunday throughout the year. I'd thought about calling her, but she liked to spend her days off with Libby as much as possible, and I needed to get my mind straight.

Bo was set to fly out later this week, and I wanted to make sure I spent time with him. After coffee, of course.

Unless it was Humphrey, the store only needed one employee to work on Sundays. We went in a rotation where each employee worked Sunday once every four weeks. If Humphrey wasn't trusted to be alone, that meant I bit the bullet and worked with him once a month. Our week was the next week. Huzzah.

Today, Miss Margaret pulled Sunday duty. If I wasn't here, the coffee bar didn't operate on Sundays. It was too much to ask one person to have coffee brewed and deal with coffee drinkers on one side of the store and readers on the other.

Margaret had just flipped on the OPEN light when I got to the front door. I used to use the back entrance at the delivery alcove to enter the store, but rarely did since discovering Paige Whitaker's body there. If another dead person got dropped off there, I'd leave it for someone else to discover.

After today, I didn't know if I wanted to get involved in any more of these investigations. Reflecting upon it, I'd been fortunate with the other cases I'd been involved in that they didn't revolve around such revolting people. Money can buy things and let you reach a certain status, but it doesn't make you a good person. In fact, I'd known good people who came into money through their careers to go bad, get into drugs and other legally questionable practices.

Off the top of my head, there were at least five crimes we'd uncovered that Zach had committed. That wasn't counting what I would consider morally reprehensible things he did.

I opened the front entrance as Margaret was walking to the book counter. Her back was to me. The bell chimed on the door, announcing my entrance.

The spry old woman spun on her heel and turned to me. "Clark! What are you doing here? Winona told us in our group chat that you were doing another murder thingy. I figured you'd be out with that pretty detective hunting down the bad guys."

Partnering with Gomez would have been preferable to spending the last thirty-six hours with Moody. Although, it was interesting working with him. He wasn't as inept as I had figured. When it was his turn to step up, his experience showed.

"Nah. I'm done with that."

"Did you get the bad guy?"

"Nah. This one is for the police. I pitched in because it happened near where my brother and I were playing golf yesterday."

"Well, you were in the right place at the wrong time then." Margaret had this droll manner about her that was at the same time endearing and snarky.

I nodded. "Yep. It was interesting for a while, but I'm not so sure I'm cut out for it. Some of the people you end up investigating are just...."

"A bunch of scumbags, huh?"

"Mostly."

"Hoo boy." Margaret chuckled. "Better the boys in blue investigate than you."

"I think you're right there."

Margaret got to work. I went behind the coffee counter and made myself a double espresso. A cup of coffee was my normal go-to, but I felt like I needed something stronger now. There were several bars a short walk away, but I didn't want to drown my frustration in alcohol. That happened occasionally after Autumn's passing. The drinking got to a point where I had to force myself to back off and not drink when I was sad or mad. Moderation was key.

I took the espresso and sat in an easy chair in front of a picture window. It had a partial view of the ocean. Sunlight glimmered off the surf. A trail of thin clouds drifted in the sky. Seagulls caught updrafts and sailed in the salty breeze, lifting my mood. Nothing like ocean therapy.

The bell on the door chimed, and I heard Margaret greet the customer. A row of bookshelves shielded me from the front of the store. I had set this two-seat grouping and the bookshelves in such a way that readers or mobile workers would have a semi-private retreat in the store.

I sipped from the espresso cup. The earthy blend from Beach Hippie Coffee hit the spot. Just what the doctor ordered.

"What's a girl gotta do to get a cup of coffee around here?"

I turned in my chair to find Detective Gina Gomez standing beside the edge of a bookshelf. My heart skipped a beat.

Talk about just what the doctor ordered.

CHAPTER
FORTY-EIGHT

GOMEZ WAS DRESSED casually in a pair of khaki shorts, matching sandals, and a navy t-shirt with a South Carolina Criminal Justice Academy logo silk-screened on the upper-left side. Adding to the casual image was the fact that she was wearing makeup and a pair of dangling seashell earrings—neither of which I'd seen her do much. She had a natural beauty about her and didn't need makeup.

Our relationship had been strained since she told me she was engaged to Lucien. It shouldn't have mattered since our "relationship" was supposed to be of a professional nature. Except for the fact that she and I had made out right before she showed me her engagement ring. Since then, we'd worked together on the Tidal Creek case, but there hadn't been any further fireworks. Besides, I reminded myself, I had a girlfriend. Andrea. I needed to spend more time thinking about her and our relationship rather than a woman engaged to another man.

Tension filled most of my encounters with Gomez during that investigation, leading up to meeting Lucien. I didn't know what to make of her surprise appearance here, knowing she was coming back from a conference and was supposed to check in with Moody and the investigation, not with me. I was no longer part of it.

"Well, fancy seeing you here out of uniform," I said, rising from my seat with the espresso cup in hand. "Let's see what we can do about getting you a cup."

We stood face to face awkwardly. I didn't know whether to hug her or shake her hand. She made the decision for me.

She wrapped her arms around me and squeezed lightly. It was a pleasant squeeze. She did a quick pat with her hands on my back either in a comforting way or to see if I wore a shoulder rig for a concealed weapon. Since we'd had a conversation about my aversion to guns, I settled for the former.

She released the hug. "Moody filled me in about the case and what happened between you and Zoe. Thought I might find you here."

"You know how I roll." I didn't know how to feel about her prediction of where to find me and what that meant coming from her.

"I wanted to see how you were doing," she said. "I feel responsible for letting you get involved in these cases, and sometimes we dig into things, or people, who get to us. I'm sorry that happened to you."

"You don't need to apologize. I knew what I was getting involved in the first time."

She cocked an eyebrow. "Did you?"

I smiled. "Alright. Not the first time, but for sure by the second."

A few minutes later, I was back in the same seat with Gomez sitting in the neighboring chair, coffee cup in hand. After taking her first sip, she said, "Ah. That's good. It was a long drive down I-95 from D.C. to here."

"I bet."

"Traffic was its normal nightmare."

"Sounds about right."

I watched her out of the corner of my eye, wondering why she was here. Why was she *really* here? She could have called me with words of comfort. Then she told me.

"I had just come into Conway when Phil called me with an update about the case. He told me what happened between you and Zoe. He confided to me that he didn't blame you for wanting to wring her neck."

"She's a real piece of work."

"That's what I heard." She sipped her coffee, stared out the window, and said, "I read all the reports before I left the hotel this morning, and Phil told me everything that happened today before Chief Miller told you to *adios*. Now, I need to pick your brain because something's happened."

My blood ran cold. "What happened?"

She reached across the gap between the chairs and placed a pre-consoling hand on my wrist. "Because someone tried to kill Paxton and kidnapped her son."

At that moment, everything clicked into place. There would be no grand summation scene where we gathered all the suspects and laid out everything that happened in the murder, leading to the reveal of the killer.

Not here.

Not now.

There wasn't time.

"Percy," I said, draining the last of my cooling espresso and getting to my feet.

Gomez raised her eyes at me. Her mostly full mug was cradled between both hands. Confusion was etched on her face. "The divorce attorney?"

"Yes. He was behind all this, and he had help. Come on. We need to rescue Ethan before it's too late."

CHAPTER
FORTY-NINE

"*LET'S TAKE MY* car," Gomez said on our way out the door. "You make your phone call."

She had asked me where we were going, but I said I needed to call Gideon first. He knew the location.

Her blue Camry was parked next to my Jeep in the employee lot behind the bookstore. I climbed in the passenger side as my phone was dialing on speakerphone mode for Gomez to hear. As I settled into the seat, the coconutty fragrance of her car freshener took me back to our journey to and from Charleston together when we were tracking down a food blogger who had killed two people on the Boardwalk and disappeared. The aroma brought other, more vibrant memories of the trip back to the rain-soaked parking lot of a random gas station.

I shook those images away as Gideon answered with a "hullo."

"Gideon—"

"Who's this?" he asked.

I buckled my seatbelt as Gomez exited the lot.

"It's Clark."

"What can I do for you?"

"Quick, something's happened. We need to know where Percy keeps his boat."

"Who's we?"

"The police and I."

Gideon cursed under his breath. "Crikey. I shoulda known. Keeps it at the Grande Dunes Marina."

"What's the name of it?"

"*Splitsville Racer.*"

"What does it look like?"

"You can't miss it, mate."

* * *

I THANKED GIDEON for the information and description of Percy's boat and ended the call. Gomez heard it all and made calls of her own. None of which were to Chief Miller. Interesting.

She took 10th Ave N to Grissom Parkway to avoid weaving through congested summer traffic, then had to merge north on the Bypass the rest of the way. She had no fear of getting a ticket, she said. Troopers would recognize her plate. A quick search on the DMV database in their patrol cars would identify her.

I explained to her that Zach was only the first domino to fall. It was a crime of passion, just not in the typical context of how a person thinks of passion.

We made a left at the stoplight just before reaching the Grand Strand Medical Center onto Marina Parkway. We went straight through a roundabout and followed the road which curved sharply to the right. Moody's Explorer waited at the edge of the Myrtle Beach Watersports parking lot near the marina entrance. The SUV blocked the entryway to the dock with lit flashers. Dozens of boats, small and large, were docked in the marina.

The large Villa Marbella Condos complex at Grande Dunes, the

Marina Inn, Ruth's Chris Steakhouse, and the Grande Dunes Tennis Club lay to our left. A walkway on the right side of the marina led to the Anchor Café. A golf course lay beyond it. Golf carts and landscapers rolled about. The sky was a clear blue. An old man with a shaved head wearing a gray jogging jacket and pants walking his chihuahua without a leash watched with disinterest.

Gomez drove around a squad car that had just pulled to a stop and jumped out of the car. She shouted to Moody to turn the flashers off. We didn't want to tip Percy off that we were here. Coming up behind us were the familiar faces of Officers Nichols and O'Brien. Moody opened the door, reached in, and extinguished the blue, flashing lights.

A gaggle of people trying to get to their crafts were told to stand aside by O'Brien and Nichols. Another patrol car arrived with Officers Dame and Battles. The more the merrier.

Gomez told Moody to go to the marina office and let them know what was happening and to close it down. He hurried off in one direction. We went in another, running along the dock, searching for Percy's powerboat.

The appearance of Battles and Dame trailing us in uniform caused boaters to stop and gawk at us.

I slowed and shouted to a group of white-haired silver spooners coming out of the E Dock entrance. "Percy Blyth and the *Splitsville Racer!* It's deep blue and charcoal gray. Have you seen them?"

A guy with tortoise shell glasses, thick silver hair, the arms of a cashmere sweater wrapped around his neck, and an agape mouth pointed down at the end of a long dock jutting off from the main boardwalk.

"Thank you!" I called out. Gomez and the others had gone

further down the boardwalk while I asked for help. I shouted and pointed, "Hey! They're down here!"

Alarms blared from the marina office. Moody appeared at the end of the Boardwalk, searching for where to go.

The roar of a speedboat starting its engines thundered forth from the end of the dock where Lifestyles of the Rich and Famous with Robin Leach had pointed.

I ran as fast as possible. Three slips from the end on the right was a 40-foot powerboat with a glittering deep blue and graphite polished metallic hull. An antenna grouping sat on top of the teak cockpit. It appeared built for speed, just as Gideon had described it.

Percy was in the process of unwinding a rope from a cleat on the edge of the dock when I caught up to him. Ethan sat in the co-pilot's seat with a thick pair of headphones on his head and a tablet in his lap, thankfully oblivious to everything going on around him.

"Stop!" I shouted at the top of my lungs.

Percy looked up, and his mouth fell. I was the last person he expected to see.

It didn't enter my mind that he might have a gun until he fired it at me.

CHAPTER
FIFTY

THE BULLET WHIZZED past my head. I ducked behind a wooden piling as another bullet hit it square in the center, throwing off a cloud of splinters.

Footsteps pounded down the dock in our direction. Gomez approached at a sprinter's pace.

"He has a gun!" I shouted to her. It should have been obvious to her after two BOOMs rang out, but I had to warn her.

Gomez got to me and ducked where I huddled behind the piling. She'd heard the shots. She wasn't armed, nor was she wearing body armor. I marveled at her. She'd heard bullets and still ran to my aid. Our bodies did their best to take up the same space. It was an oddly intimate moment at a decidedly odd moment. She gasped for breath as Dame and Battles entered the fray.

"He's armed," she called to them.

The officers drew their firearms and approached the craft just as Percy started backing the *Splitsville Racer* off the dock and into the open water of the marina. With his focus now on navigating the boat out of the marina and heading to escape somewhere along the Intracoastal, Percy didn't break his concentration on the immediate task at hand.

All two-hundred and seventy-five pounds of Officer Dame leaped from the dock and onto the side of the speedboat near the cockpit. The boat wobbled in the water at the sudden added weight.

Battles reached the end of the slip and aimed his gun at Percy. "Remove your hands from the controls!"

Percy glanced to his right, seeing Battles. Of more immediate interest was Dame. The bulky officer had gotten his balance and made his way to the side of the cockpit. He whipped out his gun and aimed it at Percy's face. "Gotcha, sucker."

I let out a breath of relief. Ethan was safe.

Gomez was in my arms. I let go.

* * *

PAXTON'S MOM CAME and picked up Ethan. With him being nonverbal, interviewers obtained little from him besides a few words from his tablet.

EMTs came and checked Ethan, Gomez, and I over. They were fine. I was uninjured but shaken after being fired at. They recommended a psychologist in case any PTSD arose from the incident. I took the card and stuck it in my back pocket. I'd been through a lot in the past year, including being thrown fifteen feet after a camper van exploded in my vicinity, but this was the first time I had faced looking down the barrel of a loaded gun.

The little boy had only seen me one time in his life before today. I may never know how much of today's events he understood or would remember (hopefully none), but he showed his gratitude with stiff hugs all around for Battles, Dame, Gomez, and myself.

We received word that Paxton was going to be fine. Percy had talked his way into their home under the guise of talking about Zach's will and to see how Paxton and Ethan were doing in the wake of his death. Percy had smashed a vase on the back of Paxton's head and had fled with Ethan in tow.

After laying out to Gomez how the murder went down on the golf course, a squad car was dispatched to Grace's residence to pick her up on suspicion of aiding and abetting a murder. I still needed to process it all, including the feelings I had when Gomez intertwined her body with mine while seeking cover behind the wood piling. Not to mention she sought me out first when arriving back in Myrtle Beach.

Moody drove me to the station to make a statement on my role in the near shootout at the marina. I spent several hours there waiting for them to complete the booking process for Percy and Grace. While I waited, I called and spoke to Andrea. She told me I was stupid for getting involved, and we'd have to have a chat about not getting involved in future cases. After dodging a literal bullet and in the heat of the moment, I didn't disagree with her.

Later, after replaying the scene over and over in my head, the part I ended up thinking about most was Gomez in my arms.

Another call went to Mom, informing her of what transpired. She said she'd seen Erica Sullivan talk about it on Channel 2 News. Thankfully, my name was not mentioned. We agreed to meet for breakfast tomorrow morning. I'd tell her all about it then.

Gomez exited an office door and closed it behind her. I stood against the wall in a cramped hallway, sipping on stale coffee from a white foam cup like the previous evening.

"Hey," she said as she stopped in front of me.

"Hey," I returned.

She tucked her dark hair behind her left ear. "How are you doing?"

"For someone who didn't wake up this morning expecting to

get shot at, decent."

Gomez attempted to smile. Her hand reached out to pat my arm but stopped halfway. She tucked it under her elbow.

"We wouldn't have gotten either of them if it weren't for you."

"You would have eventually figured it out."

"Yeah, but Percy might have escaped to anywhere, and who knows where Grace was trying to run off to. Figuring it out is one thing. Catching the criminals is another."

There wasn't much I had to say to that. That's me. Johnny on the spot. "You're welcome."

"Both Grace and Percy face life in prison."

I would explain Grace's involvement to my family over breakfast. Gomez already knew the story. "Good. Put them under the jail, the whole lot of 'em."

"Except the boy."

Her mention of Ethan brought something rare for today to my face. A smile. "Such a cool young man."

"Paxton's mom is going to take care of him while she's on the mend."

"Is she going to be okay?"

"Yeah. A couple of stitches took care of the wound. It was a wonder the vase Percy struck her with didn't crack her skull."

"She's fortunate there, at least."

"She is." She paused. "Paxton's mom tells me she really is a good mother to Ethan. She might be a little full of herself, but no one takes better care of him. Her mom said Zach had been a good father, despite his dealings and temperament."

"That's good. That little guy deserves the best."

"He'll get it too. Since Zach never got to file for divorce, Paxton stands to gain everything. She won't have to work another day in her life if she doesn't want to."

"Good for her and Ethan," I said and meant it.

We stood in silence. Neither was sure what to say. I'd only known Gomez for a little over a year, but we'd been through so much together. As it was the day I met her, her flowery perfume was intoxicating. It was amplified in this enclosed space, making me want to reach out and touch her.

"Lucien told me about you coming to the forensics lab."

"Oh? What did he have to say?"

Gomez pulled her eyes away from mine and said, "That you and him about got into it."

"Oh. You think we were posturing with each other to show who is the dominant male to gain your favor?"

She laughed. I liked the rare times when she laughed. It was a pleasant laugh. The laughs brought rare smiles. Hers wasn't one to light up a room like you read about in romance novels or see on the Hallmark Channel. What made hers so special was the way she looked at you. Like I'd won the big prize for making her smile. That prize being a scarcely seen grin. That made each one special. "No. He's just one of these alpha male types who asserts himself in a group of people. That's one of the reasons why he trained to move from patrol to forensics. He'd have his own team there."

"Like the alpha types, do you?"

"No." She shook her head. "He has a lot to offer."

I didn't want to sound like the jealous type, but I was unable to keep my mouth shut. "What do you see in him beyond his appearance?"

She crossed her arms. "What do you see in Andrea, besides her appearance?"

I opened my mouth to respond with a dozen reasons but didn't. I didn't respond to her question, but said, "Look, I asked him about Autumn's phone. He didn't like it when I challenged him about not knowing who might have stolen it."

"I asked him about it too. He didn't have an answer. I told him it was important to you, and he shrugged his shoulders like, what was he supposed to do?"

"Such a caring individual," came out in dripping sarcasm.

What had begun as a congenial conversation had grown sour since the mention of her fiancé and then Andrea. I had to control what I would say here on out. I couldn't take back my last statement, no matter how much I wished.

Gomez took the high road. Her shoulders sagged. "Look, Lucien isn't a warm and fuzzy guy. He's a tough man's tough man. He shoots straight from the hip, which is more than I can say about many of the people here who have rank. There's a good deal of workplace politics involved."

"You'd mentioned that before when you told me about how you struggled to get to your position."

Her voice lowered. "Yes. A lot of men in suits making decisions. Now, with Chief Miller here, more women are seeking and getting promotions."

"That's good." Her compliment of the new Chief raised a question. "Speaking of her, how come you didn't call her when we took up pursuit of Percy? You called Moody, but even he didn't loop her into it."

Her eyes bore into mine like she wanted to tell me something but was unable to do so. "No reason. We were doing it on the fly, and I needed to call the people in the department I trust the most."

I played that comment through my head a few times before saying, "Which means you don't trust Chief Miller."

"I didn't say that."

"You said the ones you trust the most. Your police chief should be above suspicion. Is she not?"

Gomez looked down the hall in both directions. No one was in sight. "I can't talk about it here."

The discussion had taken another unexpected turn. Before I asked her where we could talk about it, Lucien came out the same door Gomez had.

He saw us standing close to each other and from his expression, didn't like it.

"What's going on here?" he asked, walking up and prying his way between Gomez and me.

Both of us taking a step back, Gomez said, "I was just thanking Clark for helping solve this case and to let him know that Detective Moody was going to take him home within the next fifteen minutes."

"Is that right?" he said in my direction.

It took all my willpower not to turn to him and say that his fiancée and I were getting ready to arrange a private chat with each other away from his eyes and ears.

"Yep," I answered.

He said, "Very good." His eyes bore into mine, trying to intimidate me.

It didn't work. I didn't let him. I held his gaze.

Gomez diffused the situation. To Lucien, she said, "Come on. We have a few details to wrap up." To me, she said, "Thanks again for everything, Clark."

With that, they went back through the door they had appeared from. Lucien went in second with his hand on the small of Gomez's back and gave me one last dirty look over his shoulder.

CHAPTER
FIFTY-ONE

I CLIMBED INTO Moody's Explorer twenty minutes later, a complete mess.

Even during the busy season, the roads around Myrtle Beach late on Sunday evening were still quiet. A few stars were visible in the sky between sparse clouds and despite light pollution. I remembered the days of camping out at the Beech Fork State Park across the West Virginia state line near my childhood home of Proctorville, Ohio.

My friends enjoyed staying in tents. I loved crashing on a sleeping bag and gazing up at the stars at night. Days like today made me miss that. I would much rather be there than here. Either at Beech Fork or somewhere among the stars. I needed a break. I needed to get away from Myrtle Beach, even if for only a few days. Everything to do with this weekend made me want to leave. Maybe I'd hop on a plane with Bo and see his place on the West Coast. Perhaps a much-needed vacation was in order. I hadn't been on one since Autumn died.

The question that went unanswered in my mind was: who would I want to take with me?

Then all the issues of who would oversee the opening of Garden City Reads, not to mention the looming deadline I had to finish writing the next book in my series. Of course, I could use the escape to write, but that would leave Winona hanging with the new store.

Ah. Adulthood and responsibilities. I longed for the days of my childhood and none of that.

The passing lights of Myrtle Beach scrolled past the car window. Moody broke me from my reverie.

"What's troubling you?"

I tried to think of a way to put my thoughts on the case in a nutshell. "Zach seemed like a lowlife, slimeball, vengeful with questionable morals. After getting waist deep into it, I wondered why we were doing this? Maybe the world is better off without him."

In his wisdom, Moody said, "That might be true, but Zach also had a 7-year-old who loved him and will never see his daddy again. That boy, more than others, won't deal well with a big life change like this. If nothing else, you do it for Ethan. You found his daddy's killers. You did good today, kid. That boy is safe thanks to you."

Ethan being out of danger was the one consolation that came from all this. "I know."

He grunted. "Look, kid. I know I don't always come off seeming like the nicest guy, but I like you. You've been a real help to the department."

"Appreciate it."

We went over the bridge above the Farrow Parkway exit. A McDonalds and the WBTW News studio passed by on our right.

"I know you're still held up on what happened with your wife."

I took my gaze off the scenery and over at him. He kept his eyes on the road.

"I can't help it. I was almost at a point where I moved on with my life, and then Gomez told me her suspicions. After that, that's all I can think about. I *must* know."

"I understand." He took a deep breath and let it out. "Let me tell you."

"What?"

"I knew what had happened to you even before we met on that first case."

My eyes widened. "You did?"

"I did. I was supposed to be with Banner that night but had a prior engagement I was unable to break. He kept a tight lid on what had happened, but Gina and I discussed it after his passing."

On the night of Autumn's death at the courthouse, the then lead detective, Ed Banner, took Gomez along with him to investigate the scene. At the time, he and Moody were partners. If Moody hadn't had the other obligation, he would have gone along with Banner. Not Gomez. She told me that Banner had acted weird that night and made several phone calls and spoke in hushed tones. Banner died of a heart attack a few months later.

I met Banner's wife a few months ago and got ahold of his phone records from the time when Autumn had died. The phone calls he'd made were to the same unlisted phone number that sent Autumn the threatening messages the night before her death.

In the weeks and months following Gomez's revelation to me that she didn't think Autumn died of natural causes, I poured over court records and spoke to coworkers, trying to figure out if there were any cases where Autumn may have stumbled across information that someone wanted covered up. Nothing stood out. It had been a dead end.

She worked for Judge Whitaker. The judge was the one person I had yet to speak to, although I had tried.

"And then we happened to cross paths after I stumbled into your investigation of Paige Whitaker's death."

"Correct," he said. "It was clear to me that you were still haunted by your wife's death, even before Gina told you about her suspicions."

We pulled into my neighborhood. After navigating through a few turns, he made a right onto Lake View Circle. He stopped at the border of my front yard and the paved street.

He got out of his Explorer at the same time I did and walked with me stride-for-stride as I approached my front porch.

"If you walk me to my door," I said in the darkness, "I'm not giving you a kiss goodnight."

He stopped at a point midway in the front yard between the Explorer and the porch. We stood in the middle of the yard. The grass was higher compared to my neighbors, but I hadn't had time to mow it this week. When he stopped, I took it as a signal to halt.

He came a step closer, and for half a beat, I imagined him shoving a blade into my gut. After being shot at earlier, I was seeing my possible death around every corner. He didn't have a blade, gun, or even a sharp pen.

"Did you follow up on the ownership of that house on the Waterway? The one beside that kooky doctor?"

"You mean the rental?" I asked.

"Yeah. That one."

"I did. I couldn't find the name of the person who owns it. Only some anonymous holding company."

"What was the name?"

"Summit Capital Holdings."

He grunted, mumbled "I thought so," and looked over both shoulders.

"I went on the Horry County records search website that you gave me," I explained. "I punched in the address and that's what came up. It didn't allow me to dig any deeper into the company."

He said, "Going to need you to follow up on the company. Go to the Register of Deeds at the county courthouse in Conway."

"Why? The case is over. Besides, Chief Miller took me off the case."

His grunt this time was more of a long sigh. "We, uh, just want to make sure everything is covered, and I asked you to do it. We're already looking into the loan shark service. Zach's death might uncover more cockroaches hiding in the shadows. If Percy was right and Zach was doing a lot of business offshore, then that's something the Feds will want to know about."

That was an interesting comment. "You think the rental house had something to do with Zach?"

Moody grunted in disgust. "It's possible. Might have been a love nest or something. My guess is that we get in there, and we'll find the bedroom where some of those pictures were taken."

"Do you think Lucien will be able to track down the network the photos were printed from, like he had mentioned."

"Maybe. Maybe not. This is all part of the investigation."

He kept looking around like he was looking for someone watching us. His actions made me nervous. However, nothing stirred along the quiet street. I didn't know if the detective was as fatigued as I was, but what he was asking me to do sounded pointless at this point.

I said, "Can't they figure out who Summit Cap—"

Moody cut me off and drew close. His breath smelled like tuna. "Look, Clark. There's something I need to tell you. About your wife."

Why didn't he tell me in the privacy of the Explorer? With where we stood, twenty feet away from his SUV and twenty feet away from the front edge of the house, I understood. He was trying to keep whatever it was he wanted to tell me away from possible digital eavesdroppers.

I swallowed. "What is it?"

He grunted. "I can't tell you tonight."

"Then when?" I whispered with urgency. "Is it about the night of her death?"

"Not quite," Moody said. He weighed his next words before saying, "There was a reason I wanted you to hang with me on this case, but I don't want to say more than that right now."

I wanted to grab him by the collar and shake him until he told me everything he knew. I'd had a feeling since day one that he was holding something back from me. Moody had been around too long and had seen too many things to be completely ignorant. The last thing I needed this evening was to be arrested for assaulting an officer. If he wanted to tell me, he would on his own time.

"Then when?" I bit out.

"Tomorrow. Noon. Remember the place you met Gina and I when you had the OceanScapes murder figured out?"

"Yeah." I narrowed my eyes. "At the Ba—"

He cut me off. "Don't say the name. I know what you were going to say. Be there. Get Gina there. She needs to hear this too if I'm right."

"What if you are?"

His next words would haunt me for years to come.

"Then this city might burn to the ground."

CHAPTER
FIFTY-TWO

I STARED AT him for a few moments, letting the implications sink in. My heart pounded. Since Gomez told me she thought Autumn had been murdered, I'd come to understand that there was more going on in Myrtle Beach than most people were aware of. There had been whispers and rumors over the years, but nothing substantiated. Tony Bruno told me that there was someone controlling the city behind the scenes. He didn't know who it was but was aware of who the second in command was, but didn't tell me who, likely for my own protection. It occurred to me, based on Moody's actions and comments, that Zach might have been involved.

"I've been around the block a few times, and I've seen some things no person should see," Moody said. "You're fortunate that you have a nice job, nice family and friends, and a nice home. You're not used to being around the types of people I've come across."

"Agreed."

"After living on this Earth for as long as I have been fortunate to do, I've learned a few things."

Moody volunteering life advice was new territory. I had the feeling it wouldn't be sunshine and rainbows. "Like what?"

He breathed out and grunted. "It's like this. I know you like to believe in the good in people. For people out here on the streets, this world is hostile. So impossible for some. Other folks devour to survive. Some of those devourers stay hungry and will eat up everything in their paths to get on top. That's how it is. That's how it's always been."

His words made my skin tingle. "You know someone like that?"

He didn't answer the question.

Instead of answering, he grunted, and we parted ways. I remained rooted in the yard, watching him return to his vehicle.

His last words to me before climbing into the Explorer were, "Keep a baseball bat under your bed and your doors locked."

I flexed my fingers, thinking about what to do next. Whatever Moody had to tell me, he wanted to do with Gomez at the same time. Why? My only thought was, whatever he wanted to, or was ready to reveal was so earth-shattering that my life would be in instant danger by possessing that knowledge. Had I crossed a threshold with him these last two days that made him trust me more, or had I stumbled upon something relating to Autumn's death that I hadn't realized or made sense of yet?

Whatever it was, I wasn't sleeping here tonight.

* * *

WHEN I KNOCKED on my parents' front door at ten till midnight, Bo answered the door.

"Hey, bro. Didn't expect to see you here tonight."

I had a travel bag that I'd thrown a few essentials into. Changes of clothing, toothbrush, razor, deodorant, soap, and two books. They were all I thought of bringing with me on the fly. It had been over two years since I needed to pack a travel bag and fully expected to learn that I'd forgotten some important items. Obviously, I needed a vacation.

"I didn't feel like sleeping at home by myself." It was true to a degree. I also didn't like the idea of sleeping with one eye open and gripping my pillow tight while trying to get some much-needed sleep. If someone tried to get into my home tonight, they might be surprised not to find me. By staying with my parents in one of their guest rooms, I wouldn't have to register for a room somewhere and secure it with a card.

I could have stayed at Andrea's, but I figured it was too late to call her. Besides, I didn't want a repeat of the awkward conversation we had last night.

Mom being Mom, had the spare bedroom ready to go somehow in the ten minutes between the time I called and asked to spend the night and arriving.

Dad and Mom had a ground floor bedroom. They came shuffling out when they heard Bo and I speaking.

Mom came and gave me a warm hug. "I'm so glad you're safe. The news said a gun was fired during the apprehension."

The scream of the bullet *whizzing* past my right ear was something I would never forget. "Yeah, I was fortunate."

"Were they firing at you?" Bo asked.

We were all clustered in the foyer at the bottom of the stairs. They surrounded me. After the day's events and the conversation with Moody that had led me here, my knees were weak. All I wanted to do was get upstairs and crash. It seemed like they were expecting me to tell them all the details here and now. If I were in their house shoes, I would understand their excitement.

"Remember the guy wearing the Puma hat?" I asked Bo.

"Yeah."

"It was him."

His mouth fell open. "Get out of town. You're kidding."

"I wish I was."

Dad said to Bo, "Clark's tired. Let him rest." To me, he said, "I'm sure he'll tell us all about it over breakfast, right?"

I breathed out in relief. Dad saved the day. "Yeah. I'll give you all the details then."

Bo took my bags upstairs and deposited them in the other guest bedroom.

"I'm glad you're okay," he said to me before closing the door behind him. "Proud of you, little bro."

I hardly slept. The vivid memory of being shot at, the case, the moment of closeness with Gomez, and not knowing what Moody wanted to tell us had a party in my mind.

At some point late in the night, I drifted off to sleep with a bad feeling that Zach's murder investigation wasn't concluded.

* * *

I CALLED AND talked to Andrea before going downstairs to breakfast. She was getting ready to take Libby to school. I wanted to call her before she watched the news and possibly heard my name mentioned. I relayed what happened in a nutshell and told her I'd see her later. Maybe she, Libby, and I will go to dinner.

We hung up. I got dressed and walked out into the upstairs den. Bo's door was open. He wasn't inside. A glorious coffee smell drifted up the stairs from below. My nose followed it downstairs where Mom had breakfast waiting. Both being early risers rubbed off on Bo and me. We didn't have a large house growing up. No matter how quiet Dad and Mom were in trying to get him out the door in the wee hours of the morning, we still heard them.

Dad worked at various coal jobs when Bo and I were kids. He and my mom woke up at three or four in the morning five, six days a week for years. Dad had one of the most important jobs in any strip-mining operation. He ran the coal loader. If he didn't work, the coal wouldn't have been loaded into trucks. If the trucks didn't run, the coal piled up and the company didn't get paid.

How important was his job as the coal loader? I remember asking him why he didn't ever want to be the foreman on the job and run his own site. He asked, why would he do that? He made more money than the boss.

The job took a toll on his body over the years. All the vibration from the heavy machinery shot his knees. He'd had them both replaced. Now his hips were giving him problems. He recently had to take up using a cane.

It took him a minute to get seated. Although I'd arrived at their house around midnight last night, Mom had a full breakfast on the table by 6:30.

After we had gathered at the table, Bo told me he had canceled his flight. He jabbed a spoon into a juicy grapefruit. "This weekend was too short. I don't have any pressing matters awaiting me back home. I wanted to hear all about what happened to you yesterday. Besides, we never got to finish that round of golf."

I sipped from the mug. "We may never finish that round. I'm not sure when or if Swaying Palms is going to open again."

"Why is that?" Dad asked, cutting into a plate of biscuits and red-eye gravy.

"The girl running the pro shop was operating a loan shark

service," I said. "Apparently, it was a long-running scheme that the course operators knew about. The FBI has been called in to investigate."

"That blonde was hot as biscuits," Bo said, "but she looked mean."

"She's wretched," I said.

My mom loved a good mystery and had offered advice on the cases that I had worked on to date. This was the first time she was out of the loop. She was dying to know what had happened. Pardon the pun.

She raised her coffee mug to her lips with both hands. "Can you tell us about it now?"

I drank from mine, and said, "Sure. Here's how it went down."

CHAPTER
FIFTY-THREE

ON THE OTHER occasions when I've revealed how a murder occurred, there had been audiences, and the killers were present. This time, the perpetrators were behind bars, and the other suspects, if they had engaged in any illegal activity, were being taken care of.

Now, it was Mom, Dad, and Bo. I didn't have to go over each suspect and whittle away at their motives and how they may have conducted the murder.

From the start, this case had been complex. However, the nuts and bolts of it fitted together to create a diabolical puzzle.

"I'll try to go through this in the best way I can make sense of it," I said.

"No rush," Dad said, "take your time."

"Please do," Mom added. "This is always my favorite part of any book."

I checked the clock on the microwave in the kitchen. I planned on driving to Conway after meeting with Moody and Gomez at noon. It was too much to cram into the morning to go to Conway and back. There was no hurry.

"Bo was there," I said, "so it'll be easy for him to picture this. Maybe even add a few thoughts."

Bo nodded, but said like a fanboy, "This is so cool."

Mom and Dad weren't there, so I started from the beginning.

"We got to Swaying Palms a few minutes early to meet Detective Moody and his friend Tom. Our foursome had to wait to tee off, and we grabbed a few buckets of balls and headed to the driving range where the group ahead of us were finishing their practice round. It didn't take long for Zach to make his voice heard."

"He was drunk from the get-go," Bo said.

He sat opposite me at the table. Mom and Dad sat across from each other to my left and right. Their heads went back and forth depending on whether Bo or I were talking.

"Yup. He was already pounding a beer and whistling at Zoe, who runs the pro shop. It turns out they had a history together."

"What kind of history?" Mom asked.

I placed a hand on the table. "Zoe might be one of the vilest people I've ever met. She ran a loan shark service for club members who needed to pay off gambling debts amassed while playing at the course. Most of the men who play at the club are married. She let the married men pay back some of their debt by sleeping with them."

"Eww," Mom said.

Dad drank from a glass of orange juice.

"Yeah. Like Zach turned out to be, she was morally bankrupt. Used married men to suit her needs. Zach was married, but she turned him down." I sipped my coffee. "For a while I tried to make the pieces fit to where she had done it. In the end, none of it added up. She was out there hitting a few balls before she had to open the pro shop. They left the range shortly after her. They were using push carts and walking the course. We were riding in carts. While we finished hitting our balls and before their tee time, they left their hand carts by a walkway leading to the back entrance of the clubhouse.

The video feed only showed the bottom half of their bags and the legs of anyone walking past. In the video while they were all inside, a pair of shapely legs passed by and seemed to have done something with Archie's golf bag to make it wiggle.

"Here's the first wrinkle. The course superintendent and the security guy were in the monitor room when we were watching the video, and they both said those were Zoe's legs. She had gone out to ask the starter if his wife could come in for a lesson before opening the shop, so she was out there. But she didn't return the same way. She came back through an employee entrance at the front. That part bothered me. Either she was openly lying," I wiggled a finger, "or it wasn't her at all."

"Who was it?" Dad asked.

"Grace, the beverage cart girl. She's not very attractive, so neither of the guys watching the video thought it was her. They never gave her a second look. When I met her, it was apparent that she had other quality features, just not above the neck."

"Oh," Bo said. "She looks good from far, but far from good."

The same may be said for people from either sex. "Yes, something like that. It occurred to me that they might have been her legs, and not Zoe's, who might have messed with Archie's bag. More on her in a bit. They come out, get their carts, and roll up to the first tee where they had to wait for the first group in front of them to clear the landing area. We pull up behind them, close enough to hear their conversation. Zach and Archie start wagering on who is going to win the hole. The other two guys kept out of it."

"Weren't you there with that detective?" Mom observed.

"I was, but he didn't say anything about it." I ran my finger around the mouth of the almost empty cup. "Said it happens everywhere. They'd have to spend too many man hours investigating all the golf courses here."

"Of course," Bo said, "they might have to now, after uncovering the loans."

"That's going to require assistance from the federal level," I said. "They might pursue it, but to what end? I'm sure it would hurt tourism if guys in suits started patrolling all the courses."

"The powers-that-be wouldn't want that to happen," Dad said.

I said tongue-in-cheek, "I bet. I mean, it's the bulk of this area's economy. Anyway, Grace has a small tattoo of a bear on her ankle that they went back and found after I put their forensics folks onto Grace. After the first few holes, Archie couldn't find his 3-wood and asked the other guys if they'd seen it. Which they hadn't."

"You should have seen Clark bumping into this guy in the clubhouse after the ninth hole," Bo said.

"What happened?" Mom asked.

I shrugged. "I went to the counter to grab my food, bumped into Zach, and exchanged a few words. I didn't take him seriously because he was drunk. It was no biggie, but a sign of things to come."

"Where does Percy come into this?" Dad said.

"Okay, so these guys have been playing together at this course for years. They have a standing tee time as a group. They're familiar with each other's playing styles and habits. They know that Zach a) likes to bet, b) likes to show off how far he can drive the ball, and c) gets drunk while playing. They'd played the 11th hole dozens of times. Percy knew that if Zach was inebriated enough and the amounts of the bets were high enough, he'd try to hit it over the sand trap in the corner of the dogleg hole.

"That's exactly what happened," Bo said. "The guy who got killed and this other guy —"

"Zach and Archie," I said.

"Right. Zach and Archie. They had been getting into it the entire time. Archie won a bunch of money on the previous hole and Zach bet him double or nothing on the 11th."

Dad rested his elbows on the table. "Ooo. This is good."

"It made for good theater while we were playing," I said. "Here is where it got interesting. Percy was playing a bet of his own."

"What kind of bet?" Mom placed both hands around her mug.

"That Zach would get overzealous and hit it over the sand trap," Bo said.

I placed both hands on the table and opened them. "Which he did. It's entirely possible he and Grace did this a few times before Zach ever actually hit it there, since they played once a week. His competitor, Archie, gets up and hits a perfect drive. That put Zach under pressure to one-up him. The only way to do that is to hit it as close to the bunker as possible without it going in. He tees it up and whacks it right over."

"I bet that made him madder," Dad said.

Bo snorted. "Nuclear."

"He was," I said. "He grabbed his cart and stormed down the fairway. Clouds were starting to gather on the horizon at this point. Etiquette required him to wait until his three mates had hit their second shots. His went the farthest and would have had to walk past all three. Gideon was the closest to the bunker. Archie and Percy hit their second shots. Archie ended up near the hole, and Percy's ball landed near the trees on the right side after the swing of the dogleg."

"Ah," Bo said, "probably right where he wanted it."

"Bingo," I said. "With his ball close to the trees, and while they waited for Zach, with the help of Gideon, to find his ball and play it, he had an excuse to duck into the trees and search for lost balls. At least, that's what he said he was doing."

"What was he doing?" Dad asked.

I turned to him. "Making a bee line for a cart path that runs around the perimeter of the golf course."

"Why?"

"To meet Grace."

CHAPTER
FIFTY-FOUR

"What was she doing there?" Mom asked. "How did she know to meet him?"

"A matter of timing," I said. "They left the clubhouse at 10:30. She was there when we were and knew when they left so she could time her role. The golf course knows how long it takes on average to play each hole. If it takes twenty-four minutes to play the 10th hole, then she would know they would be coming around the dogleg on the 11th between ten and fifteen minutes later. All she had to do was load up Archie's stolen club and swing by to pick up Percy. She would have been waiting for him when he emerged from the trees. She drove him the one-hundred yards from where he met her to where the cart path met the edge of the course before curving back to the clubhouse around the 10th.

"We discovered tire prints in the grass near where we believe they hid. We found footprints, and we were unable to tell if they belonged to someone on the landscaping crew or Grace and Percy. But they were there. The tire marks showed where the cart came to a stop and later turned around and went back where it came from. I figure she picked him up before they did the deed and dropped him off in the same spot on the way back."

I paused to drain the last of my coffee.

"Want another?" Dad asked.

I pushed the empty cup across the table. "Please."

He took it and made me another Newman's Blend with their Keurig. Not my favorite blend or brewing method, but when in Rome...

"Thanks," I said when he set it in front of me.

He retook his seat. "Go on."

The coffee was hot, strong, and bitter. After yesterday's events, two out of three coffee's attributes I enjoy aren't bad.

"How did they do it?" Mom asked once I'd wet my whistle.

"Here's what I believe happened," I said, holding the mug on the table with both hands. "Percy had witnessed Zach hitting the ball into those trees before and was familiar with the buttons to push to agitate him enough to make him hit the ball as hard as he could."

"The entire morning," Bo said, "Zach and Archie had been having a contentious back-and-forth. Percy would pipe up occasionally and stoke the flames."

"Right," I said. "He was fully aware of what he was doing. Zach predictably hit the ball into the woods. Percy is good enough of a shot maker to place his second shot on the left side of the fairway close to the woods. It might have been better if he hit it there to begin with so he wouldn't have had to lie about searching for balls."

I batted a hand. "Anyway, Grace acts in an all-girl comedy troupe with Percy's daughter. Since Grace is the more, uh, mannish of the group, she gets all the male parts. Her job was to distract. Percy hops in her cart, and they speed to the area between the woods and the two homes where no one was watching and hop out. We found one set of footprints in the grass, but it turned out to be two. One made cleat marks. The other didn't. One came from Percy's golf shoes. The other from Grace's sneakers. There was a random Srixon ball we found in the trees near where Zach and Gideon split up their search."

"What if Gideon saw or heard Percy and Grace?" Mom asked.

"Yes. Another risk Percy took. He wouldn't have known Gideon would follow Zach to aid in his search."

Mom considered that. "What would have happened if he did see them?"

"A couple of things." I set the mug on the table. "If he saw them, then they would see him. They could have either called it off at that point or tried to kill him too. Or Percy might have played it cool and said he came back to aid in the search."

"Oh," Mom said. "They didn't, which was either good or bad depending on which way you want to look at it."

"Correct," I said. "He didn't. Gideon and Zach split up their search, and he wandered far enough away that he thought someone else was there, but not close enough to make out details. Gideon said he heard a man's voice say something to Zach after his initial yell. He probably heard Grace impersonating a man's voice to throw him off. The medical examiner told us that Zach had a big welt in his back. I think either Grace or Percy, likely Grace, threw the ball and hit him. He was already flustered that Archie had beat him on the previous hole. He stood to lose a lot of money on that one hole. Zach yelled in rage and took off to see who threw the ball at him. He found Grace, and they had words with each other. Percy was hiding behind a tree and waited for Zach to pass by. While Zach yelled at Grace, his back was to wherever Percy hid. Here, he tried to trick us. Zach had dropped his 3-iron in the brush when Grace hit him with the ball. Percy picked up the club and Grace had given him Archie's 3-wood."

I swallowed before continuing. "Percy had both clubs and emerged from hiding. The medical examiner's report said the killer used the iron and hit Zach in the back of the neck, breaking it and knocking him to the ground. Then he took the bigger club and whacked him on the side of the head like a ball sitting in the rough. That's what killed him."

"Oh my," Mom said with a hand pressed against the side of her face.

Dad's head bobbed up and down. He saw action in Vietnam and had seen worse things happen to a person.

"I'll never forget hearing him scream," Bo said.

I raised my eyebrows. "Me neither, Bo. Me neither."

A clock ticked on the wall as we played the scene in our heads. The hum of a car passed on the street. The aroma of coffee, biscuits, gravy, and bacon lingered over the dining room table.

Mom broke the silence. "Why did he do it?"

It was a question I asked myself during the night that my mind sorted out in my sleep. "Love."

"Was he in love with Zach's wife?" Dad asked.

"Nope. Their son, Ethan." I explained about Percy losing his autistic sister and how Ethan also had autism. That, and he's just a cool kid. Percy had this lingering sense of loss (which I understood from personal experience) with his sister and knew that Zach was about to file for divorce, wanting full custody. Percy had been a friend long enough to know that if they split, Ethan would suffer. "As a single parental unit, Zach and Paxton worked well in caring for Ethan. As individuals, they were so selfish and self-absorbed that Percy had to feel that Ethan would suffer, and he didn't want that for the child. Besides, Percy was aware of his client's illegal dealings and had known that Zach might face prison time if caught. He killed Zach to protect Ethan and tried to do the same to Paxton."

"That's so sad," Mom said.

"Agreed," Dad, Bo, and I said together.

"What do you think his plan was after kidnapping Ethan?" Dad asked.

"Not sure to tell the truth," I answered. "Percy might have had an escape plan, or he might not have been in his right mind. Driven by emotion."

"And he'll plead insanity if that's the case," Mom said.

"That would be my guess." I drank from the mug. "The part I haven't figured out yet was the lockers."

"What about them?" Mom said.

"We found the murder weapon in Archie's locker."

"Makes sense," Mom said. "Tried to frame him. Archie had been at it with Zach all morning, as you said, and killed Zach when he had the opportunity. There's your motive."

"Exactly what Percy was going for. Logistically, it didn't work. Archie was the farthest away from Zach when he was killed. Also," I paused because another piece of evidence fell into place. "Also, it was the back of the club face that had blood on it."

"I get it," Bo said. "Archie is left-handed. Percy is a righty and naturally swung the way he was used to, but with the back of the clubhead facing forward."

"Bingo," I said, shooting a finger gun at my brother.

"Clark," Bo said, "I gotta tell you. That's one of the most impressive things I've ever seen. You figuring all this out? I can't tell you how much I admire you for it. Wow."

Growing up, Bo rarely gave me any type of praise. Most of the time, he picked on me and put me through the school of hard knocks, like a typical older, cooler brother.

"Thanks," I said.

"Just think," Dad said to Bo, "he's done this five other times."

"I know," Bo said. "Wish I'd been here for them."

"Meh," I commented, "you had other things you've been doing with all your globe-trotting and adventure seeking. I bet that was fun."

"Sure was," he said and glanced back and forth between Mom and Dad. They looked from him to me.

There was something else going on here that I was clueless about. I asked, "What is it?"

Bo cleared his throat. Tears formed in the corners of his eyes. "I uh. I uh, don't know how to say this."

When he couldn't continue, Mom said, "Bo is going to be staying with us for a while, isn't that right?"

He used a finger to wipe away the tears. Despite the breakfast digesting in my gut, I felt an empty feeling there. I feared the worst. That he was going to say he was sick and needed to be taken care of. That was the only thing that sprung to mind.

"Uh, Clark." Bo cleared his throat. "I'm broke."

I know three things about Bo. He was super smart. He liked to have fun. Money burnt holes in his pockets. It somehow didn't surprise me that he lost millions of dollars since leaving Uber. He bought a multi-million-dollar home, traveled all over the world, and lived a lavish lifestyle.

Here's the thing. He didn't consult a financial advisor nor invest any of the money when he received his windfall. Bo figured that he would be able to live off the interest. He wasn't exactly broke, but he no longer had enough to meet his expenses. He'd put his house up for sale and hoped someone would purchase it before he got foreclosed upon.

I just shook my head.

We talked about that for a while before I had to leave and meet Gomez and Moody.

I told Bo as I walked out the door that we would play that round of golf this week.

Little did I know, but this was about to be the longest week of my life.

CHAPTER
FIFTY-FIVE

WHEN I PULLED into the Bar-B-Cue House parking lot, Gomez's blue Camry was already there. Outside of the gray police-issue Explorer, I wasn't sure what Moody drove as a civilian. He might be here already. I didn't see him as the most punctual person, so the odds were that he hadn't arrived. Which meant a possible awkward moment with Gomez while we waited.

I wasn't sure about my feelings toward that.

As I worked with Detective Moody over the last two days, it occurred to me that my earlier judgment of him was incorrect. Despite the gruff exterior, he was a good man. He'd shown a fatherly side I hadn't seen before. My respect for him had gone up, and I considered us friends.

The restaurant didn't seem busy yet. They opened at eleven. Only two other cars dotted the parking lot.

When I had figured out who murdered Paige Whitaker, I had called Gomez and Moody to meet me here to tell them what I believed happened, which ended up being correct. I had flubbed up an earlier attempt at fingering the murderer but was embarrassingly wrong. Sorry, Chris.

It was then that I first saw Gomez out of her regular navy pantsuit. At that time, she was fresh off a jog and was wearing skintight workout clothes. It was also the first time I'd seen her with her hair down. I was still getting over the loss of Autumn, but it was the first time since her death that I looked at another woman and thought, "She's *fine*."

I got out of the Jeep and entered the restaurant to find Gomez alone in a corner booth, far away from the other customers. A cup of sweet tea sat in front of her. Despite not needing to, she waved me over.

Before I sat down, the server took my drink order. Sweet tea as well. If you go to a BBQ joint in the South and you don't have sweet tea, you're doing it wrong. Unless you have Cheerwine. That works too.

"Hey," she said as I sat down across from her. She wore one of her nice pantsuits with her hair pulled back into its customary ponytail.

"How's it going?"

"Just waiting for Phil. Haven't heard from him yet today."

"Is that normal?"

Her forehead creased. "For Moody to not be in contact? Yes, that's normal. He'd go all day without speaking if possible."

"Hmm. That's not how he was this weekend. He was surprisingly talkative."

"Yeah. That's because he's coming around to you." She leaned forward. "I think he's gotten used to you ending up being around and doesn't mind it."

I smiled. "You feel the same way?"

The corner of her mouth curved upward. "Similar."

While we waited, she told me that Percy wasn't talking. True to form, he'd lawyered up.

While Grace and Percy were being processed at the station, they had sent the forensics team back to Swaying Palms to search Grace's beverage cart.

"They find something?"

She leaned back. "Oh, yeah."

"Like what?"

"Packaging for a padlock."

"That's interesting."

"Yup. Grace sang after that."

"I imagine so."

Gomez explained that Grace said Percy's plan all along was to set up Archie. Not that Percy didn't like him. Of the four, Archie was the easiest one to pick on. Even he would acknowledge that he wasn't in the same league intelligence-wise as Zach, Gideon, and certainly Percy. He was the one they tended to pick on, but Archie was good-natured about it. He didn't care.

"Why did she help him?" I asked.

Gomez shook her head. "He promised her a paralegal job when she graduated and to pay off her student loans at the community college."

"That doesn't sound like a reason why I would want to help with a murder."

"Me neither," she said. "With as much as these people slept around, I wouldn't put it out of the realm of possibility that there was something going on with her and Percy."

"To each their own."

Gomez continued to tell me, "Percy's locker was beside Archie's. He watched his friend spin the combination on the lock many times and memorized it. One time, when no one else was in the locker room, Percy snapped a picture of Archie's lock with his phone. He went to a hardware store, matched it up, and paid cash. After they killed Zach, Grace's job was to get into Archie's locker, swap out the locks, and stash the murder weapon in it."

"Why swap the locks?" I asked.

"Percy's reasoning was, if Archie happened to come back, open his locker, and find the club, he would say it was planted there. On the other hand, no one would believe he didn't know his own locker combination. So, when they got it open and the club was there, it made Archie look guilty."

"Ah, that's devious."

"Yup," Gomez agreed. "Some friend, huh?"

"They're all a bunch of scuzzballs."

"Seems like it."

"I've been thinking about it."

"The murder? I'm sure."

I ran a thumb along the edge of the table. "These investigations."

"What about them?"

"I hope this is the last time I have to do this."

Her lips pressed together. "Oh."

We both understood the implication. If I didn't do this anymore, we would have no reason to see each other. She was engaged to a man who didn't like me, and I had a girlfriend who was uncomfortable about my relationship with Gomez.

I explained, "I hated having to be around those people. I understand you can't pick who you investigate, and I've gotten off lucky in the ones I have that the suspects around the cases weren't completely terrible people like the ones here." There have been others along the way, and murder is despicable, but in this case, I granted an exception for Gideon. He seemed like a cool dude, and

I loved his accent. "I totally admire the work you do, but this, this isn't for me."

Gomez's head tilted. Her eyes narrowed. I didn't know what, or if, she had any emotions toward me at this point.

"Maybe you missed your calling," she said.

"What's that?"

"You would have made a great detective or private eye if you didn't have the bookstore. When you do that, you can be choosier with the people you have to be around."

Being PI wasn't something I'd considered, but it might have been right up my alley.

Her cell phone lay on the table. It vibrated before it rang, breaking our conversation.

I glanced at my watch. It was half past twelve.

Gomez picked up the phone and studied the screen. "Hmm."

"Who is it?"

"Moody's wife. Hold on."

She answered the call. Listened. Her eyes went wide. Then her lips trembled followed by a sharp intake of breath.

"Okay. Okay. Thank you for calling. Please, let me know if you need anything. I mean that. Anything."

She ended the call and laid the phone on the table. I felt queasy.

I said, "What is it?"

Her voice started to break. Tears pooled in her eyes.

If the table was not between us, I would've pulled her to me to comfort her.

"It's Moody." A tear trickled down her cheek.

I swallowed. The way she said that gave me chills, and I knew before I asked the question what her response would be.

"What about him?"

"He's dead."

To Be Continued...

ACKNOWLEDGEMENTS

In case you didn't notice, this was the longest book in the series so far by a wide margin. To get it into your hands required much help. I'd like to thank my wife, Tasha, for all her support. My sharp-eyed beta readers, Angie Barnhardt, Darren Bourne, Jatana Royster, CariAnn Sparks, Karen Polhemus, and Haley Mellert help catch mistakes that fall through the cracks.

Dr. Stephanie Rose is always a big help when it comes to answering medical questions and how to tame down the cause of death descriptions. Cozy they are not.

I again enjoyed working with my editor, Lisa Borne Graves. She does a wonderful job of offering kudos when needed, but in rounding the stories into their finished form. Her Welsh husband, Matthew, aided in nailing Gideon's accent and detailing the inner workings of golf courses.

As always, thank you to Myrtle Beach and the Grand Strand where inspiration is around every corner.

Now if you'll excuse me, I'm going to go write the book that exposes Autumn's killer once and for all. Even that might not be the end of it . . .

All books in the series are available on Amazon, Barnes and Noble, Books-a-Million, and wherever books are sold. Don't see them in your local store or library? Ask the bookseller or librarian to order them for you.

Learn more on his website at calebwygal.com.

ABOUT THE AUTHOR

Caleb is a member of the International Thriller Writers and Southeastern Writers Association, the author of ten novels, social media marketer, woodworker, occasional golfer, reacher of things on high shelves, beach walker, shark tooth finder, and munchkin wrangler.

His two Lucas Caine Adventure novels, *Blackbeard's Lost Treasure* and *The Search for the Fountain of Youth*, were both Semi-Finalists for the Clive Cussler Adventure Awards Competition.

He is currently at work on the next book in the Myrtle Beach Mystery Series.

He lives in Myrtle Beach with his wife and son (the munchkin).

Visit Caleb online at

www.CalebWygal.com

*If you enjoyed this story please
consider reviewing it online and at Goodreads,
and recommending it to family and friends.*

Printed in the USA
CPSIA information can be obtained
at www.ICGtesting.com
LVHW040107140424
777255LV00001B/4